Named a Best Book of 2012 by *The Huffington Post*, *St. Louis Post-Dispatch*, and *The Kansas City Star*

"We want stories to stir our desires. We also want them to lead us to places we don't recognize and build us a temporary residence there. Bergman provides alluring glimpses into the strangeness, the ruthlessness, of the animal kingdom."

—*The New York Times Book Review*

"A fine, moving debut collection . . . [Bergman] draws scenes and characters with a quick, incisive touch. . . . This is a poignant prose menagerie."

—Associated Press

"Compassionate . . . Bergman has a flawless feel for our connections to other creatures."

—*The Miami Herald*

"*Birds of a Lesser Paradise* is an astonishing debut collection, by a writer reminiscent of such greats as Alice Munro, Elizabeth Strout, and even Chekhov. Expertly delivered, Bergman's stories bloom from the minutiae of life. They confirm the inescapable power that nature—and our own biology—has over us."

—Sara Gruen, author of *Water for Elephants*

"Megan Mayhew Bergman apparently possesses, all in one sensibility, Ralph Waldo Emerson's love of a back-to-the-land self-sufficiency, Amy Hempel's infinite tenderness toward animals, and Tillie Olsen's fierce sense of the emotional intensities of motherhood. *Birds of a Lesser Paradise* features characters who, even understanding it as well as they do, want to mother the world, and their stories are rendered with dazzling compassion, intelligence, and grace."

—Jim Shepard, author of *You Think That's Bad*

P9-DLZ-781

"A big-hearted collection of stories—each one a precise and compassionate study of human life, the changes and obstacles—all carefully housed under the miracles and marvels of nature. Megan Mayhew Bergman is a brilliantly gifted writer who recognizes and highlights life's fragilities in a way that will leave your heart aching while also finding those bits of hilarity and absurdity that bring uniqueness to each and every creature."

—JILL MCCORKLE, AUTHOR OF *GOING AWAY SHOES*

"I predict that astronomers will soon be renaming the star Sirius to Megan Mayhew Bergman. *Birds of a Lesser Paradise* offers us a spectacular new voice in the world of American short fiction. The characters in these stories—each one—perform as beacons on who we are and how we should act, all without pretense or exhortation. This is a first-rate collection."

—GEORGE SINGLETON, AUTHOR OF *THE HALF-MAMMALS OF DIXIE*

"Bergman's excellent stories are hard-earned and well-honed. Her characters speak as if their very lives depend upon getting it right, getting it down, facing the toughest stuff that tumbles down with equal toughness and enduring resilience. A very fine and impressive debut."

—BRAD WATSON, AUTHOR OF *ALIENS IN THE PRIME OF THEIR LIVES*

"Extraordinarily powerful and beautifully written."

—JON KATZ, AUTHOR OF *A DOG YEAR*

"A stellar debut . . . Bergman writes straightforward, elegant prose that dovetails nicely with swampy Americana, and possesses a great facility for off-kilter observations."

—*PUBLISHERS WEEKLY*, STARRED REVIEW

"A top-notch debut . . . that deserves big praise. The beginning, one suspects, of a fine career."

—*Kirkus Reviews*

"Many of these stories have climaxes like the tail of the scorpion: they curl back on themselves with a powerful sting. Readers will be shocked, amazed, and always entertained by the work of this accomplished writer of short fiction."

—*Booklist*

"An immensely appealing collection with a rare clarity and cohesion and the capacity to appeal to a wide-ranging audience."

—*Library Journal*

"A tender collection . . . the prose is tightly packed and graceful."

—*The Huffington Post*

"Megan Mayhew Bergman's stories are as technically skilled as they are emotionally affecting."

—Rebecca Joines Schinsky, Book Riot

"Bergman's stories are swarming with nature—with oceans, wildlife, biology, the whole mess of planet Earth—but their real strength comes from how they're always able to distill it down, again and again, to us: our own, singular, one-shot human lives, and the people we share them with."

—*BookBrowse*

"Bergman excels at a mundane kind of gothic that is both familiar and frightening. . . . A curious triumph of heart and storytelling."

—*Paste Magazine*

"*Birds of a Lesser Paradise* is a fine example of writing that is both intimate and vast in scope. There is always more to each of these stories than meets the eye. . . . Most impressive of all is how Mayhew Bergman's writing is unflinching but tender. She allows that unexpected combination to coexist and in doing so, she has written one of the finest short story collections I've read."

—Roxane Gay, *The Rumpus*

BIRDS *of a* LESSER PARADISE

Stories

Megan Mayhew Bergman

Scribner
New York London Toronto Sydney New Delhi

SCRIBNER
A Division of Simon & Schuster, Inc.
1230 Avenue of the Americas
New York, NY 10020

This book is a work of fiction. Names, characters, places, and incidents either are products of the author's imagination or are used fictitiously. Any resemblance to actual events or locales or persons, living or dead, is entirely coincidental.

Copyright © 2012 by Megan Mayhew Bergman

All rights reserved, including the right to reproduce this book or portions thereof in any form whatsoever. For information address Scribner Subsidiary Rights Department, 1230 Avenue of the Americas, New York, NY 10020.

First Scribner trade paperback edition November 2012

SCRIBNER and design are registered trademarks of The Gale Group, Inc., used under license by Simon & Schuster, Inc., the publisher of this work.

For information about special discounts for bulk purchases, please contact Simon & Schuster Special Sales at 1-866-506-1949 or business@simonandschuster.com.

The Simon & Schuster Speakers Bureau can bring authors to your live event. For more information or to book an event contact the Simon & Schuster Speakers Bureau at 1-866-248-3049 or visit our website at www.simonspeakers.com.

Designed by Carla Jayne Jones

Manufactured in the United States of America

3 5 7 9 10 8 6 4

Library of Congress Control Number: 2011019400

ISBN 978-1-4516-4335-0
ISBN 978-1-4516-4336-7 (pbk)
ISBN 978-1-4516-4337-4 (ebook)

Some of these stories have been published in slightly different form: "Housewifely Arts" in *One Story* and *2011 Best American Short Stories*, "The Cow That Milked Herself" in *New South* and *New Stories from the South 2010*, "Another Story She Won't Believe" in the *Kenyon Review*, "Saving Face" in the *Southern Review*, "Birds of a Lesser Paradise" in *Narrative*, "The Urban Coop" in the *Greensboro Review*, "The Right Company": portions of this story appeared in *Shenandoah* and *Oxford American*, "Every Vein a Tooth" in *Gulf Coast*, "The Artificial Heart" in *Oxford American*, "The Two-Thousand-Dollar Sock" in *Ploughshares*.

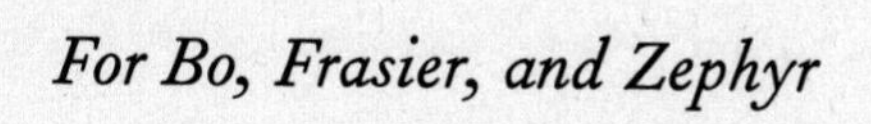

For Bo, Frasier, and Zephyr

We will now discuss in a little more detail the Struggle for Existence.

—Charles Darwin, *On the Origin of Species*

Contents

Housewifely Arts

I am my own housewife, my own breadwinner. I make lunches and change lightbulbs. I kiss bruises and kill copperheads from the backyard creek with a steel hoe. I change sheets *and* the oil in my car. I can make a piecrust and exterminate humpback crickets in the crawl space with a homemade glue board, though not at the same time. I like to compliment myself on these things, because there's no one else around to do it.

Turn left, Ike says, in a falsetto British accent.

There is no left—only a Carolina road that appears infinitely flat, surrounded by pines and the occasional car dealership billboard. I lost my mother last spring and am driving nine hours south on I-95 with a seven-year-old so that I might hear her voice again.

Exit approaching, he says from the backseat. Bear right.

Who are you today? I ask.

The lady that lives in the GPS, Ike says. Mary Poppins.

My son is a forty-three-pound drama queen, a mercurial shrimp of a boy who knows many of the words to Andrew Lloyd Webber's oeuvre. He draws two eyes and a mouth on the fogged-up window.

Baby, I say, don't do that unless you have Windex in your backpack.

Can you turn this song up? he says.

I watch him in the rearview mirror. He vogues like Madonna in his booster seat. His white-blond shag swings with the bass.

You should dress more like Gwen Stefani, he says.

I picture myself in lamé hot pants and thigh-highs.

Do you need to pee? I ask. We could stop for lunch.

Ike sighs and pushes my old Wayfarers into his hair.

Chicken nuggets? he asks.

If I were a better mother, I would say no. If I were a better mother, there would be a cooler with a crustless PB and J in a Baggie, a plastic bin of carrot wedges and seedless grapes. If I were a better daughter, Ike would have known his grandmother, spent more time in her arms, wowed her with his impersonation of Christopher Plummer's Captain von Trapp.

How many eggs could a pterodactyl lay at one time? Ike asks.

Probably no more than one, I say. One pterodactyl is enough for any mother.

How much longer? Ike asks.

Four hours, I say.

Last night I didn't sleep. Realizing it was Mom's birthday, I tried to remember the way her clothes smelled, the freckles on her clavicle, her shoe size, the sound of her voice. When I couldn't find those things in my memory, I decided to take Ike on a field trip.

Four hours 'til what? he says.

You'll see, I say.

I haven't told Ike that we're driving to a small roadside zoo outside of Myrtle Beach so that I can hear my mother's voice call from the beak of a thirty-six-year-old African gray parrot, a bird I hated, a bird that could beep like a microwave, ring like a phone, and sneeze just like me.

In moments of profound starvation, the exterminator told me, humpback crickets may devour their own legs, though they cannot regenerate limbs.

Hell of a party trick, I said.

My house has been for sale for a year and two months and a contract has finally come in, contingent on a home inspection. My firm has offered to transfer me to a paralegal supervisory position in Connecticut—a state where Ike has a better chance of escaping childhood obesity, God, and conservative political leanings. I can't afford to leave until the house sells. My Realtor has tried scented candles, toile valances, and apple pies in the oven, but no smoke screen detracts from the cricket infestation.

They jump, the Realtor said before I left town with Ike. Whenever I open the door to the basement, they hurl themselves at me. They're like jumping spiders on steroids. *Do* something.

Doesn't everyone have this problem? I said. The exterminator already comes weekly, and I've installed sodium vapor bulbs.

This is your chance, he said. If you clear out for the weekend,

I can get a team in for a deep clean. We'll vacuum them up, go for a quick fix.

I thought about Mom, then, and her parrot. With a potential move farther north in the future, this might be my last opportunity to hear her voice.

Okay, I said. I have a place in mind. A little road trip. Ike and I can clear out.

I'll see you Sunday, the Realtor said, walking to his compact convertible, his shirt crisp and tucked neatly into his pressed pants. I'll come over for a walk-through before the inspection.

That night, Ike and I covered scrap siding in glue and fly paper and scattered our torture devices throughout the basement, hoping to reduce the number of crickets.

I hope you're coming down later to get the bodies, Ike said. Because I'm not.

He shivered and stuck out his tongue at the crickets, which flung themselves from wall to ledge to ceiling.

The cleaners will get rid of them, I said. If not, we'll never sell this house.

What if we live here *forever?* he asked.

People used to do that, I said. Live in one house their entire lives. Your grandmother, for instance.

I pictured her house, a two-bedroom white ranch with window boxes, brick chimney, and decorative screen door. The driveway was unpaved—an arc of sand, grass, and crushed oyster shells that led to a tin-covered carport. When I was growing up, there was no neighborhood—only adjoining farms and country lots with rambling cow pastures. People didn't have fancy landscaping. Mom had tended her azaleas and boxwoods with halfhearted practicality, in case the chickens or sheep broke loose. The house was empty now, a tiny exoskeleton on a tree-cleared lot next to a Super Walmart.

I pull into a rest stop, one of those suspicious gas station and fast-food combos. Ike kicks the back of the passenger seat. I scowl in the rearview.

I need to stretch, he says. I have a cramp.

Ike's legs are the width of my wrist, hairless and pale. He is sweet and unassuming. He does not yet know he will be picked on for being undersized, for growing facial hair ten years too late.

I want to wrap him in plastic and preserve him so that he can always be this way, this content. To my heart, Ike is still a neonate, a soft body I could gently fold and carry inside of me again.

Ike and I lock the car and head into the gas station. A man with black hair curling across his neck and shoulders hustles into the restroom. He breathes hard, scratches his ear, and checks his phone. Next, a sickly looking man whose pants are too big shuffles by. He pauses to wipe his forehead with his sleeve. I think: These people are someone's children.

I clench Ike's hand. I can feel his knuckles, the small bones beneath his flesh.

Inside the restroom, the toilets hiss. I hold Ike by the shoulders; I do not want him to go in alone, but at seven, he's ready for some independence.

Garlic burst, he reads from a cellophane bag. Big flavor!

I play with his cowlick. When Ike was born, he had a whorl of hair on the crown of his head like a small hurricane. He also had what the nurse called stork bites on the back of his neck and eyelids.

The things my body has done to him, I think. Cancer genes,

hay fever, high blood pressure, perhaps a fear of math—these are my gifts.

I have to pee, he says.

I release him, let him skip into the fluorescent, germ-infested cave, a room slick with mistakes and full of the type of men I hope he'll never become.

The first time I met my mother's parrot, he was clinging to a wrought iron perch on the front porch. I was living in an apartment complex in a neighboring suburb, finishing up classes at the community college. After my father's death, Mom and I had vowed to eat breakfast together weekly. That morning I was surprised to find a large gray bird joining us.

The house was too quiet, Mom said. His owner gave me everything. I didn't even have to buy the cages.

You trust him not to fly away? I said.

I guess I do, she said.

When she first got him, Carnie could already imitate the sound of oncoming traffic, an ambulance siren, leaves rustling, the way Pete Sampras hit a tennis ball on TV. Soon, he could replicate my mother's voice perfectly, her contralto imitations of Judy Garland and Reba McEntire, the way she answered the phone. *What are you selling? I'm not interested.*

A month later, during breakfast, the bird moved from his perch to my shoulder without permission.

Mom, I said. Get this damn bird off of me.

Language! she warned. He's a sponge. She brought her arm to my shoulder and Carnie stepped onto it. She scratched his neck lovingly.

I was still grieving Dad, and it was strange to watch Mom find so much joy in this ebony-beaked wiseass.

What are you selling? the bird said. I already *have* car insurance. Carnie spoke with perfect inflection, but he addressed his words to the air—a song, not conversation.

You can't take anything personally, Mom warned.

The man of the house is *not* here, Carnie said. He's dead.

You really take it easy on those telemarketers, I said, looking at Mom.

Dead, dead, dead, Carnie said.

That night, he shredded the newspaper in his enclosure, which smelled like a stable. Lights out, Mom said, and tossed a threadbare beach towel over his cage. Carnie belted out the first verse of Patsy Cline's "Walkin' After Midnight," then fell silent for the evening. His parlor tricks seemed cheap, and I hated the easy way he'd endeared himself to Mom.

The next week, Carnie became violently protective of her. Wings clipped, he chased me on foot through the halls and hid behind doorframes, not realizing his beak stuck out beyond the molding. As I tried to shoo him from the kitchen counter, he savagely bit my wrist and fingers. Then, days later, as if exchanged for a new bird, Carnie lightened up and preened my hair while perched on the back of the couch.

I'll take him to the vet, Mom said, mildly apologetic for her bird's bipolar antics. She was a perfectionist, and I knew she wanted a bird she could be proud of. But I think part of her was flattered by Carnie's aggressive loyalty.

Show me how you pet the bird, the vet, a behaviorist, had said.

Carnie, inching left and right on Mom's wrist, cocked his head to one side and shot us the eye. Like a whale, he gave us one side of his face at a time, revealing a tiny yellow iris, ensconced in a white mask the size of a thumbprint, one that looked out at the world with remarkable clarity.

Mom ran her index finger down Carnie's chest.

I don't know how to tell you this, the behaviorist said, but you've been sexually stimulating your parrot.

Mom blushed.

Inadvertently, the behaviorist said. Of course.

He thinks I'm his mate? Mom asked.

Less cuddling, the specialist said, more cage time.

I called three places to find Carnie—the plumber who took him, the bird sanctuary he'd pawned the parrot off on, then the roadside zoo. Now the car is too warm and I'm falling asleep, but I don't want to blast Ike with the AC. He's playing card games on the console.

Are we leaving so that people can move into our house? Ike asks.

We're going to Ted's Roadside Zoo, I say.

Go fish, Ike says. What's at the zoo?

There's a bird I want to see, I say.

What, he asks, is gin rummy?

We pass a couple in a sedan. The woman is crying and flips down her visor.

It's hard being a single mom, but it's easier than being a miserable wife. I hardly knew Ike's father; he was what I'd call a five-night stand. We used to get coffee at the same place before work. The director of the local college theater, he was a notorious flirt, a married one. Separated, he'd claimed. He sends a little money each month, but doesn't want to be *involved*. The upside to our arrangement is simplicity.

I put some pressure on the gas and pass a school bus.

Did I tell you about Louis's mom? Ike says. How she got on the bus last week?

Louis's mom is a born-again Christian with two poodles and a coke habit, the kind of person I avoid at T-ball games and open houses at school.

Tuesday afternoon, Ike says, she gets on the bus with her dogs, raises her fist, and says something like, Christ is risen! Indeed, He is risen.

No, I say. Really?

Ike pauses for a minute, as if he needs time to conjure the scene. Really, Ike says. Louis pretended not to know her when she got on, but his mom held on to that silver bar at the front of the bus and said, Lord, I've been places where people don't put pepper on their eggs. Then she started to dance.

Ike waves his arms in front of his face, fingers spread, imitating Louis's strung-out mother. I see the rust-colored clouds of eczema on his forearms. I want to fix everything. I want him to know nothing but gentle landings. I don't want him to know that people like Louis's mom exist, that people fall into land mines of pain and can't crawl back out.

When Ike was almost a year old, I brought him by for Mom to hold while I emptied the old milk from her fridge and scrubbed her toilets. I tried to come at least once a month to tidy the place and check in on Mom. The living room was beginning to smell; Mom was not cleaning up after Carnie. Suddenly the woman who'd ironed tablecloths, polished silver, bleached dinner napkins, and rotated mattresses had given up on housekeeping.

Would you like to hold Ike while I clean? I said.

Mom sat in a brown leather recliner, Carnie in his white lacquered cage a foot away from her—always within sight. Mom was losing weight and I worried she wasn't eating well. I brought her cartons of cottage cheese and chicken salad, only to find them spoiled the following month.

Are you trying to sell my house? she said. Are you giving Realtors my number? They're calling with offers.

There's a shopping center going in next door, I said. This may be your chance to sell.

I placed Ike in her arms.

It's not hard to lose the baby weight, Mom said, eyeing my waistline, if you try.

I was determined not to fight back. There was heat between us, long-standing arguments we couldn't remember but could still feel burning—should we sell Dad's tools? Should she go to the eye doctor? Who would care for her goddamned bird? Didn't I know how hard they'd worked to give me the right opportunities? Our disagreements were so sharp, so intense that we'd become afraid to engage with each other, and when we stopped fighting, we lost something.

You're like your father now, she said. You never get mad, even when you want to.

It was true—Dad was hard to anger, even when I'd wasted fifteen thousand dollars of his hard-earned money on my freshman year of college at a private school they couldn't afford. When I came home for the summer, he'd sat with his hands in his lap and a face that was more sad than disappointed. Mom stood behind him, silent and threatening. I knew later that night she'd berate him for taking it easy on me, and I hated her for it.

I guess you'll need to get a job, he said.

Dad, I said. I made a lot of mistakes this year—

I wanted to give you a good chance, he said, looking down at his fingers.

I remember feeling relieved that he wasn't yelling at me. Now I wish he had.

I'd do it again, he said. But you understand, there just isn't enough money to take the risk on another year.

Now I tortured myself imagining each of his hours. He worked at the same plant for twenty-six years making industrial-quality tools—hammers, chisels, knives, clamps. Every day he ate a cold lunch on a bench caked with pigeon shit. I could almost hear the echoes of men moving and talking, their spoken lives bouncing from the plant rafters as their hands worked. The black hole of his effort, the way it would never be enough, or easy—it hung over me, a debt I couldn't pay.

Mom ran her fingers over Ike's cowlick. I emptied the trash can in the kitchen, then the living room.

While you're at it, she said, would you change the newspaper in Carnie's cage? And top off his water?

As I approached the bird's cage, he let out a piercing scream, his black beak open. I held my hand up as if to say "stop." Cut the screaming, I said.

Put your hand down, Mom said. You're scaring him.

Carnie continued to scream. It was a pleading, horrifying sound, like an alarm. He cocked his head and danced across his bar, shrieking. Ike began to cry.

Never mind, Mom said. I'll do it.

She thrust Ike in my arms and marched toward the cage. She opened the door and Carnie scampered onto her finger. She brought him to her shoulder. He was silent. Mom pulled the newsprint from the bottom of his cage with bare hands. Dried bird shit fell to the carpet; she didn't seem to notice.

Let me help you, I said. Sit down. I can do this.

Sit down, Carnie said. Sit down. Sit down.

Mom ignored me and walked to the kitchen, stuffing the soiled papers into the trash can.

You should wash your hands, I said.

Don't tell me what to do, she said.

Sit down, Carnie said. Sit down.

I found Carnie's high-volume pleas disconcerting and worried they agitated Ike, who clung to my shoulder. There were things, once, that I thought I deserved. My parents' money, and certainly their unconditional love. But as years passed, our love had turned into a bartering system, a list of complicated IOUs.

I'm sorry, I said. I don't know about birds.

You'll learn, Mom said. Soon.

Ike and I arrive in Myrtle Beach at eight p.m. I know the zoo will be closed at this hour, so we find a Days Inn. There's something about the hum of an ice machine and waterlogged Astroturf that takes me back to childhood.

Ike face-plants onto the bed before I can remove the comforter.

Wait a second, baby, I say. Let me get that dirty thing off.

We get in bed and flip through channels on TV. Ike holds the fabric of my pajama legs with one hand, wraps the other around a blanket my mother crocheted for me when I was in college. His travel blanket. I feel sad every time I see it: the coral and black starbursts, the tight knots. I remember a hotel I stayed in with my mother during her own mother's funeral. Downtown Norfolk, 1986. There was a rotating bucket of chicken on a sign pole below our window. I watched it spin. Even when the lights were off, and my mother cried into her pillow, I watched that bucket of chicken rotate like the world itself.

I remember thinking that moms were not allowed to be sad, that surely women grew out of sadness by the time they had children.

Mom, Ike says. I don't want to move.

His eyes flicker and he fades. The news is on. A lipstick-shellacked anchor tells of a new breed of aggressive python in southern Florida that strangled a toddler in his sleep. Maybe one will come to our hotel, I think. I will have to fight it off with my pocketknife, club it with the glass lamp on the bedside table, offer it my own body.

On our second date, Ike's father showed me a video of an infant in Andhra Pradesh. The child had rich brown skin and curious eyes. He pulled himself across a grass mat while a cobra, hood spread, hovered above the boy's soft body. The baby grabbed after the cobra's tail while the toothless snake struck him repeatedly on his downy head, snapping down upon his body like a whip.

This, Ike's father said, is how you cultivate the absence of fear. Don't you wish someone had given you that gift?

Fear keeps me safe, I said.

Snakes. Why do I think of these things before I try to fall asleep?

I put one arm across Ike's chest so that I will know if he moves. I can feel the pattern of his breath, the calm and easy way he sleeps, the simple way he dreams.

When I move out, Mom had said, I need you to take Carnie.

It was the hundredth time she'd asked. We had her bills and bank statements spread out on the coffee table. Her eyesight was failing and we knew she couldn't live alone much longer. It was time to plan.

Carnie hung upside down in his cage. Empty seed casings and shredded newspaper littered the floor. Occasionally he pecked at his image in a foil mirror, rang a bell with his beak.

I don't want the bird, I said. He hates me. He's drawn blood, for Christ's sake.

If you loved me, Mom said, you'd take him. I can't sleep without knowing he's safe and taken care of.

That's what you get, I said, for adopting a bird with a life expectancy longer than your own.

You know, she said. Then she stopped, as if she was afraid of what she'd say next.

I'd always felt Mom's vision of perfection was outdated. I was never the ruddy-faced, pure-of-heart Girl Scout with 4-H-approved sheep-grooming skills that she'd been. I failed home ec and took a liking to underground hip-hop and traveling jam bands, dyed my hair blue with Kool-Aid one high school summer. In college I got a tattoo of a purple Grateful Dead bear on the back of my neck that had infuriated Mom when she saw it. When Ike was little, he used to lift my hair to find the purple bear hiding underneath. At least someone liked it.

In Mom's eyes, atonement was more than walking the line, more than surfacing from the typical angst-ridden throes of adolescence and early scholastic failures. Atonement included my adoption of a bird I couldn't trust around my son. A bird I'd hated for over a decade.

I don't trust the bird around Ike, and I can't handle the mess, the noise—

Mom was silent. I'll give Carnie to the plumber, Mom said, collecting herself. He's always liked Carnie. He mentioned he was looking for a bird for his kids.

I wish I could take him, I said.

Lying doesn't help, Mom said.

Even before I see it, Ted's Roadside Zoo depresses me. We park outside. The entrance is a plaster lion's face. We walk through its mouth. On the lion's right canine, someone has written: *Jenny is a midget whore.*

This place smells like pee, Ike says.

It's nine a.m., but it feels like Ted's place isn't open. I've yet to see an employee, not even a ticket seller. We walk a sand and gravel path, faux palm trees overhead.

I've heard stories about these places, how they keep big cats in small enclosures. How the animals often have ingrown nails and zero percent body fat.

I have the urge to call out, *Mom?* as if I'm coming home after a long day.

We find a man feeding a seal.

Where are your birds? I ask. Specifically, your African gray?

We have two, he says. Over by the vending machines.

I need the one named Carnie, I say. The one you received from the Red Oak Bird Sanctuary.

I think it's the one on the left, he says. They all look alike, you know?

Ike and I find the birds. I can't help but feel guilty that Carnie ended up in a place like this. There's gum stuck to the bars of his cage.

I home in on Carnie's knowing eye, the white mask. He looked like the same bird, though his gray feathers had worn thin around his neck.

Carnie, I say. Carnie. Carnie. Good boy. What do you want for dinner?

I pull out a pack of sunflower seeds I purchased at the Zip Mart down the road.

I look at the white down on the bird's chest and think: *Mom's voice is in there.*

Ike closes in on the cage. He waves his hands in front of the parrot's face.

The sign on Carnie's cage reads: *African gray parrots are as smart as a three-year-old.*

I don't believe it, Ike says.

Carnie? I ask. Want to sing some Patsy?

For a half hour, Ike and I coo and speak and dance, but the bird doesn't say a word. Beneath this wall of gray feathers is the last shard of my mother's voice, and I feel myself growing increasingly desperate. How thick was her accent? Was her singing voice as beautiful as I remember? She always spoke sweetly to Carnie and I wanted to hear that sugary tone, the one she hadn't used with me in her last years.

How do you know this is the right bird? Ike asks.

I did my research, I say. And he hates me. He's spiting me with silence.

Please talk, Ike says to Carnie. Carnie bobs his head up and down and bites his leg, a gesture that strikes me as the bird equivalent of thumbing one's nose.

Just say something, I think. Anything. Just let me hear her again.

I'm surprised when I remember phone numbers and the alphabetical order of all fifty states, the way I can summon Deuteronomy like a song during a long run. But I can't recall the funny way Mom said "roof" or "Clorox." Not the rhyme she made up about bad breath or the toothpaste jingle she had stuck in her head for two years, not the sound of the way she said good night. The longer Carnie goes without talking, the more I miss her.

A month after we decided to move Mom into a home, the plumber came for Carnie. Mom's possessions had been boxed up and her furniture sold. She'd prepared a box for Carnie that contained his food, toys, water dish, spare newsprint, and a fabric square from one of her dresses. So he remembers me, she said.

The kids are excited, the plumber said. He was tall and large and moved quickly. I was thankful for his efficiency.

I'll be in the car, Mom said, letting herself out of the house. The screen door shut behind her with metallic resonance, as it had thousands of times. I didn't like letting her descend the steps on her own, but I knew, in this moment, she'd refuse help. I took the box of Carnie's things and followed the plumber to his car, dropping a towel over the cage in the backseat of his truck.

I'm always walkin', Carnie sang, *after midnight. . . .*

I couldn't look at Mom as I turned to wave at the plumber as he pulled away. I knew she was crying. I was relieved to see Carnie go, to have the burden of his welfare hoisted onto someone else's shoulders. But I couldn't escape the sadness of the moment. There was an air of finality—my mother grieving in the car, our small home empty.

After the plumber's car was out of sight, I walked through the house one last time. I could almost hear the place settling, breathing a sigh of relief, coming down from a high. Still, there was a palpable residue of our past lives, as if old fights and parrot tirades had left their marks. I paused over my father's plaster fixes and custom molding, things shaped by his hands that I couldn't take with me. Empty, the house reminded me of a tombstone, a commemoration of my childhood. With the shopping center going up next door, I had the feeling no one else would ever live there again.

I joined Mom in the car. I imagined that her stillness and set face belied inner fragility, that beneath the crust lay a deep well of hurt. As I turned onto the highway, I saw her touch her shoulder, the place where Carnie had so often rested, his remembered weight now a phantom presence on her thinning bones.

We've been driving on I-95, toward home, for five hours. Ike has been in and out of naps. We pass a billboard that says *Jesus Is Watching*.

Jesus makes me nervous, Ike says. Jesus is a spy.

I laugh and then pause, thinking how the statement would have made Mom uncomfortable. The night sets in and Ike grows quiet. I watch his eyes in the rearview. I wonder what he's thinking about.

Will you love me forever? I think to myself. Will you love me when I'm old? If I go crazy? Will you be embarrassed of me? Avoid my calls? Wash dishes when you talk to me on the phone, roll your eyes, lay the receiver down next to the cat?

I realize how badly I need a piece of my mother. A scrap, a sound, a smell—something.

I hunger for the person who birthed me, whose body, I realized after becoming a mother myself, was overrun with nerve endings that ran straight to her heart, until it was numb with overuse, or until, perhaps, she felt nothing.

One more stop, I say to Ike.

We pull into the dark gravel driveway of my mother's house. There's no neighborhood, no signage. It's just a plain, deserted house for plain folks on what is now a major highway. The white paint peels from the siding. I remember pulling into this driveway when I was past curfew, the light in my mother's bedroom glowing, the way I could simultaneously dread and love the thought of slipping through the front door, pouring a glass of water, and crafting an elaborate lie to explain my late arrival.

Ike is sleepy. He's wearing my rain jacket and has the hood cinched tightly around his face, though it's barely raining. RVs are pulling into the Walmart parking lot for the night. The smell of wet leaves makes me sick to my stomach with nostalgia. The boxwoods are overgrown and shapeless.

Hold my hand, I say to Ike. Stay close.

The screen door is intact, though the screen itself is punctured and webbed over. I hold it open, stare into the dirty glass of the front door. I try the knob—locked.

I have to go in, I say. Close your eyes.

I break the front door pane with the butt of the knife I carry in my purse and carefully reach in through a mouth of glass teeth to turn the doorknob.

This is weird, Ike says. I'm scared.

I clench his wrist. My knuckles are cold and I worry that my grip on Ike's arm is too tight. But I do not let go.

The damp carpet heaves underneath my feet. The house smells like a cave, and yet, like home. I walk around, inspecting things, Ike close behind me. Checkered contact paper still lines the pantry shelves. Windows are cracked; sills are covered in dead wasps and crumpled spiders. There is mold on the drywall and water spots on the ceiling. Someone has taken red spray paint to the fireplace and living room wall. The stove and toilet have been ripped out. Ike starts to cry.

It's okay, I say. I just want to stay here a minute.

I lead him to the back of the house, down the hallway that still feels more familiar to me than any other. My bedroom, with its teal carpet and pale pink walls, looks small. Barren. At first, it is so quiet my teeth ache. My ears strain.

I'm sad that you lived here, Ike says.

It wasn't that bad, honey, I say. This was a beautiful house.

The crown molding my father installed lines the ceiling, though one loose piece sags. I remember him getting up early so that he could work on it before heading to the plant. It was my mother's birthday present—crown molding for my room.

My father died on the steps of the tool manufacturing plant, not ten minutes down the road. A heart attack. The doctors said it was a birth defect, that he was born with a weak heart. Now the building is empty, abandoned, as if all his work was for nothing. Mom's grief was as long as a river, endless.

I walk back to the kitchen and climb onto the green plastic

countertop. Ike watches me, curious and confused. I remove the valances Mom made in the early eighties; dried bugs fall from the folds of the fabric into the sink below. These are the things with which she made a home. Her contributions to our house were humble, projects that took weeks of stitching and unstitching, measuring, cutting, gathering. I realize now how much of our house was crafted by hand. My father had laid the carpeting and linoleum. Mom had twice painted and reupholstered the dining chairs. My parents were quick-fix averse, always in for the long haul. When the country road in front of their house had been widened to a highway, they complained but never entertained the idea of moving.

I scan the kitchen and picture Mom paying bills at the table, her perfect script, the way she always listed her occupation with pride: homemaker.

I feel a new respect for thrift and permanence.

Next I pull scraps of peeling wallpaper from unglued seams and corners. I pull it slow and steady like skin after a sunburn; the old adhesive gives easily.

Mementos, I tell Ike. I close my eyes. Now I can hear my mother everywhere—in the kitchen, in my bedroom, on the front porch.

Turn off the television.

Warm up the stove.

Brush your hair.

Put your father's shoes where I can't see them. In the trash.

On Sunday, as promised, my Realtor arrives a half hour before the potential buyers and their home inspector.

Your house should look as perfect as possible, he'd said before I left for the weekend. Ask yourself: What would Jackie Onassis do?

When I see the Realtor's convertible in the driveway, I ask Ike: Think you can box up the mini NASCARs and finger puppets?

Sorry I'm late, our Realtor says. He is a slightly overweight cosmopolitan type who wears ostrich-skin loafers and tonic in his hair.

He rushes to the kitchen, as if he has immediately sensed disorder. He strokes the valance over the kitchen window. I remembered last night, as I was hanging it, that Mom had found the pattern in *Southern Living*.

Is this velvet? he says. Are these . . . cobwebs?

I have placed scraps of rogue wallpaper next to my stove and another in the bathroom—a repeating pattern of pale brown cornucopias and faded fruit I took from my mother's house.

These must come down, the Realtor says. Now.

He pinches the curling shreds with his thumb and forefinger.

Leave it, I say. They add charm.

You'll never sell this house, he says, shaking his head in despair. Crickets on speed and a curtain that Elvis made in home economics class. Get serious.

Apple pie? I ask, pulling out a day-old pastry I had purchased from the market's discount bread bin that morning. I've steeled myself against critique. There are too many things I can't fix.

A couple in a minivan pulls up in front of the house, followed by the home inspector in a pickup truck. They come to the door, their faces already twisted with scrutiny. She is small and blond and he is thick like an old football player.

Hi, I say. Welcome. We're about to head out; the house is all yours.

I stuff some magazines and soda into a canvas bag and look around for Ike. I hear him running up the basement steps.

Ike presents a scrap of siding that is covered in glue and cricket exoskeletons. It is not, I suspect, a winning move. Apparently, enough crickets survived the Realtor's quick fix only to meet their end on our glue board. The couple exchange a glance. The inspector scribbles a note.

I crouch down to the floor and touch Ike's cheek. You're brave, I say. Thank you.

Ike grins. Together, we can make a solid grilled cheese, prune shrubs, clean house. Together, maybe we're the housewife this house needs. Maybe we weren't made for Connecticut's long winters. Maybe our best life is here. On a good day, we're just one man short of a catalog-worthy family.

A week before she left for the nursing home, we packed my mother's belongings. Ike had just started kindergarten. Leaving him at a friend's house to spend time with Mom on a Saturday was a miserable trade-off. I wanted to soak up every last bit of innocence he had left, answer every question, scoop him up for hugs when he'd allow it. But I was the only person Mom would allow in the house; there was no one else around to help.

I held up various tchotchkes for Mom's approval.

Take or toss? I asked.

Mom sat in her recliner. She wore a light blue dress she'd made herself. The fabric was so worn it was nearly transparent. Carnie rested comfortably on her shoulder. I worried that his talons would break her thinning skin, but she moved as if she hardly noticed his weight.

I held up a box of ornaments, plastic apples I'd hand-painted for her as a child.

Toss 'em, she said.

I began to wrap her glassware in newspaper.

Make sure to leave plenty of print for lining Carnie's cage, she said.

My mother cupped Carnie with both hands and brought him to her lap. She crossed her legs, then scratched the finger-wide point between Carnie's wings. His eyes, like little black seeds, fell to half-mast as she stroked him. They were accustomed to each other, a pair of sad habits. He was more familiar with her voice and touch than I, more dear to her everyday existence. His transgressions—dirty cage, the occasional nip of her finger—were met with gentle understanding.

Don't call here again, he said. Don't call.

Remember, I told my mother. I'm not obligated to look after that bird.

Well, she said, I'm not *obligated* to look after you.

You are, I thought, her words a splinter in my chest. You have to be.

In that moment, I withered. I hated her for her coldness, her stubborn rationale, her ability to come up big in a fight even when she was dog-tired and bird-boned and couldn't see the food on the end of her fork.

There she sat, outmoded in her homemade dress, bird in her lap, shit on her shoulder. Steamrolled by the world, but in the face of defeat she threatened us all.

Carnie moved back to her shoulder and buried his head into

her thin hair, almost as if he was taking her in, making a memory. It occurred to me that with her voice inside of him he would always have more of her to remember.

You don't want to keep these? I asked, giving her a second chance on a box of photographs.

My heart, she'd said. I can turn it off.

For years, I'd believed her.

But I know the truth now. What maniacs we are—sick with love, all of us.

The Cow That Milked Herself

First, he showed me his kidney.

This, Wood said, is the cranial pole. He pointed to the C-shaped edge of his organ.

My turn, I said.

He moved the ultrasound probe to my belly, rolling the small tip across my hardening stomach.

I think we cleaned this after the rottweiler, he said. He squinted at the probe.

We were in the veterinary clinic after hours, Wood still in his white coat, stethoscope around his neck. I was seated on a steel table, the metal cold against the backs of my knees. Wood had missed my last ob-gyn appointments and wanted to see the fetus for himself.

Don't drop it, he said, handing me the probe while he dimmed the exam-room lights and warmed the transmission gel. This thing costs twenty thousand dollars.

I'd been lonely at my OB appointments, but Wood had an obligation to his patients. There were dogs with shattered elbows, cats with failing livers, cows with mastitis. Crying women in the waiting room cradling arthritic shih tzus, one-eyed ferrets. Malamutes with slipped discs, terriers with severe allergies to carpet cleaner. I believed they needed him more than I did.

He pressed the probe into my abdomen.

Here is the gestational sac, he said. And this flash here—this is the heart.

We were speechless then, watching the beginnings of our child thrive on-screen. Two freshly neutered Labradors whined from their cages outside.

Every week there was a patient at the clinic Wood forbade me from seeing, knowing I'd be unable to resist and would come in anyway, heart bleeding. Last week it had been a cancer-stricken golden-crowned sifaka who was the last of his kind in captivity. Despite the pain he must have been in, he had been gentle with his keeper, raising his bony arm so she could stroke his side. Her touch seemed to comfort him.

This week it was Cerulean, a tripod rottweiler.

Too hard on the heartstrings, Wood said.

Take me to see her, I said.

She's not pretty, he said. She's been self-mutilating. *Down there*. He raised his eyebrows.

Cerulean had come in that morning. Wood was an ultrasound specialist, and her owners had hoped he would be able to reveal a tumor or kidney stones—something specific that would explain why she was hurting herself.

You don't want it to be behavioral, Wood told me. Always harder to treat the mind than the body.

But he had found nothing. Her scan was clean.

No mineralization, no masses, Wood said, disappointed.

Cerulean sat on the concrete floor and leaned against the cinder-block wall. Her black fur shone in the fluorescent lights. Her ears were small. I could not bring myself to look at her eyes. She had mussed the towels into piles. Her feet made me want to cry, the pads of her three remaining paws plump and worn.

At three months I just looked fat. Like I had eaten four sandwiches instead of one, I told my mother. I could cup my belly in one hand, swing my forearm underneath the slight mound the book said should be the size of a grapefruit. I couldn't bring myself to say the word *womb*.

Wood came home in his white coat, smelling of formaldehyde and anal glands. He asked "What's for dinner" but did not listen for the answer. Instead, he stuck his head inside the refrigerator.

How was your appointment? he asked, peeling off his white coat, pulling off his left shoe with the heel of his right.

I made three-bean chili, I said, shooing the cat from the stove.

I wiped buttered paw prints from the glass.

Wood cracked open a beer.

I was palpated today, I said. Like that thing you do to cows, when you feel for lumps in their abdomen.

I can tell when a woman is pregnant by finding the ridge of her uterus, my OB had bragged. I touch a thousand tummies a year, for God's sake.

On the screen, the fetus had doubled over, then stretched, a sun salutation with no sun.

I couldn't help thinking, I told Wood, that the nub of his or her vestigial tail looked a lot like the end of a cocker spaniel.

Incessant waggers, he said. Submissive urinators.

Loving, I said. Warm on your lap.

The following day, the picture of my fetus, taped to the kitchen cabinet, made my niece cry.

I'm scared, too, I said.

I meant it.

The black-and-white photograph showed the baby's skull and vertebrae, eye sockets like moon craters.

Somehow, it wasn't enough. It didn't tell me what I wanted to know about my child, what I *needed* to know to sleep at night. No photograph could say: Everything will be perfect.

Later that evening, Wood rubbed my back, sutured the dress straps I had snapped with my swelling bosom. I could feel his breath on my scapula, his needle stitching cottonlike skin.

Friends came over for dinner that night bearing presents, pop-up books and sock monkeys. I put out a plate of crudités but noticed too late the dog hair wound into the broccoli florets.

Wood spoke of his upcoming conventions, the paper he'd coauthored on using ultrasound to monitor the morphology of female jaguar reproductive tracts. It was hard to trump frozen jaguar sperm.

In captivity, the jaguar mother is capable of devouring her own cubs, he said.

I blushed at Wood's lack of faith in mothers. It was as if he saw, at the heart of all women, an animal. Primality.

Here, Wood, I said. Open this package from your aunt. It isn't just *my* baby, you know.

Wood slipped his finger underneath the wrapping paper.

A breast pump is an awful lot like a vacuum milking cup, my husband said, untangling the gifted contraption. He held the suction cups to his chest.

Soon she will be the cow that milked herself, he said.

Our friends howled.

A week later, Cerulean came back to the clinic for observation.

She smells like pepperoni pizza, Wood said over the phone. I can't explain it.

I hated the thought of her on the cold cement floor, the cage bars obscuring her view, the indignities of her mysterious condition.

Can I bring you lunch? I asked.

I drove to the clinic with sandwiches and a bag of soft dog toys.

What is this? Wood asked, holding a headless hedgehog.

Let me put one in, I said.

Wood placed a hand over his eyes and left me alone with Cerulean.

Hi, I said to her.

She looked at me from the corners of her eyes, shy and damaged. I sat on the floor and tucked my legs underneath my body. I wanted to massage lotion into her feet, stroke her back.

Here, I said, handing her the hedgehog through the bars of the cage, then the stuffed cat.

I want to mother the world, I thought. I have so much love.

Then—I have no business being a mother. I am a selfish woman.

Then—I can do this. Millions of women have been mothers.

Then—I feel very alone. I do not know what I'm capable of.

My fetus grew arms, carried a yolk sac like a balloon.

These, the OB had said, pointing to a white Cheerio on the screen, are the sex cells of your grandchildren.

Tell them I'm sorry about all the weed I smoked in high school, I said. And that time . . . well, there were a lot of times.

I wondered if I would fill the shoes of the mythical matriarch, if suddenly my pancakes would become legendary, my dresses tailored, my back rubs soothing.

When I first told Wood I was pregnant, he had taken off his sweatshirt and placed the cockatiel to which he was administering medication on the exam-room counter.

I think the bird pooped in my hood, he said.

Wood's cheeks were flushed. I touched his shoulder. It was a Saturday morning and I was helping him with his early-morning rounds. I liked those mornings when the clinic was quiet and it was just the two of us feeding schnauzers and ferrets in between sips of coffee and exclamations about the morning paper.

I *am* excited, he clarified, minutes later. He wrapped his arms around me and kissed the crown of my head.

I wanted to be as interesting to Wood as a urinary bladder wall tumor, lab work. I wanted to be pored over, examined by his hands, researched, discussed, diagnosed. I wanted to keep him up late, bring him in early.

Cerulean likes the stuffed cat, Wood said on the way to our birthing class.

Then he reminded me that he had to leave class early. Gall bladder infection in a Chesapeake Bay retriever, he said.

The instructor wore fleece leggings and a purple spaghetti-strap top.

Some women, she said, hands cupped as if she were holding a beach ball, achieve orgasm during birth.

I may have to poke out her third eye, I said to Wood.

Wood did not understand my anxieties—miscarriage, autism, premature delivery.

I wish it would come out like a goat, I told him. Sturdy, hooved, walking.

Every spring we helped the veterinary school calve and foal. The meat goats bloated with twins, the petrified sheep with their petrified lambs, limp and gentle on the mud floor. We picked the weak ones up and held them to the mother's teat, removed the small bodies from the piles of hay when they did not thrive, bottle-feeding them if there was any hope of life.

You'll do fine, he said, patting my stomach. Rugged stock.

But I knew how I would do. I would take my maternity leave and he would come home for dinner at night, late. My milk would let down when the cat cried at the moon from the staircase window. I would wake up sticking to the sheets. I would love and complain with equal vigor.

I'm sorry I missed the asexual revolution, I said. Aphids, bees, captive hammerhead sharks—they know they're on their own. They don't expect understanding.

What the cape bee gains in martyrdom, she loses in genetic potential, Wood said.

Self-reliance, I began.

Take last week's sifaka, Wood said. He was the last of his kind. He needed others.

I'd been thinking about nativity scenes. Camels leaning over the manger like my cat nesting in the crib. The way Joseph pretended his hands were tied, that he wasn't responsible in the first place.

The birthing class instructor passed around a wooden bowl of mixed berries. Wood held up one hand in protest.

I don't need to look, he said. I know how this works.

In your last weeks of pregnancy, the instructor said to the class, the cervix softens like ripe fruit.

These women don't know much about birth, Wood whispered. I'd like to take the class on a field trip. I'd like to take these girls to a farm during calving season.

This is different, I said. Your child will not be a ruminant.

Remember, the instructor said. It may take days to fall in love with your newborn.

The next Saturday Cerulean's cage was abandoned. The stuffed cat, overturned in the corner, was missing an eye.

Don't tell me how this ends, I said to Wood.

Later, as the sun rose, Wood rolled me onto my side and warmed the transmission gel. The exam table was cold.

He pressed the probe into the taut skin stretched across my womb like canvas. In the treatment room his fingers were deft and comforting. His eyes focused on the baby beneath my skin. I could feel his anticipation. It washed over me like love.

The ultrasound excels at imaging the heart, Wood said. The heart is a fluid-filled organ.

States away, a woman gave birth to octuplets like pups. Perhaps another arched her back in ecstasy as a head fourteen inches in diameter emerged from her cervix. An endangered lemur picked at her barren womb in the confines of the zoo hospital. Me, I watched a heart, small but fast, beat between the shadows of our daughter's ribs. I hope you never break, I said, though I knew it would, again and again.

With his finger, Wood traced the outline of our daughter's organs on the screen.

Tell me again about jaguar reproduction, I said.

The baby gestates for a little over ninety days, Wood said. If her cubs are taken from her in the wild, the mother will chase them down for hours, roaring continuously.

I would do that, too, I said. I promise.

Birds of a Lesser Paradise

I fell for Smith the day my father hit his first hole-in-one on his homemade golf course. Dad had spent years shaping the earth in our backyard until he had two holes that landed somewhere between an extravagant minigolf spread and a Jack Nicklaus par-72.

Mae! my father yelled, hoisting his nine-iron into the air. I did it!

He was a couple hundred yards away, and because I didn't think my voice would carry, I jumped up and down a few times and clapped my hands, trying to appear visibly thrilled. But I was self-conscious with Smith standing behind me, his hands stuffed into the pockets of his army-green cargo pants, an anxious scowl on his almost beautiful face.

Dad sauntered off to pluck the winning ball from the hole, long, white beard trailing in the wind, his spaniel, Betsy, two steps behind. It was hardly fifty degrees out, but Dad was wearing shorts and hiking boots. He was nearing seventy, but he had the bulging calf muscles of a man half his age.

I want to see birds no one else has seen, Smith was saying. I printed out the checklist for North Carolina. How soon can we mark these off?

Slow down, I said, smiling.

I don't know if I can tell a common goldeneye from a loon, he said. Is that important?

He followed me to our picnic table, which was soft from rot and green with moss.

Smith stuck his fingers into his bramble-thick hair, hair the color of sea grass. It seemed inclined to one side, like a plant reaching for the sun. He wore a paint-flecked T-shirt covered in a school of dolphin fish.

First, I said, let me tell you what we can see here in the Great Dismal Swamp.

I opened our brochure, pushed it toward him like a menu. We had a chunk of land outside of town that had been in my father's family for two generations. We lived in his ancestral home and ran Pocosin Birds, our bird-watching business, from the property.

In April, I began, birders can expect to sight fifty to one hundred bird species in the swamp.

Are you reading backward? Smith asked.

I have it memorized, I said.

I studied his face. His left eye was deep brown, his right hazel. For a moment, I wondered if he had a glass eye.

Eyes like David Bowie, I said, nodding my head in approval.

Are you going to take me into the swamp? he asked. He smiled. He was lean and dark from the sun. I couldn't tell if he was twenty-five or just short of forty, impoverished or on the receiving end of a trust fund. When he smiled, he looked like too much fun to be thirty, as if he wasn't tired of the world yet.

Typically, I said, we help our clients assemble the correct gear and map a course. We drop you off at daybreak.

I took a red pen from my pocket and circled an area near Lake Drummond.

The best nesting sites for warblers are here, I said. What do you know about songbirds?

I want to go in with *you*, he said.

Dad was born on the outskirts of the swamp at a time when it was desolate, hard, and flecked with ramshackle hunting cabins. His father had been into timber, and Dad was raised wild—the kind of man who could pick up a snake by its neck with the confidence I'd exhibit picking up a rubber version in a toy store. He was sentimental about his family home and the town. Anything he was used to having around he wanted to *keep* around. So when the town got too small to sustain a post office, he converted the blue mail drops into composting hubs in the back corner of our lot. He bought the abandoned elementary school at auction for almost nothing—no one wanted to pay the taxes on it, and looters had already taken the copper pipes and pedestal sinks. He rented it out for birthday parties, weddings, and to local artists for studio space. When a developer leveled the city park, Dad reassembled the jungle gym in our side yard near the garden and let the scuppernong vines go wild.

We lived in a dying town with a dwindling tax base. I never thought I'd come back, but the swamp was in me; if Dad was half feral, I was one-quarter. I liked the way the water tasted, the sound of birds outside my window in the morning. A few years in Raleigh studying conservation biology at the state university and I needed to find a place where I could look out my window and see nothing man-made. I missed the smell of things rotting, the sun bearing down on a wet log.

Nothing in the city seemed real to me—it was fabricated, plastic, artificial, fast. After years of biology classes, every come-on was a mating call, every bar conversation a display—a complicated modern spin on ancient rules. I didn't believe in altruistic acts—I could find a selfish root to anything. Eventually I felt as if I was looking out at the busy world and I could see nothing but its ugly bones.

I was taught that at the heart of all people, all things, lay raw self-interest. Sure, you could dress a person up nice, put pretty words in his mouth, but underneath the silk tie and pressed shirt was an animal. A territorial, hungry animal anxious to satisfy his own needs.

At least in the swamp, there was no make-believe chivalry, no playing nice. It was eat or be eaten out there, life at its purest, and it's where I wanted to be.

Another thing—I loved my dad. I'd never known my mother—she'd died just after giving birth to me—so he was all I'd ever had. He was honest, fun, and unapologetically himself.

I'm not *asking* you to come home, my dad said, when I approached him with the idea. You won't find a husband here, he added.

I don't want one, I'd said—and for a while, that had been the truth. Perhaps it was all the years I'd watched my father carve out a happy life alone.

Your old room is packed solid, he'd said. I disassembled a tobacco barn. Numbered the slats. You can't move in 'til I sell it.

I'll take the room over the garage, I said. I have some money to fix it up—I'll put in a shower.

Aside from serving in Korea and a short stint living on a houseboat in his twenties, Dad had remained hidden from the world in the swamp, inhabiting the same house, trapping the same illegal lines, fishing the same shallow waters.

We didn't watch the market or follow politics. That was part of the appeal, for me anyway. For centuries people had used the swamp to hide from their problems. Runaway slaves, ruthless fugitives, shell-shocked soldiers, and cheating wives—all had hidden in the swamp at one time.

When I moved from the city to the swamp, the things I could not have became special again. Cappuccino was special. Driving forty minutes to eat second-rate Indian food was special. Planning a day around the "good" grocery store—special.

You got about half fancy living out of town, Dad told me.

I was a thirty-six-year-old single woman living in a poor man's theme park, running birding trips into the swamp. Most of my binocular-laden clients were pushing sixty and just as concerned with sunscreen and hydration as they were with spotting a pileated woodpecker. I drove them into the swamp in Dad's pickup, left them with a map, a bagged lunch, water, a GPS device, and a phone, and picked them up at twilight in a place that seemed less wild every day.

For the most part, I was happy.

Can I offer you some water? I asked Smith, walking toward the main house, the farmhouse in which my father had been born.

What I don't understand, he said, is how you band a royal tern.

Netting, I said. Fine netting. Or find the juveniles before they flee the nest, which they do, quickly.

I brought Smith into the kitchen. Even though our house was a mess the old juniper paneling made it smell clean.

The downstairs consisted of three rooms. Dad had taken out walls and combined the kitchen and living areas. On the countertops, cups brimmed with pens and cooking utensils. We'd piled old quilts on top of threadbare chairs and sofas for the cats and Dad's dog, Betsy, to nest in, dirty paws and all. Photographs were tucked into the dusty frames of older pictures. The doorway was lined with mud-caked boots and waders. Coon, fox, and rabbit skins were pinned to the paneling. Dad kept a bulletin board heavy with dried snakeskins, maps, and articles on the ivory-billed woodpecker.

He still believes they exist? Smith said excitedly.

Some days, I said. But most people know they're extinct. *I* know.

There are sightings, Smith said. Mostly Florida, right?

They're just seeing the pileated, I said. Or maybe a sapsucker. People catch sight of a big bird like that and they see what they want to see.

At that moment, Dad came in. As he opened the door, the maps and clippings on his bulletin board flapped wildly.

Who's this? he said.

Smith extended his hand.

Smith Jones, he said. Bird enthusiast.

If you like birds, Dad said, moving toward his computer, you'll love this video.

Dad had just discovered the Internet. He pulled up a clip that set the ardent mating displays of birds of paradise in New Guinea to Michael Jackson's "Billie Jean."

The birds, dripping in vibrant plumage, skated across branches, flicked their heads, and called like wild flutes to the heavens. Dad slapped his thighs and his laughter filled the house. His laugh was unmistakable, almost an affront. Smith smiled; he didn't look uncomfortable.

Want a beer? Dad asked.

Smith nodded.

As Smith brought the bottle to his mouth I noticed his full lips. I imagined them sliding down my neck, grazing the back of my hand. I pressed the cool bottle to my forehead. I had to laugh at myself, the way lust crowded my judgment. Still, I was lonely enough not to take a good-looking stranger for granted. It could be years before one appeared again.

That a spaniel? Smith asked, nodding at Betsy.

Something like that, my dad said. Gun-shy and made of God knows what mutts.

Eyes like a woman, Smith said, reaching down to scratch her chin.

Betsy shoved her tender brown nose into Dad's thigh. She rarely left his side, except on bird expeditions, when she was crated. She was a slave to her instinct—the spaniel in her needed to flush birds. The woman in her wanted to please my father. Her eyes were a piercing amber, knowing. Dad rubbed her ear, gently pulled a burr from her coat.

What's this? Smith asked, touching a black-and-white photo on Dad's bulletin board.

Broken-necked bear, Dad said. Fell from a tree slicked up with honey.

There are hundreds of bears in the swamp, I said. Go in for a few days and you'll see one, I promise.

Maybe ivory-billed woodpeckers, too, Smith said, raising his eyebrows.

It's possible, Dad said, his voice quiet and serious.

I shook my head. Not a chance, I said.

I've seen one, Dad said. Years ago, when I had been out in the swamp for three days. I had started to feel a part of it, then. I hadn't spoken to another human being in hours. I was ready for it, know what I'm saying?

Soon it was like listening to two men speak excitedly of buried treasure; their shared enthusiasm was evident. Smith and my father conceived a weeklong expedition in the swamp. If there was an ivory-billed, they would hear it, find it, and record it.

There's a reward, Smith said, scanning a site he'd pulled up online. Fifty thousand bucks.

Nothing short of three days in the heart of the swamp will do, Dad said.

While we're at it, I said, why don't we look for unicorns?

Get excited, Smith said. It could be the definitive canvas of the Great Dismal. We could know for sure.

We already do, I said. There's no question. They're gone.

It's possible, Smith said. Give us that.

It's not, I said.

Don't be a black cloud, honey, Dad said.

It always sucked to be the realist.

I put out olives, crackers, and a block of cheese for supper. Dad passed out a second round of beer.

Eventually Dad excused himself; he liked to read for an hour before going to bed. I dug out the Scrabble board and unfolded it on the floor.

You play? I asked.

I will, Smith said.

He sat cross-legged on the floor, his beer beside him. He cocked his head to study the board before laying down his letters. He wasn't clean-shaven; his whiskers were ash blond and gave him an innocent look.

I flipped on the radio; the silence was too provocative. Dad kept it on the oldies station—he loved Motown—but lately it had occurred to me that the men singing these songs, these songs Dad and everyone else had been listening to as long as I could remember—"I'll Be Around"; "Be Young, Be Foolish, Be Happy"; anything by Ben E. King—were dead or dying. These men could sing about love better than anyone, but now they were long past loving women, and their impotence depressed me.

"Bernadette" by the Four Tops was on. To be Bernadette, I thought. To be a muse, to inspire jealousy, to make a man shout into the microphone: *You're the soul of me*.

Another beer? I said, walking over to the refrigerator.

Please, Smith said.

There were interludes of mindless banter between plays. Smith inched closer to me. I noticed the strings tied to his wrist, the tan line on his arms revealed by short sleeves.

L-A-U-P-E-R, he spelled.

As in Cyndi, he said.

Not sure that counts, I said.

Where do you live? I asked. I'll pick you up in the morning to shop for provisions.

An unfinished neighborhood, he said. Builder put in all the

septic, cleared the lots, put up a clubhouse and a pool and built three spec homes, and then—boom—foreclosure.

Did you buy the house? I asked.

What do *you* think? he said, laughing. Squatter's rights.

I shook my head. I had no idea what this man was capable of, what his values were. Perhaps he'd known about the reward for an ivory-billed sighting, and that's why he was here. The swamp was as good a hope as any. My attraction to him was instantaneous, and I worried it was palpable.

He moved in close, as if he was going to kiss me. Perhaps he read the panic on my face, because he pulled away.

I went to school with the builder, he said, standing up. See you in the morning. Turn right two lights after the old post office and you'll see signs. There's only one inhabited house. You can't miss it.

I drove into Smith's abandoned neighborhood at nine. The sidewalks were overgrown and the swimming pool was green with algae and thick with debris. The clubhouse at the heart of the development was unfinished—the windowsills were unpainted; the screen door leaned against the stained stucco. Sewer pipes were stacked next to grass-choked *For Sale* signs on weedy empty lots. A sign advertising the development featured a toddler in sunglasses reclining on an inner tube, and a slogan: *Home is HERE.* It also said *Satan Lives* in red spray paint.

I couldn't see Smith when I pulled up to his house, so I idled the car and dug out an old tube of lip gloss. The car door opened while I was homed in on my face in the rearview.

It's not like the world can't tell what's hiding underneath,

Smith said, sliding into the passenger seat. And besides—you have nothing to hide.

I didn't see you coming, I said.

That, he said, pointing to the clubhouse as we drove out, is my command central. I put a minifridge and my radio in the office there. I don't cook, though—the oven isn't real. Just a plastic facade the builder put up when he ran out of money.

It's quiet here, I said.

I have my cats, he said. I let them hunt the place.

You like it? I asked.

No real expenses, he said, shrugging his shoulders. I got a car out back—no plates, though. Drive at my own risk. Got an old cow skull glued to the front. He laughed.

Do you have waders? I asked. You're gonna want something like that to keep the mud out of your pants in the swamp. And, you know, in case you surprise a snake. There *are* snakes.

We drove to the army/navy store. Dad has a tent you can borrow, I said, before going in.

Smith shopped quickly. He high-fived the seventy-year-old buzz-cut clerk and paid cash for a pair of cheap gaiters and insect repellent. We started the drive back to his house.

You know the elementary school? I said.

The empty one?

Dad owns it. Got it for a thousand bucks, I said. It's beautiful inside. Wanna see it?

We parked in the untended lot, now raised and broken by tree roots. My heart raced as I unlocked the enormous double doors. Smith ran his fingers down the marble stone with the date the school was built: 1917.

The sun wasn't on the building yet and the brick walls kept

the place cool. Our voices bounced off of wooden floors the color of honey, floors scarred and gashed by hundreds of small shoes, sliding desks.

Smith grabbed my wrist and pulled me into a dark classroom where the ceiling tiles heaved with moisture and outdated maps curled against a chalkboard.

After years alone and long stretches of celibacy, I'd forgotten how it felt to be flipped on like a light, to try to concentrate when your blood and heart were screaming inside you.

I leaned against the cinder-block wall. Smith put one hand above my head and closed in on my face. I hadn't been touched this way in years.

I gave him my mouth and tilted my head back to keep the hot tears in my eyes from spilling down my face. I wanted to keep them to myself. I worried they came from something awful, like gratitude.

The next morning, Smith met us at dawn. He was all arms and legs and his pack rattled when he walked—too many useless carabiners dangling from straps and zippers. I found my skepticism of Smith renewed, despite our strong attraction. What did he want from me? I thought. From us?

Let's bring that old dog of yours, he said to Dad. I'll hold her leash if you need to approach any birds.

She *does* like adventure, Dad said. And it's not too hot. I've got a packable water bowl.

Dad was always looking for an excuse to have Betsy along. She rode in the back of the pickup, which we left at the head of an old logging road a mile into the swamp.

The spring sun was already warm as we threw on our packs, which were stuffed with sleeping bags, tents, food, and a few changes of clothes.

Dad, I said. Can I dab sunscreen on your nose?

He closed his eyes like a relenting child and kept talking while I smeared lotion across his face. His skin was porous and age spots were beginning to form on his forehead.

I can't help but be excited, he said.

The trail was sandy and flat and the tree cover was thick; the thin trunks of young pines and oaks arced over our heads. The farther we went in, the more my ears grew attuned to birdsong. Dad kept a water bottle in one hand and led the procession with a fast pace, which made him wheeze. His excitement and hope began to nag at me. I didn't want to see him let down.

Smith handed me a bag of homemade trail mix.

The good kind, he said. Minimarshmallows, chocolate, peanuts, and dried cherries. Every few steps he tossed a peanut to Betsy, who had left my father's side and now followed Smith with food-driven devotion.

Who is this man? I wondered. Where had he come from?

Where'd you go to school? I asked.

Middlebury, he said. For two years. Took some biology.

We kept walking. I could smell my hot skin. My pack was too heavy, but I wasn't going to admit to such a novice mistake.

The male ivory-billed, Dad said, has a black chin and a red crest. Juveniles and females have a black crest, but the bill is chalk white. The call sounds like a horn.

Smith turned to smile at me over his pack. A navy bandana covered his wild hair. I felt guilty sharing a secret with him, that my father was unaware of what had taken place between us.

Smith stopped, midtrail, and put his hand on my father's shoulder. He placed his finger to his lips and cupped his ear.

Listen, he said. From over there.

Dad paused.

It must be a double drum, Dad said, shaking his head. That's a single. Not the one.

I glared at Smith.

Look, Dad said. It's probably not going to happen, and if it does happen, it won't happen this soon.

He trudged on, a little heavier, a little more tired. After a few hours Dad's neck was drenched in sweat and he wiped his forehead often.

Can I carry your camera for you? I asked Dad.

Did you bring the woodpecker call? he asked.

I nodded. We walked on, hot and hungry. I was ready for a break, but I'd go as long and as far as Dad wanted.

Don't get his hopes up, I whispered to Smith. This might be fun for you, but it means something to him.

Smith looked like I'd sucker-punched him.

Sorry, he said.

It was just after six when we settled in to camp. We found a small clearing, the site of an old logging camp. Its remains, mostly rusted tin roofs, lay in overgrown heaps in the woods beyond the tree line. The maple and swamp gum around us were choked with smilax. The cicadas were humming and the evening sky was still blue as we threw up three tents. I could hear the frogs tuning up; we were just north of Lake Drummond, near the old lumber canal. Dad opened his tent for Betsy, but she remained with Smith, who tossed sticks into the woods for her to chase.

I was tired and a blister was forming on the back of my right heel. While Dad started a fire to keep bugs away, I set up the camp stove and heated water for tea. I unwrapped the sweet potatoes I'd baked earlier and mixed them with roasted garlic and black beans and heated them in a skillet over the stove.

After eating, Dad thumped his chest and squirmed.

Feel okay? I asked.

Heartburn, he said. Just need some water.

Smith sat quietly and stared at the fire. For a few minutes the flames held us like a magnet, a false sun. It was as if we were early hominids or starved settlers, fugitives pausing to rest.

Come help me, I said, touching Smith's arm and handing him the discarded tinfoil from supper. I led him a few yards away from camp. Are you mad? I whispered as we tied up our food in bear bags. I didn't mean to snap at you earlier.

Nah, he said. I get it. You're protecting him.

Throw this line over the tree limb, I said, handing him a rope with a sack of rocks on one end.

Dad, who was now nothing but a silhouette in front of the fire, choked a stick with his hands and practiced his putting stance. He sent clumps of pine straw flying with imaginary golf balls.

I read somewhere, Smith said, that they've found the ivory-billed in Arkansas. Maybe we could head down there sometime.

But I'd stopped listening. I was rushing toward Dad, who had crumpled and lay heaving on the ground. He clutched his chest and shoulder and tried to sit up. Betsy lay down beside him.

Breathe, I said, coaxing him to lie back down on the ground. Breathe, Dad.

Even as I tried to calm my father, I could feel panic overtake me. I couldn't let Dad die out here. I had to be rational, make the right decisions.

Elevate his head, I shouted to Smith, who stood behind me, as if waiting for instruction.

Smith dropped to the ground and put Dad's head in his lap.

Do you have aspirin? I asked.

Dad shook his head. Smith, too.

Don't worry, I said, though I felt as if someone had hit my skull with a blunt shovel.

We have to get him out, I said to Smith. I think he's had a heart attack. Or a stroke. I don't know.

You run, I said. Grab a flashlight and my phone and run until you have service. Tell them we are roughly one half mile from the place where the groomed trail becomes a footpath near the old logging camp.

Smith stood up. He looked drunk, tired, shocked.

Go, dammit!

I hated myself then, for letting a stranger into our life, for having to trust this stranger to save my father. Smith sprinted into the woods. Betsy hesitated, then followed him.

I sat Indian-style on the sandy soil next to the fire and cupped Dad's head, bringing it gently into my lap. I massaged his temples and jawline.

You're going to be okay, I said. You have to believe that.

I'm sorry, he said. His voice was small and strained.

Don't talk, I said, trying to sound calm. Just rest. Rest and breathe.

When you camp in the swamp at night, you know there are bears. There are hundreds, and they smell you, and they're curious.

Everything sounds large at night—raccoons, squirrels, a startled deer.

But nothing was as fierce and wild as me. I was furiously alive.

Dad told me once that he knew how to do many things—rig a trap for a prize mink, field dress and butcher a buck, navigate by the Southern Cross, but when I was born he didn't know how to feed or burp me. Your diapers were in a knot, he said, or sliding down your legs. I forgot to brush your hair. I couldn't keep your face clean. Your mother was dead. Those were hard times.

He was sorry, but I wasn't. I couldn't picture that grieving, incompetent father. I remembered the stacks of bird books, flash cards, and faded Audubon prints. Stories of him looking for Carolina parakeets as a boy, begging his father to stop logging, hoping he'd still find a viable pair in the swamp.

Remember, he'd tell me. Birds *need* dead trees for nesting and foraging.

What I never told Smith was that Dad had left years earlier for Arkansas at the news of a possible discovery of the ivory-billed. He'd driven his pickup to the protected tract and quietly trespassed for two weeks, tape recorder in hand. For most of his life, he'd been desperate to believe in the bird's existence.

Your mother believed, too, he'd said.

I tried to find my mother in my dreams. In college, when I got high, I'd sit on the roof of my dorm with my eyes closed and search for pieces of her inside myself. I figured that the parts of me I didn't understand—those I couldn't trace to the bearded man knee-deep in juniper water back home—were her. My perfectionism, my temper, my love of heat—and, as my father reminded me, the way I sang to myself—off-key, pitchless, hopeful.

I don't like thinking about those four hours in the pitch-black swamp night. The fear in my gut, Dad's arrhythmic breathing, the sounds of snapping limbs and rustling leaves. Suggestions.

An emergency squad rode into the swamp on two ATVs. I heard the sounds of their machines and voices and as soon as I saw their lights, I cried. They loaded Dad onto a stretcher but didn't have room for me, so I left our gear in the middle of the woods and jogged after the ATVs with my flashlight. The sound of the ATVs quickly disappeared and I found myself running, tripping over tree roots, tears mingling with the sweat on my face, sand in my teeth, the rocks hard underneath my boots.

As the swamp opened up to the logging road, and the logging road opened up to the highway, I looked for Smith and Betsy, but I was alone.

I brought Dad home from the hospital two days after the heart attack; he was to rest before the quadruple bypass his doctors had scheduled. I hadn't heard from Smith after sending him into the woods, but when we arrived home, Betsy was tethered to the front porch, a bowl of water at her feet. She quivered and cried until I unleashed her. She put her paws on Dad's knees, desperate for acknowledgment.

I'd been home that morning preparing for Dad's arrival. Smith had apparently dropped Betsy off while I was gone. Perhaps he'd been watching the house or seen my car. I hoped he wasn't avoiding me.

That Smith fellow tried to run off with my woman, Dad said, scratching Betsy's head.

Easy, Dad, I said. Let me get you inside. I guided him to his bedroom and helped him onto the bed.

Will you keep the business up, Dad asked, until I can get back to work?

Of course, I said.

Betsy claimed a spot next to him, circling until she found the place where she could rest her chin on his knee. I dragged the television into his room, but he didn't want it on.

Can you make me a fruit salad? he asked. And a fried egg sandwich?

I nodded. That afternoon, I nailed a platform underneath Dad's bedroom window where I could spread birdseed.

Eventually, Dad said, I should get out of your way, go somewhere with railed showers.

You're staying here, I said. You're going to be as good as new.

New was never all that good, he said.

You'll be *fine,* I said.

Despite our verbal optimism, we felt our lives turning. We felt the beginning of something sad.

Dad shook the newspaper—a habitual motion—as I placed a dinner tray over his lap. He pointed at the obituaries: It's my generation's time, he said. Natural progression.

Don't rush, I said.

The next morning, we quietly ate breakfast on the front porch. Dad looked out over the property.

There's crabgrass on my course, Dad said, surveying his green.

Dad reread biographies on Jefferson and Roosevelt and tried his hand at the *New York Times* crossword puzzle. His complexion was sallow and he moved stiffly.

I want to be outside, he said after two days. He looked out the window like a sad dog.

Give it time, I said. But part of me felt that depriving him of the outdoors—the sulfur smell of the swamp air, his putting green, the trails he walked daily behind our house—was akin to starvation.

The next morning, I made him breakfast and opened his windows. Then I walked down our gravel driveway to organize the latest team of bird-watchers and drive them into the swamp. I emulated the speeches I'd heard from Dad: *Try to become part of the forest. Be patient and humble. Find the dead trees.* He had a way of exciting our customers; I felt condescending.

The night before, I'd dreamed that Smith had climbed into my bed while I was sleeping. It could happen; we never locked the doors, no one in our town did. At first, the idea of him in the house at night was petrifying, but the imagined trespass only underscored his air of mystery.

I wanted to lay eyes on him, thank him for what he'd done for Dad.

But maybe Smith had no intention of coming back. He had the inherent toughness a thing must possess to survive on its own. Perhaps I was romanticizing him because he was my only option, the one piece of luck I'd brushed up against in this lonely place. You don't know him, I reminded myself. You don't know the ways he'd change your life.

After dropping the bird-watchers off at the swamp, I went to fill Dad's truck with gas. The station attendant was holding court behind the counter.

You could take each one of these small Carolina towns, the man said, these towns without stoplights and no tax base and no real post office to speak of, turn 'em upside down, and shake 'em. All sorts of characters would fall out. Nazi war criminals in Burgaw. Hoffa in Wilson. Earhart in Duck. At least when I was a boy.

I put a ten-dollar bill on the counter and let the screen door slam shut behind me. Outside, I took a deep breath. I could hear the man laughing, decades of tar in his dark lungs. *What better place to hide?*

Across the street: a tobacco warehouse, lumber supply company, and garden center. Bulldozers moving earth for a shopping mall. In a few months, men would come here for hunting licenses. I wouldn't leave the house without an orange cap. I'd tie orange ribbons to Betsy's collar, keep the cat inside. The smell of woodsmoke would fill the town. Pickup trucks would roll by, still-warm deer piled in truck beds like trophies.

The only ivory-billed woodpeckers I'd ever seen were stuffed and mounted on dry branches. I wondered, if he could go back to that day in the swamp, would Dad have put a bullet in the bird's heart to prove he'd seen it? To watch it longer, watch the life fall out of it?

For thirty years, he'd wanted to know for sure that what he saw was the real thing.

Days after seeing Smith for the last time, I knew I was waiting for someone I didn't understand. Maybe I'd spend the rest of my life waiting, another refugee made into myth by the swamp. Maybe it was for the best; some people and places are better left unchanged.

The night before his surgery, Dad went to bed early. I cleaned the kitchen and stared at his closed door. I missed him. Already. I walked down the hall and knocked.

Can I come in? I asked.

He was propped on his pillows, Betsy sleeping against his feet. She looked up as I entered. His television was not on; there was no book in his hands. He'd placed a picture of my mother on his nightstand. I opened a window.

For the morning, I said. So you can hear them sing.

He didn't speak, but reached for my hand.

The air was too warm, but we were used to it. The crickets were loud and I let their noise chip away at my worries. I rubbed my father's rough hand with my thumb.

I did see one, he said. Once. I'm positive. It was the real thing. A bill the color of chalk.

Somewhere in the distance, a train ran over the old swamp tracks, tracks Dad had followed in and out of the swamp as a boy, tracks he'd known before he fell in love, before he spent two years grading our backyard into a golfing green.

He'd seen the last wild things, the early hunting cabins, the last virgin timber, and maybe even the last living ivory-billed. He'd seen the last great bucks, the last great hunters, the skin-laden trappers emerging from the woods at dawn smelling of sulfur and musk.

His family had made it through the Depression selling mink; I'd once watched Dad carefully tug the mangled body of one from a chicken-wire fence, desperate to save the skin. He still ate the chickweed and creasy greens that had been self-seeding in the backyard since his father's time. Dad's old-school frugality was harsh, endearing, maybe a lost art.

Will you put socks on the bed, he said, in case I get cold?

The rhythm of the crickets outside muffled traffic, and every now and then the clear note of a jay cut through the air like a circular saw. Maybe it wasn't the same as it had been when I was a child, but the swamp remained a wild place, wild enough to hide whatever wanted to be hidden.

You had a good childhood here, he said.

It was the beginning of a good-bye that I didn't want to hear. Even if he made it through the surgery, he'd be a different man. Older. More careful.

I could smell the swamp rose, harlot pink and fragrant in the hot night. Dry magnolia leaves scratched against the vinyl siding of the house. Dad relaxed into his pillow. Betsy fell asleep, no longer on guard.

For minutes, maybe an hour, I held his hand, and I think he slept.

I wished for things to stay the same. I wished for stillness everywhere, but I opened up the rest of the bedroom windows and let the world in.

Saving Face

Lila had two things to do that day: have dinner with her fiancé, Clay, and evaluate the working farm at Sandhill Prison. She put on her work boots, the steel-toed ones with worn and hay-packed heels, stuffed a change of clothes into a bag, and threw a box of shoulder-length gloves into the back of her pickup.

After her work at the prison was done, she'd join Clay in a diner car some urbanite had turned into a second-rate wine bar. She'd put the wedding on hold a year ago; now he wanted to discuss the future, reach a final decision. Because she didn't know what she wanted, she was dreading the meal the way she dreaded obligatory Sundays at church with her mother, or the therapy sessions she'd started recently. But she packed a black dress and the only tube of lipstick she owned.

Lila drove the flat, pine-shadowed highway toward the correctional center. She kept her windows down and public radio on.

Most buildings in this part of town were churches or sad municipal structures, some vacant, some half used, mildewed, ugly, and too expensive to fix.

It's the kind of year you keep your old shoes, she thought, passing a man in a lawn chair on the side of the road who'd been begging as long as she could remember. His sign said: *Vietnam Vet. 1 Wife, 2 Kids, 3 Skinny Cats. Need Food and Bud Light*. Betcha can't hit me with a quarter! he shouted at the passing cars, a cigarette between his teeth.

Lines were long at the dollar hot dog stand downtown, while tables at Brodie's Italian Bistro sat empty. Her mother was cutting coupons again. Her father had offered her a spare bedroom in her childhood home in case she wanted to drop her lease, but her veterinary practice was breaking even, and she valued her independence.

Lila had an apartment downtown over a bakery. Every night her three cats climbed into bed with her, kneading her arms, legs, and chest. They were not demanding companions. They settled into the nooks of her knees and at her feet. The white noise of their purring sent her to sleep feeling less alone.

It was summer, but Christmas decorations still hung from the lampposts surrounding Hoke County City Hall—no one wanted to pay to have them taken down. The green tinsel had faded in the sun and birds had nested in the hollowed-out candy canes.

Tacky, her mother said, but sooner or later you stop noticing.

That's life in Raeford, Lila said.

Lila drove her pickup past the barbed-wire fence line and the brick prison and down a dirt road toward the prison farmhouse. In recent years someone had tacked vinyl siding to the house. The facade was dented and yellowed by the dry dirt that rose from the road. Sorry-looking air-conditioning units sagged in the windows.

Sandhill Prison had been many things. The Tuberculosis Sanitarium for Negroes. The Mary Hobgood Training Center. Now it was a low-security prison with a working farm. The administration was thinking of closing the farm and selling the land and had called Lila in to evaluate the health of the livestock. Lila checked her notepad: seventy jersey cows, five pigs, and one horse.

We don't need any bleeding hearts, the warden had said. Just a real good evaluation of health. In other words, how many of these things can we sell?

Lila slammed her truck door shut and walked to the farmhouse. She knew the farm well; she'd been called out for cattle vaccinations and difficult births over the years. She looked backward, nervous. Prisoners who worked the farm roamed the land freely. She could see a handful in their orange jumpsuits raking through the compost pile in the distance.

Hey, Doc, the warden said, sticking out his hand. He wore pressed khakis and a short-sleeved button-up.

She hated the way people looked at her face, like they were sorry.

The wolf hybrid had taken most of her upper lip. He'd roused from his anesthetic haze earlier than expected as Lila was pulling quills from his muzzle. It had not hurt at first; the shock had delayed the pain. It was two in the morning and she was the only one in the surgical suite. She remembered blood on the mounted telephone as she dialed for help.

After a year of plastic surgeries, two seams remained where grafts had been placed underneath her nose. A cosmetic surgeon had tattooed a rose-colored line where the edge of her upper lip once appeared.

You were so beautiful, her mother had said in the hospital, giving Lila milk through a straw that leaned against the corner of her broken mouth.

Her mother had been reluctant to hand her a mirror in the days that followed.

I want to see, Lila said.

A few days will make all the difference, her mother said, falsely cheerful, turning away to riffle aimlessly in her overnight bag.

Give me a mirror, Lila said, gripping her mother's arm.

And what Lila saw she did not accept, not at first. The sight of her blue and inflated face took her breath away and terrified her, the suture creeping across her mouth like a strange vine. The swelling and bruising hid a reality, she knew. She tried to demolish the hope that crept up, the banal optimism that promised she could return to life as a pretty girl. The fresh injury was obvious, but in time it would heal and then the scarring would beg the question: *What happened to you?*

Though he waited in the hospital for three days, Lila would not let Clay into the room after the accident. He was a firefighter and carpenter who made custom cabinets from reclaimed wood. Lila liked the way he told stories and the breakfasts he made on the weekends—French toast and scrambled eggs he got from the farm down the road from the firehouse. They'd known each other in high school and gotten reacquainted when Lila came back home after veterinary school—her mother had given him Lila's number in the wine aisle of the grocery store.

Tell him he can go, she scribbled, handing a notepad to her mother in the hospital room. He's not obligated to stick around.

He wants to see you, her mother had said, taking her hand.

I don't want to be seen, Lila wrote.

You're due to be married, Lila's mom said. In four weeks.

Days later, despite her mother's and Clay's protests, Lila canceled the reservation at their reception site, called off the caterer and the florist. Someone else could have the peonies and white roses, she thought.

Clay had called constantly, and while she would talk to him, she would not permit him to see her. Eventually he resorted to waiting in his truck outside of her parents' house until she finally let him see her face, two weeks after the accident, when the stitches had come out and the initial swelling was down.

Please, he said, taking her arm in her parents' living room. This doesn't matter.

It matters to me, she'd said, turning away. I'm not the person you fell in love with.

He'd spent the past months trying to convince her that nothing had changed. But she worried he was softhearted and sympathetic, not sincerely attracted to her. She'd figured he would end things after she put the wedding on hold, but he hadn't.

We can take it slow, Clay had said. I don't mind waiting.

Recently, he'd grown more impatient, lamenting the minimal physical contact Lila permitted.

I just want to be close to you again, he'd said a few days before requesting the dinner date.

I know I owe you that, she'd said. And it's not that I don't want it. I just can't do it; I can't stand the thought of not being beautiful to you.

You are—

Don't say something you don't mean, she said.

Lila had practiced faces in the mirror for months after the accident. How to stand at an angle. How to show her best side in a photograph. How her mouth looked when she talked, took a drink. She began wearing nice slacks and lost weight. She blew her hair straight in the mornings.

But still she felt she was wasting time. Even with expensive makeup she could not cover the scars above her mouth. The more time she spent on her appearance, the more frustrated she felt. Why invest time in something so damaged?

Clay constantly reassured her that she was beautiful, but she didn't believe him. Wouldn't it just be easier to start from scratch? she thought. Begin again with someone who'd never seen her before the accident? Then there would be no doubt about the attraction; it was the doubt she hated.

Once you'd been a pretty girl, Lila thought, you had to drag around your clubfooted vanity for the rest of your life, watch it wane and suffer. She remembered the way men had looked at her in the past, and knew they would never do so the same way again. She'd had male professors who had—she was almost sure of it—inflated her grades in veterinary school. The cashier at the country store used to give her free coffee in the morning, wave her through the line with a wink. He still waved her through, but she suspected his generosity now came from pity.

She'd never obsessed over her looks; she'd never had to. She was naturally pretty and had never worn much makeup or watched what she ate or taken a long time to get ready. But now that her face was altered, she felt she was walking through life relying on a different set of tools. She'd have to depend on her smarts, she thought, her own resourcefulness. She'd always been good at her job, but now she worked longer and harder. Part of her had always assumed she'd live a life in a partnership, with a dual income to fall back on; now, even with Clay insisting things were fine, she began to calculate the savings she'd need to buy a house and reach retirement on her own. Her self-confidence was as crippled as her face.

Since the attack, Lila had made one rule: Don't get close to *anything*.

There was a day in the airport she remembered. She'd seen two young girls standing behind a deaf woman and her mother. The deaf woman had a twitch. The girls made garish, frantic signs at each other and jerked their shoulders to their ears behind the woman's back. At the time, she'd done nothing. Now Lila wanted to go back to that day and grab the girls by their collars. But every time she pictured bringing her face close to theirs, her imagination stopped cold.

I worry the inmates are enjoying themselves, the warden said, leading Lila to the barn.

This is prison, he said. Not 4-H club. The board of directors felt a working farm would be part of rehabilitation—get these guys ready for the working world. But it's a money pit. Too easy on the prisoners, too much free time.

Lila had a stethoscope around her neck and a canvas bag slung over her shoulder. It was filled with calipers, vaccines, palpation sleeves, dewormers, euthanasia solution, lube. She kept a penlight clipped to her pants pocket.

Twenty-two hundred and fifty gallons of milk a week, an

inmate in the entrance of the barn said, loosening the twine around a bale of hay.

This is Rom, the administrator said, holding his hand out as if he were showing her through a door. Been with us for years.

Romulus Candle, the inmate said, sticking out his hand. His skin was calloused and he had a long, white beard, which he'd braided down to his sternum. His eyebrows were wild and curled. Lila could see the pores in his nose when she shook his hand.

Seven hundred and fifty gallons of yogurt, he continued, pointing at a pressurized silver vat.

Then he opened a stall door and pressed his face to the cheek of a chestnut-colored horse.

Ah, Debra, he said, breathing her in.

Rom took his pointer finger and ran it underneath the horse's lip and across the gum line.

She likes this, he said, and Lila could tell that he was right. The mare flared her lips, then nosed Rom's shoulder.

Rom will show you the place, the warden said. Take as long as you need—I'll go over the results with you later.

He disappeared. Lila could see dust falling in the strips of light that shone between the barn siding. She could smell the slightly sweet aroma of hay.

We gotta get this place making money, Rom said, turning to Lila, his voice suddenly desperate. We can't shut it down. We can't sell.

Ever think of suggesting an in-house butchering operation? Lila asked.

What kind of people do you think we are? Romulus said, raising his eyebrows.

Lila ignored him and began making notes; later she'd have

to calculate average milk production ratios, average age of livestock, levels of concentrate in the feed.

Let's have a look at the jerseys, she said, striking out of the barn and walking toward the cattle grazing in a small pasture.

When I get out of here, Romulus said, I'm going to start a business. You see, Raeford's just crawling with kudzu. Every place that's not a place, as far as I'm concerned, is crawling with kudzu.

Pick it up, Lila said, waving at Romulus to keep pace with her. The ground was dry and hard under her work boots. They approached a series of old outbuildings next to the pasture.

What I'm going to do is this, Romulus said, as he jogged to catch up with her. I'm going to start a kudzu clearing service. Cows'll eat kudzu faster than anything. And I'll have a pack of border collies that'll keep 'em in line and off the road.

Crazy, she thought.

Lila could see the sweet, empty eyes of the jerseys huddling near the trough. Hair curled over their foreheads like small toupees. Their ears hung to the side, clipped with yellow plastic tags. She would kick their teats, test for mastitis and infection, examine the piles of feces on the ground, but she had a feeling none of this data would matter in the end. Soon they'd be three hundred pounds of boneless meat apiece.

Suddenly Romulus grabbed her arm. His fingernails were long and pinched her skin. Her pulse quickened and she felt for the pocketknife she kept in her pants pocket.

I need to show you something, he said, shoving her into a shed.

Lila's darkest moments had occurred when she was alone after the accident. She lay in bed, her apartment quiet, the street below vacant after business hours. Her face throbbed, the healing skin itched, and the suture site burned. When she wanted to punish herself, she didn't take her pain medication. She wanted to feel the mistake, get to know it.

I'm ugly, she thought, and stupid.

She split into two those nights, looking upon herself with someone else's cruel eyes.

She pictured her failure, the important one: the wolf-hybrid's large body draped across the metal table, his pink tongue riddled with porcupine needles, the bright surgical light shining onto his thick coat. She thought she had time, that she'd administered enough anesthetic. But maybe she hadn't reached the dog's anesthetic plane, or maybe he'd metabolized the sedative differently than expected.

Damn the extra time I took, she thought. She regretted the care with which she'd tugged the quills from the dog's lips—the same lips that opened to reveal brutal teeth, the teeth that had torn into her face with an almost feral abandon as the dog unexpectedly came to.

I was so casual, she thought. I didn't protect myself.

She'd treated the dog with tenderness. What did I expect in return? she wondered. Gratitude?

There were no promises, no obligations between living things, she thought. Not even humans. Just raw need hidden by a game of make-believe.

Treat yourself with compassion, her therapist had said as she packed to leave the hospital.

But the most tangible feeling for Lila was anger, anger at herself for misjudging an animal, anger at Clay for making it hard, for constantly prodding her from the solitude in which she found safety.

Lila's eyes adjusted to the dark shed. Small patches of light fell on the hay. If she'd had hackles, they would have been up. Adrenaline shot from one end of her body to the other.

Let go, she said, shaking off Romulus's grip.

Look, he said, gesturing to the corner of the shed.

Lila saw a calf on the ground, a few weeks old at most. Its back end was atrophied.

What's this about? Lila said. She tried to convince herself she was in control. Still, she was cautious and backed farther away from Romulus.

Rom took a handkerchief from his jumpsuit pocket and blew his nose.

I kept her a secret, he said, nodding at the calf. I been bottle-feeding her all along.

He got down on the ground. The calf nuzzled him.

I need you to take this one with you when you leave today, he said, turning to Lila with pleading eyes. Please.

In bed at night, Lila often thought of the times she'd broken someone's heart. She'd kissed Paul Devaney in high school but didn't let him go up her dress. She refused to dance with Rahul Kanwar at prom. In college she had given men wrong numbers when they asked her out. She'd cheated on her boyfriend in veterinary school with a swine professor.

Until the accident, she'd always been good to Clay. He was strong and honest and they had fun together.

She missed falling asleep on his slick chest on humid nights with the bedroom windows open. She missed canoeing the Tar River, visiting his family, eating his mother's deep-fried cooking and receiving her handmade birthday cards in the mail. She missed hitching rides in the fire truck, sanding cabinets at two a.m. before a big order was due, drinking wine and laughing at one of Clay's stories.

One night he'd been telling Lila about visiting his grandmother in the trailer park and going to Myrtle Beach with his brother. Then he paused and walked across the shop floor, picked her up, and placed her on top of the cabinets they were working on. She felt the sawdust on the side of her face and in her hair as he pulled her legs open and slid her to the edge of the cabinets.

What if we break them? she'd said, laughing.

I trust my craftsmanship, he said. Plus, it's worth it.

The first night in the hospital after the accident, Lila had pictured herself lying across those cabinets again, Clay hovering over her and coming up to kiss her mangled mouth. It made her sick.

I work hard, Romulus said. I been here years mending fences, planting soybeans. I get up and milk at five in the morning.

Romulus pressed his forehead to the space between the calf's eyes.

I have to do my job, Lila said, looking away.

I'll pay you, he said, when I get out. I'll make it up to you, take care of the bills, the feed. I will.

And you get out when? Lila asked.

The calf stretched its front legs and rested its nose on a pair of mud-caked hooves.

I don't know, Romulus said softly.

Lila knew what would happen to the farm. The land would be sold, the animals put on the open market. Romulus's calf would die on its own within the month.

I have my professional credibility left, she said to herself. That is how I walk into goddamn places like this with my head held up. I can't compromise.

Lila left Romulus on the ground with the calf. The calf sucked at Rom's thumb while he brushed the mud from her coat. She went outside, bent over to touch her toes, and raised her arms to the sun, exhaling loudly. She tried to calm herself, her body still electrified from Romulus forcing her into the shed. She hated looking at the calf, hated the way her profession thrust her into ethical dilemmas on a daily basis.

This is not a difficult decision, she reminded herself. The calf is suffering.

One of the hardest parts of her job was learning to trust her rational self, taming the compassion that had led her to become a veterinarian in the first place.

Part of her hated the thing she was about to do, the same way part of her hated getting up in the morning, brushing her teeth and washing her face, spending time with her reflection, looking at Clay's letters, wondering what life would be like if she'd only given the wolf-hybrid more anesthetic. But life in Raeford was like that. Washed-out. Full of regret. People in old shoes, tough jobs. Lila reached in her bag for a syringe. Everyone was sorry about things. They were sorry about the tinsel fading on the lampposts. They were sorry about the empty tables at Brodie's downtown. They were sorry about her face. People were sorry. And they'd keep on being sorry and watching lives fall apart at close range.

Lila walked back into the shed. Romulus peeled himself from the calf's body, where he'd draped himself like a shroud.

I'm sorry, she said, her voice cold and practical. We need to do what's right for the calf. She's in pain.

I'm afraid I can't let you, Romulus said.

He stood up. He held something in his hand. Her knife.

She felt as if someone had thrown a bucket of cold water over her head. She began to back up but was disoriented.

Stay right there, he said evenly. She stopped moving. Her heart raced. She made a mental note of all the doors and windows in the shed, looked around for something she could use to defend herself.

His black eyes studied hers. He was breathing hard, but there was a calmness about him. He was sure of himself.

Lila imagined another scar on her face, imagined the tip of the knife cutting into her patchwork skin. Did it matter? It did. There was always more to lose.

Romulus stepped toward her. A swath of light landed on his orange jumpsuit.

I don't want to fight you on this, Lila said, trying hard to project a sense of authority she did not feel. I just want to do the right thing.

I never loved anything this way, Romulus said.

He brought the knife in front of his body. Lila felt a surge of energy and anticipation.

I'm serious, he said.

Lila did not doubt him. She listened for other inmates, the sound of the warden coming back. Nothing. She'd have to reason with him; she had no choice.

The calf looked up at them with big eyes.

Romulus ran a hand over his hair and took a deep breath.

Here's what I'm going to do, Lila said evenly. I'm going to fill this syringe and leave it for you.

No, Romulus said.

There's nothing else I can do here, Lila said. You have to trust me.

Tears began to well in Romulus's black eyes.

She placed the syringe on an overturned milk crate.

Put it in her neck, she said, pointing to a spot on her own.

Romulus dropped the knife into the hay. His body sagged. He picked up the syringe.

For a moment, Lila wondered if she should watch, make sure Romulus did the job. But she turned around and ran as fast as she could back to the farmhouse, pausing a moment to grab her bag. She decided that she wouldn't speak of the incident, that she was tired of people worrying, feeling sorry for her.

Lila thought of Romulus in the shed with the calf. He'll do the right thing, she told herself. People almost always do.

Lila pulled out of the prison gates, her body still humming with adrenaline. She didn't have enough time to go home before meeting Clay at the wine bar in town, so she pulled the truck over on the side of the road near the old Edgerton place. The road was empty and she couldn't see anyone around, so she got out of the car and opened the passenger-side door, which faced the tree line.

Lila stepped out of her boots and work pants and for a second exposed the naked body she was still proud of. She slipped the black dress over her head, the soft fabric sliding down her back and falling into place.

She used the passenger-side mirror to do her lipstick, careful to cover the pink, tattooed lines where the swollen flesh of her lip used to end.

To her right, wild turkeys ran through barren fields, fields that once grew cotton and tobacco, fields that someone was too poor or too old to tend. She wiped the lipstick from her teeth.

Maybe tonight would be different. Maybe Clay would take her hand and she'd let him. Maybe, after wine, they'd eat a big meal at Brodie's, tip like movie stars.

But what kind of woman found a happy ending in Raeford? Lila drove the deserted country road toward the dying town she called home. She imagined Clay's strong hands on her body again and wished she was more beautiful than proud.

Yesterday's Whales

I've been told self-righteous people always have it coming, that when you profess to understand the universe, the universe conspires against you. It gathers and strengthens and thunders down upon you like a biblical storm. It buries your face in humble pie and licks the cream from your nose because when the universe hates you, it *really* hates you.

What? Malachi shouted through the door in a panicked voice. That's impossible.

I burst out of the bathroom and wagged the positive pregnancy test wand in front of his face.

Immaculate conception is out, I said. God and I aren't on good enough terms.

My heart was pounding and my voice was too loud. What I wanted to do was sleep and talk about this another time, a time when I had a better idea of how I felt, how I would handle the news. Though I suspected we were both looking for our moral footing, we jumped into the conversation, eyes afire.

This is a really big deal, Malachi said, sitting down on the bench we kept in the kitchen. He put his face in his hands, then peeked out like a sheepish toddler. This is just—

What? I said. You think that because you're the East Coast's predominant voluntary extermination proponent that we're magically infertile? Because you tell other people they shouldn't have children you—

There's a clinic downtown, he said, nodding his head as if he was agreeing with himself. I know the guy that runs it. Sam Wise. He was at last week's conference. I'll call—

We're not even going to talk about it? I said, moving closer to him. We're not even going to give it the weight we give a decision about what we're going to have for dinner? We just spent fifteen minutes in front of the produce section at the market. We just tested our peaches for bruises. We debated what type of olives—

I have strong beliefs, he said. *You* have strong beliefs. Your decisions are hormone-driven right now, and I understand—

You do *not* understand, I said, gripping the countertop and closing my eyes.

Malachi began backing away to the French doors that opened onto the slate patio, where he was grilling eggplant steaks. He was a vegetarian epicure who snuck bites of bacon out of salads and quiches when he thought I wasn't looking. His senior year at Yale, he'd started a nonprofit he called Enough with Us, or EWU—an earnest throwback to Wordsworth's poem "The World Is Too Much with Us." In the eight years since, he'd put out two books and worn a path along the liberal college and Unitarian lecture circuit, advocating the end of humankind, sacrificing the human race to let nature reclaim the earth.

I was proud of him. I thought he was right. I'd grown up under two biology enthusiasts in rural Maine, where people were scarce and wilderness still had an edge. I wanted nature to win, too.

Malachi dreamt of thick forests and megafauna consuming urban landscapes, nothing but our plastics and waste scarring the earth centuries after our disappearance. He pinned lush pictures of Borneo to our bedroom walls, cliffs with rivulets of water spilling down, visions of earth with no evidence of man's hand.

Five years ago, I met Malachi at a vegan cooking class on P Street. We made a savory vegetable pot pie and went out for wine afterward. We moved in together within a year. He knew a lot about food, poetry, music, and politics, and I introduced him to the outdoors—camping, hiking, foraging. On weekends we cooked for friends, volunteered at events for the local animal shelter, saw live music, and took long walks in Rock Creek Park.

In our house, the word *breeding* was said with the same vitriol used when mentioning Republicans, Tim Tebow, and pit bull fight clubs. Women churning out multiples were breeders, and when they were profiled as heroes in newspapers and television shows, Malachi wrote editorials that usually went unpublished. *We are parasites on the world, all of us,* he'd written. His thoughts—our thoughts?—were not palatable to most people, including my family. I'd learned voluntary extermination was not fodder for pleasant table conversation; two years ago Malachi blasted my mother over pumpkin pie for expressing her hopes for grandchildren.

You'd give them a death sentence, he said. Massive water

shortages and die-offs are imminent. It's selfish to make more of ourselves; the desire to see your genes replicated in the world is a crude biological impulse.

Before you got one one-hundredth of the world to take you seriously, she said, and that wouldn't be enough, the earth would already be shot, done for. There may be time to turn things around.

There isn't, Malachi said.

You are one hundred thirty pounds of FUN, Mom said, mocking Malachi's slight frame. He scowled.

You think I like the fact—

Look, Mom said. When it comes to mass annihilation, put your money on a rogue black hole or nuclear winter. You're pinning your hopes on the very people you'd like to extinguish.

My mother, the longtime director of one of Maine's conservation organizations, was no softhearted bridge player who pined for craft time and sing-alongs. She wore no makeup and kept her gray hair cropped short in a pixie cut. At fifty she'd hiked the Long Trail on her own, kayaked whale-watching expedition routes off the coast of Lunenburg in Nova Scotia. Compared to Malachi, she was no less ardent an environmentalist, just hopeful.

Malachi paced in front of the patio doors, one hand in his hair, then on his lips. Hand me a plate, he said.

Where are you going? I said, something feminine and hysterical brewing inside me.

I'm not walking away from you, he said. I'm walking *toward* the eggplant. I need to be outside to think.

When he opened the door, the city screamed and the post-work din of Washington's Dupont Circle spilled into our town house. Busy people walking, talking, eating, spending. The door shut behind him, and it was as if I were standing in a soundproof room. Or drowning.

Maybe I'd missed a birth control pill. Maybe my body had imposed its will and bypassed my medication and social convictions. Maybe the universe was making an example out of me: *You are an animal. You are a mammal. This is what your body wants.*

I guess all the cerebral striving in the world couldn't combat the biological basics.

I'd begun suspecting pregnancy earlier in the week. My breasts were sore and Tuesday morning I'd nearly blacked out in the shower; the scent of my mango shampoo turned my stomach. I had no interest in morning eggs. I worked as a veterinary technician at the zoo and was asked to assist with the necropsy of an oryx; I begged off as soon as the veterinarian began to split the animal's flesh with his scalpel. I was exhausted and wanted nothing more than to read a book on the couch the last few evenings, a time when Malachi and I often went out to coffee shops and bars to recruit new EWU members.

What if? *What if?* All the sermonizing I'd done to friends, on the phone to my sister. *If we all begin to make these sacrifices . . . it's about better decisions. . . .*

As I unwrapped the pregnancy test, I'd thought: Just because you signed the No Breeding Pledge doesn't mean you can't create a life within your own body.

And so I had.

Malachi came back into the kitchen with the plate of eggplant steaks. They were drizzled with olive oil and topped with crumbled fresh feta cheese, roasted garlic, and rosemary, which we grew in a planter outside.

I can't eat, I said, waving him off and moving to the couch, a secondhand green corduroy sectional. Our living room and kitchen were essentially the same room, set apart by a large, potted jade plant Malachi had maintained since college. One wall was exposed brick. Custom shelving lined the fireplace and held carefully selected books—Edward Abbey, Thoreau, Emerson, Rachel Carson, Sibley Guides. There were books on debt forgiveness, foreign travel, languages, seal hunting—all ready for the sporting scrutiny of our dearest friends, who came over on weekends wearing chic vintage and bearing artful hors d'oeuvres.

Are you going to call your mother? he said. Because I think you should wait. She'll—

I'm going to distract myself, I said. Sit with the information a little longer.

I needed to be still, slow down, press pause, because I'd never entertained the idea of becoming a mother. Well, I hadn't entertained the idea since college, when nearly all my friends assumed we would one day have children. But it wasn't *real* then. Children were only a far-off given, a thing that happened to you, like wisdom teeth. It wasn't until I met Malachi that I began to feel the weight of human guilt.

Malachi set the plate down and made me ginger tea with a splash of agave nectar. He delivered it to the coffee table next to me without asking, as if to underscore his utility and devotion as a partner. Then he fixed himself a plate and sat properly at the table, cutting the entire eggplant steak into cubes before taking a bite. I propped myself on a pillow and began reading a book on the intelligence of pigs. Except I wasn't reading.

The book reminded me of the slick and waxen fetal pig I'd refused to dissect in high school biology, how I couldn't bring myself to cut its perfect skin. There'd been what looked like a smile on its nascent face, as if it still expected to be born, and was hopeful for what life would bring—green pastures, slop, other warm bodies. The teacher subtracted points from my participation grade and granted me access to a virtual dissection, where I dragged a pixilated heart across the screen of a second-rate Toshiba.

Just before lab, a kid in my class, a farmer's son, had said: Pigs sing to their children.

Now, as a veterinary technician, I regularly assisted with necropsies at the zoo. I'd picked apart red pandas who'd died after ingesting pesticides. I'd gone elbow-deep in an old camel, pocketed a worn tooth from a geriatric albino tiger. My constitution was stronger than when I was younger. I was solution-driven, fascinated by what ailments plagued these exotic animals, always eager to pinpoint the previously undetected tumor, the birth defect, or rotted intestine.

Pigs might be better stewards of the earth when we're gone, Malachi said, noticing the book in my hands.

I closed my eyes and laced my hands over my chest.

Can I get you to try some of this eggplant? Malachi said. You haven't eaten much today.

I sat up with the intention of standing but felt as if I couldn't leave the couch.

Do we have any saltines? I said. Gatorade?

No, Malachi said. But I'm happy to run out and get some for you.

Don't come back with any organic stuff, I said. *Please*. I need the real thing. No weird crushed-wheat crackers.

Malachi frowned, stuffed his wallet into the pocket of his slim jeans, and disappeared, letting the soundscape of the street enter again for a brief moment until he closed the door behind him.

I felt guilty. I'd let him down by getting pregnant. As if it was something *my* body had done. On top of the guilt, I was panicked and unleashing it on Malachi, who, despite his firm convictions, had a sweet temperament. Or a mostly sweet temperament. He could be utterly single-minded about his cause, stonewalling my friends from college who chose to have children, or speaking harshly about his cousins and their broods of kids. He had clear views on sustainable fish and could come off as heavy-handed at dinners out, advising our friends what to order—*you've got to cut out the farmed fish*. He wasn't shy about telling you when you used too much water washing dishes, and he collected discarded wrapping paper on holidays with a pained look on his face. I wish you wouldn't wrap my presents, he told my family last Christmas.

I dealt with his need to advise and control because it came from a good place—his love of the world—though my mother said she found his self-righteousness appalling. I admired his principled way of living. I agreed with nearly every stance he took, but for good or bad didn't take myself as seriously. I didn't feel the searing conviction he felt, and sometimes when we were out at coffee shops recruiting for EWU, I realized I was there more for Malachi's company than for the cause itself.

Malachi was often serious and prone to bouts of melancholy about the environment—but he had a sense of humor. He joked with his friends over beers at the pub down the street or brought them home to drink scotch and listen to his collection of vintage

Richard Pryor albums. He liked to play his mandolin on the back porch and make up songs about people passing by:

Mustache man, mustache man, he walks to the metro as fast as he can.
Come hell or high water, he'll bring donuts to his daughter,
Oh sweet-talking mustache man.

He came back from the store with the sort of products he despised—commercial bastions. But he covered my feet with a throw made by Peruvian widows, poured me a glass of hyper-red Gatorade, and massaged my temples.

Thank you, I said, aware that we were playing a game of goodwill, trying to rack up a surplus of kind deeds before the unavoidable argument came.

Later that night, he came to me and said: I called the clinic, and whenever you're ready, they can give you a pill . . . if we act early enough. What do you think about tomorrow?

I didn't respond; I wasn't sure how to. It was another example of Malachi's earnest principles at work, but now they were directed at me and it hurt.

I shrugged, then excused myself. I'm going to get ready for bed, I said.

The look on his face—it was as if he'd done something kind.

I sat up in bed after Malachi turned off the lights, suddenly angry at his swift response, his inability to imagine a child in his life.

I can't go tomorrow, I said. I'm not ready to do that.

You're considering it? he said, disbelieving. You're considering having a baby?

Our baby, I said. And yes.

I *cannot* do my work with a pregnant girlfriend, he said, let alone a child. This is my credibility. You know—

You eat bacon, I said. There are holes in every principle, exceptions to the rule, ways around, contingency plans.

Not with this, he said. Not for me. If you and I feel entitled to produce another carbon-producing life, we can no longer advocate for restraint with credibility. There is a moral imperative here you're ignoring—

Morals are man-made fabrications, I said. What isn't natural about a baby?

You didn't feel that way yesterday, he said. Or last year. Or five years ago.

Can't we just explain that it's an accident? I said. The US birthrate is down—

Human extinction is my most fundamental belief, he said, sweeping his hand across the air as if to say that arguing was worthless.

Hearing him speak was like listening to our writer friends moan about their need for solitude and time because they thought maybe, just maybe, they were doing something important for the world.

And maybe they were. But I was tired of people being so goddamn serious about their ideas.

I felt that Malachi was afraid to touch me, and I was afraid to sleep, afraid to sink one day further into a pregnancy he did not support. I watched him, first with his eyes half open, then closed as he gave in to sleep. He was a heavy sleeper. His hair was thick and dark, good Jewish hair, he called it, though he wasn't Jewish. He wasn't sure what he was. A classic American mutt, he said.

He'd come from a large family down South that he hardly spoke to, rural Virginia folks whom he claimed had two babies each by the time they were sixteen. I'd never met them. Malachi was a self-starter, a plucky faux orphan.

I stroked his hair; I'm not sure why I felt I should comfort him. I was the one hurting.

I'll go away for a while, I told him, many hours later, when I wasn't sure if it was night or early morning. I'll go to my grandmother's summer house in Maine.

Malachi stirred. Did you hear me? I said.

It isn't summer anymore, Malachi said, his brown eyes opening into slits and closing again.

They haven't shut it down for the season yet, I said. I'll go, and I'll think.

He put his arm around me and fell back asleep. I could hear the clock ticking, stores beginning to open up outside, the righteous clang of a delivery truck's back door. People up early, being people, being busy, being commercial, doing what people do.

I was angry at Malachi for his harshness, for putting his ideas above me. I was tempted to let loose—to cry and itemize what we owed each other. But it would have been like entering the front lines unarmored, naked—not knowing what you wanted in an argument with Malachi was a waste of time. He always knew what he wanted—upscale Thai, an IPA, the Sunday *New York Times,* a bookstore without a children's section.

The covers were distributed as they always were, sheets pulled toward Malachi's side, the comforter stuffed between my knees. There were unspoken routines and rituals, shoes underneath the bed and books on the nightstand that reminded us what kind of people we were, should we forget for a moment, or be tempted to change.

Sadness and euphoria collided in my chest, waves of each washing over the other, until I felt only confusion and fatigue.

I wondered: What am I prepared to lose?

The next morning I packed a suitcase and made blueberry smoothies for Malachi and me.

Did you wash the blueberries? he asked, artfully pouring his fair trade coffee into a thermos made of corn plastic.

Always do, I said.

Are you sure this is what you need? he said, kissing my forehead.

I nodded. I was flying into Portland and renting a car. I was already looking forward to the drive from Portland to Camden; the road was quiet and old and flecked with lobster shacks and motels, sailboats hoisted into the air for hull repair, the barnacled landscape of my youth.

I wish I was going with you, Malachi said. He looked sad that I was leaving, or maybe sad to be facing a decision he so easily advised others to make.

Was there a part of him that looked at my abdomen wistfully? I wondered. That imagined a child of his own, with his hair and big ideas?

I called the zoo to let them know that I was sick and would likely be back next week. I had a good relationship with my boss and plenty of time off stored up; my absence wouldn't be a problem. You're missing an Asian small-clawed otter this morning, my boss said. Renal failure.

There'll be others, I said absentmindedly.

I hope not, my boss said.

Malachi carried my bag and followed me to our car—a silver 1984 Mercedes wagon that ran diesel. We kept it parked in an underground garage a block from our town house like something we were ashamed of. That had been part of moving to a city, after all—more recruits, smaller individual footprint.

Around us people in suits were walking to work and the metro station. Most of them wore practical shoes, sipped coffee, and glided thumbs across the screens of their phones.

Malachi packed the car for me, topped off the wiper fluid, and set a roll of crackers in the front seat. He held my waist and kissed me.

I'm only driving to the airport, I said.

The wagon was hot inside and the scent of strange things baked into the upholstery across decades began to fill the air—orange juice, sweat, paint. I stuffed a cracker into my mouth to distract my senses.

We'll figure this out, Malachi said through the open window. His body language oozed anxiety. He fumbled with the buttons on his denim shirt and I pictured him smoking on the back porch when he got home. He was okay with smoking and other vices, anything that would do us in faster.

Malachi waved as I backed the wagon out of our small parking spot, our fifty-dollars-a-month plot. He blew me a kiss that I pretended not to see and stuffed his hands in the pockets of his jeans.

When someone's ideal is the absence of all human life, romance is kind of a joke.

My uncle had driven up to my grandmother's cottage in Camden that morning to make sure the heat was on. He lived nearby and had become the de facto caretaker once Grandma B moved into a nursing home. He'd left dahlias the size of dinner plates in bud vases throughout the house. Their yellow petals were beginning to brown. I lifted a vase to mop a damp circle from an antique pine sideboard with my sleeve.

I'd not yet called my mother, afraid she'd hear something new in my voice. I wasn't ready for her to be there—not when I wasn't sure about my decision. I'd call later; she'd hear about my visit from my uncle soon enough.

My grandmother and grandfather had built the Camden cottage in the 1940s when they were first married. He'd been a dentist in town; Grandma B had taught high school biology. Even now, as she was losing her faculties, she could still explain the Krebs cycle and attributed rapid aging to her "bum mitochondria."

Her cottage was gray and shingled with a pale green door and mature gardens. There was a water pump covered in thick black paint outside the front stoop. The antlers from a buck my grandfather had shot before he died hung over the garage entry. In the backyard, there was a small orchard of old apple trees that we stripped of fruit in the fall for cider.

I pulled my rental car into the gravel driveway and gathered my bags. Inside, the cottage smelled of old trunks and, like most historic shore houses, mildew. The original wallpaper was still up—a cream-colored base flecked with clusters of red apples and blue flowers. All of Grandma B's sticky notes, dog-eared cookbooks, test-tube shot glasses, and ceramic animals were in the kitchen as she'd left them. The late-afternoon sun fell on the honey-colored kitchen table. I put water on and made a cup of lemon tea.

The apples are early, my uncle had written on a napkin. *Cider's in the freezer. Take some home with you.*

I'd brought Malachi here a couple of times. He loved the solitude of Maine. It's almost postapocalyptic, he'd said, as if that were a landscape he might enjoy, a place he might take vacations.

Last November the family had gathered to do a final Thanksgiving dinner in the house with Grandma B before she moved into the nursing facility. The fall sky had been bleak and Grandma sat near the woodstove. My mother, trying her best to ignore Malachi, had doted on her mother, caressing her worn hand, topping off her wine, placing a generous dollop of crème fraîche on her strawberry rhubarb pie.

Are you tired? Mom had asked her.

Just a little oxidative stress, Grandma B said, pulling her thick black glasses low on her nose and raising her eyebrows playfully.

Now the house, without my family, was bare and hushed. Yet I felt connected to my grandmother, my mother, this rugged line of hardy women with sharp ideas and heirloom casseroles, so in love with the world. Their nails packed with garden dirt, their speech full of sayings from old songs and relatives: *Does last night's fun bear the light of morning's reflection?*

I wanted, then, to become what I most admired, what now seemed most real to me. I wanted to be that exalted, complicated presence in someone's life, the familiar body, the source of another's existence. But I knew what I wanted was not always what I needed.

Between the cat-worn sofas and antique lamps there were long shadows in the house, filaments of lives. Maybe I'd rent the house for the year, take a leave from my job, hunker down with family support and raise a child. But was it practical?

I'd be coming into motherhood alone. This would not be my mother's life, or my grandmother's marriage. There would be no family portraits, no husband to share in the late-night shifts or stomach flu. No partner, at least in the immediate future, to trade anxieties with—worries about vaccines, the school bus, dwindling water supplies, pollutants from small-engine vehicles and lawn mowers.

I envied my mother's childhood, the awe with which she'd turned to her country and the world, the confidence she'd had in her right to exist and bear children. The world and mothers alike, I knew, had lost a little freshness.

It was four in the afternoon, and I had roughly two and a half hours before sunset. I threw on an extra sweater—something of Grandma B's that was left in the closet—grabbed a few apples from the tree in the backyard, and drove the car through an old campground to the summit of nearby Mt. Battie. I ate an apple as I drove, juices running down my hand and wrist.

The view from the mountain had always been one of my favorites. Below, rocky beaches framed the Atlantic into Penobscot Bay, a blue expanse punctuated by sailboats and the humps of small islands, hundreds of them, covered in evergreens.

I pictured Mom steering her red kayak around the islands, watching serenely as a humpback or minke lunged and dove before her, coming up to blow near the bow of her boat. She'd told me two things about whales last summer. One was that today's whales sing lower songs, and no one knows why.

I drove into Camden through inn-lined streets. The town's window boxes were full of late-summer flowers and creeping Jennie. The leaves on the trees were tinged with yellow, a suggestion of the bright foliage to come. Chalkboards advertising lobster rolls and bisques flanked restaurant doors.

I remembered the second thing she'd told me, her hand placed on the small of my back: When a calf is born, she said, the mother pushes her baby above the surface of the water to breathe.

I'd rolled my eyes then, at her motherhood propaganda. Now it made me want to cry. Everything did, for that matter.

Back at the cottage, I avoided calling Malachi. Instead, I daydreamed about marrying into a big French family, and what it would be like to eat dinner with them, lamb on our forks, babies at our feet. I imagined a man who'd fill the roles Malachi didn't want.

But finding a new man was out for now. Funny how pregnancy validates and neutralizes your sexuality at the same time.

I made a tomato sandwich and brought it to Grandma B's desk, a small walnut heirloom pushed into a sunny nook at the top of the steps. I opened the drawers and sifted through paper clips, expired oatmeal coupons, and stickers until I found a stack of letters, roped and set aside. I slid my finger underneath the rope and tried to open the first envelope. It was postmarked 1976, Charlottesville, Virginia—my mother writing home from college. The lip had refastened itself; I gently pried it open and pulled the letter out.

Dear Mom, it said. *My roommate is allergic to cats, but I'm feed-*

ing one on the back stoop anyway. I miss having cats around. I'm homesick—for the cats, you, Maine. . . .

The next letter was written when she'd moved to Steuben with my father and I was little, maybe four.

I took Lauren to her first swimming lesson today. She hated it, wouldn't put her face underwater or blow bubbles, and kept pulling the front of her swimsuit down. God bless her; I love that little face. She tells me she's afraid of "shawks" in the water.

I read a few more.

How do you explain Boy George to a six-year-old?

The flea beetles have taken the kale this year. What do you recommend?

Grandma B had saved them all. Though Mom had not lived with her since college, their intimacy never faltered. The letters were full of play-by-plays, carefully selected anecdotes in familiar handwriting.

I closed the desk, gently wrapping the red rope around the letters, leaving them the way I found them, the way I knew someone else would find them when Grandma B died, or her house was sold. I walked to my mother's old bedroom, sat on her bed, and called Malachi. He answered on the first ring.

Lauren, he said. He sounded spent, his voice hushed. What have you—

I haven't made a decision yet, I said, but I'm thinking about going through with it.

You *can't*, he said. Listen to me. It doesn't make any sense, bringing a child into this world.

I can't live my life waiting to die, I said.

What, he said, you're pro-life now?

This isn't a political act, I said. It's a vote of confidence.

It's selfish, Malachi said. Grossly selfish.

It's like something within my biological makeup wants me to have a child, I said, and maybe I trust that more than—

Than who? Malachi said. It's about good decision making, and *I* can help you—

I'm a thirty-year-old woman with a steady income and supportive family, I said. I'm not ready to admit the world is dying. I can't go on believing that.

Believe it, Malachi said. Another ice shelf the size of—

Look, I said. I'm plenty scared. You don't have to pile it on.

I can't believe you're doing this, he said. He was beginning to choke up. I'll call you back, he said, and hung up the phone.

I lay back on my mother's bed and cried until it felt like a needless thing to do. Her vintage Nancy Drews lined the wooden shelves. Her blue and red ribbons from years of horse shows were still pinned to the walls. A Fleetwood Mac concert poster hung from pushpins over the bed. Something in Stevie Nicks's eyes told me sex was better in the seventies, when people weren't waiting for the world to end.

It was almost nine o'clock, and the house had darkened considerably. Energy conscious, I'd neglected to turn on the lights. My back and head ached.

I called home. My father answered. Hi, Daddy, I said. Can I speak to Mom?

One minute, he said. I think she's outside with the dog. How are you, honey?

Dad was infinitely reliable, the quintessential father. The type who sent me flowers on my birthday, called regularly, kept my elementary-school art framed in his office. At that moment, hearing his voice, I wanted to be ten again, ignorant about the world, safely ensconced in my backyard watching Mom garden and Dad grill burgers, worrying about spelling homework or riding the bus. Or hiking with them in the Camden woods, riding in the backseat on a drive down the winding Kancamagus Highway with public radio on.

I'm okay, I said. Just okay.

"Just okay" sounds like a conversation for Mom. I'll yell for her. Thisbe, he shouted. *Thisbe*. Lauren's on the phone and she's *just okay*.

Lauren? Mom said a moment later. Her voice was high, on alert, already leaping to conclusions. What's wrong?

I'm at Grandma's house, I said. I need to talk to you about something. I hate to ask, but can you come down?

I'll be there in the morning, she said.

I fell asleep in Mom's old bed. I woke hours later to the whoop-whooping of coyotes. The harvest moon was low in the sky, and the entire yard was gray but illuminated. Looking at the moon, I felt something ancient and indefensible stirring within the pit of my body.

I woke up when Mom walked through the front door of the house at six a.m., meaning she'd left home at four. I heard her clogs on the wooden stairs, the familiar rhythm of her steps that used to wake me on Saturday mornings when I wanted nothing but to sleep in.

Before I could get up, she was there at the bedroom door. She wore yoga pants and a thick sweater.

My eyes were tired. I sat up; she came to the edge of the bed, ran her thin hand over my hair, and hugged me. We had not been this way in years. Living apart, we talked frequently but with busy ambivalence; we saw each other on holidays. Our intimacy was rusty, but only for a moment. Mom's embrace tightened. She knew something was wrong.

She pulled away. Our eyes were wet.

Thanks for coming, I said.

Mothers, I believe, intoxicate us. We idolize them and take them for granted. We hate them and blame them and exalt them more thoroughly than anyone else in our lives. We sift through the evidence of their love, reassure ourselves of their affection and its biological genesis. We can steal and lie and leave and they will love us.

I'll put tea on while you get dressed, she said. I brought muffins.

I pulled on a pair of sweatpants and brushed my hair, which had gotten long, because Malachi liked it that way. I headed downstairs. Mom handed me a warm muffin and a thermos.

I'm five weeks pregnant, I said, leaning over the kitchen island.

She took a deep breath and nodded. She wrapped her arm around my shoulders and pulled me close. For minutes we stood that way, her warmth the most comforting thing I'd felt in days.

And Malachi? she said. Is he supportive?

No, I said, closing my eyes to keep the tears from spilling out.

Are you going to keep it? she asked.

I don't know, I said.

I drove myself home from the airport. Dulles was black and wet from a fall rainstorm; street and landing lights made disconcerting signals in the dark. Malachi, I knew, would be hosting his weekly

EWU meeting at a friend's place, a run-down subdivided Victorian house on the edge of Adam's Morgan.

I parked the car outside on the slick ebony street and let myself in through the heavy mahogany doors. It was a cold sixty degrees out; the rain gave the air a chill. An old chandelier with missing and cobwebbed bulbs hung over me in the pastel yellow foyer, which was crowded with bikes and shoes.

I let myself in to our friend's apartment and sat in a folding chair in the back row. There were twenty or so attendees, most of them thin and hip with snug jeans and black winter hats pulled down over their hair.

These people who professed to love nature, it seemed to me, would be quickly lost within it.

Malachi, riffling through papers at the front of the room, nodded solemnly at me, eyes widening as if surprised by my presence.

He rose, cleared his throat, and began the meeting as he always did, with a reading of Edna St. Vincent Millay's "Apostrophe to Man":

> Detestable race, continue to expunge yourself,
>   die out.
> Breed faster, crowd, encroach . . .

Have you thought of protesting at the fertility clinics? one guy asked, raising his hand, scanning the room for approval. All the multiples—

It's an idea, Malachi said, but probably not the best place for recruiting sympathizers.

I cringed, picturing the scene, the people so desperate to conceive a life, their insides poked, tested, and fragile. I knew, then, that the secret I was carrying made me an outsider at EWU, forever sympathetic to the enemy cause.

What we're trying to cultivate is awareness, Malachi said, the realization that every human life drains the earth's limited resources. Our reproduction is excessive and disgusting.

Yes, someone said. Amen.

The people gathered in the room sipped their tea and took notes. We wanted the same thing, I think, an earth less taxed by human presence. But giving up on life now, I felt, was like leaving the party early.

Would there be water shortages? Yes. More starving babies? Unfortunately. Would our quality of life soon be diminished by global warming? Probably. But who, I wondered, but the strongest among us could hold those ideas in their heads and find happiness? Get out of bed in the morning?

Remember, Malachi said, not having a child is the best thing you can do for the planet.

As the meeting ended, people mumbled about Freitas's notion of ecophagy, nanotechnology gone wrong. They spoke of ecocide by asteroid, sterility by route of too frequently ingested GMOs.

Afterward, Malachi stood behind me and massaged my shoulders. His flannel shirt was missing buttons and he hadn't shaved in days. He kissed the back of my head.

Come with me, he said, leading me to the empty dining room. The fireplace was cemented over. A beer-pong table was shoved into a corner, and the smell of old beer in the carpet began to turn my stomach.

You're here, he said, smiling, though I knew his pleasure would be short-lived.

It's not as easy as you think, I said. You herald the natural world, then dismiss the power of biology over our bodies and minds.

Lauren, he said, you're a smart girl. You can control your biological urge.

I don't want to, I said.

Take a step back, he said, smiling. You can live without this.

What are you going to do, Malachi? I said. Die forty years from now with a smug grin and the satisfaction of knowing you convinced twenty people not to breed?

Your carbon footprint will be hard to live with, he said. Trust me.

His once appealing certitude was ugly, a barrier to my happiness. Malachi cleared his throat and crossed his arms in front of his chest.

I pictured the mother whale, exhausted from labor, pushing her calf up to the skin of the water. The miracle of breath in the face of predation, life in the wake of whaling ships.

I know what I want to do, I said. I looked down and saw the hope within my body as I began to explain, my raw and stupid hope.

Another Story She Won't Believe

We are the bad mothers, the moose and I—me for drinking, the moose for abandoning her yearling to attend her newborn.

I'm reading about moose in a coffee-table book someone gave me last Christmas. I ogle the pictures of moose racks, felt peeling off the antlers like downy rags. *Beware the behavior of yearling moose freshly abandoned by their mothers,* the book warns.

The storm of the decade rages outside. Four inches of snow top the previous night's frozen rain. It's too much for skinny pines and sandy soil. The trees bend and snap and fall down across the roads, ice needles shattering like glass. I suppose the barometric pressure will put women in labor across the South, jump-start a run on milk, bottled water, chicken pot pies.

My television flickers. I have it on because I'm lonely and like noise. I've forgotten what I'm watching. A tampon commercial comes on. Girls in high heels. Girls on Vespas. Menstruation is fun, the commercial seems to say. I haven't menstruated in seven years.

The power goes out. 4:43 is a long minute; I watch it on a battery-powered clock bought when I could still afford frivolity. 443 began my first phone number, a number I memorized with pride, a number that belonged to a brick ranch in a new neighborhood that abutted an old farm. A number I wish I could call now and hear my mother on the other end. I can still feel the fat of my lip tucking beneath my adolescent buck teeth when I mouth the number four.

I call my daughter, Leslie. She doesn't answer. I guess I called knowing she wouldn't.

Leslie believes the world will end in one year. She lives with a man with no education who wears work boots and stiff canvas pants. They live in his parents' basement and watch informational videos about the apocalypse online. His mother bakes herself in a tanning bed in her garage, right next to her husband's rusted-out Chevrolet. She's the color of red clay.

I tell the girls at work that Leslie's boyfriend, Zach, is like the stud pony they use to get the mares going at the reproduction barns—all prance, five hands short his filly.

Leslie's like a yearling moose, all legs, ungulate eyes with too much hope in them. Beautiful, well bred, wasting away. Hard to find.

I'm leaving school, she told me this fall. There's no point.

What else have you given up on? I'd asked. Do you still brush your teeth?

The phone rings. I don't answer. Suddenly I'm not in the mood to talk to Leslie anymore. I don't know what to say. The machine picks up.

Suzanne? a voice says. This is the Lemur Center calling. You're a volunteer with us?

I pick up. The answering machine screams like a banshee.

You live within walking distance of the center, correct? she says. I need you there now. Our power is out and it's too cold for the lemurs. The aye-aye, too.

I'm in my pajamas, I say.

The anxiety in her voice worries me. She's going to involve me in a desperate act. I can feel it.

This is a life-or-death situation, she says. With the ice and trees on the road it will be hours before we can get there.

I'm sorry, I say.

Call me when you get there, she says. I'll walk you through what to do.

I pull jeans over my pajamas and a hat over my uncombed hair. Over that, an old Burberry trench given to me by my ex-husband when I was in what I call my Gene Tierney stage—good cheekbones, groomed eyebrows. I grab sheets and towels from my linen closet and wrap an afghan around my neck like a scarf. The truth is, I have nothing better to do.

On Tuesdays and Thursdays I run the Feed an Aye-Aye a Raisin program at the Lemur Center. Every recovering alcoholic knows it's best to live within walking distance of work; it's easier to assume one morning I'll be too tanked to drive. My sobriety is fragile. I've been sober going on forty-six days, but it's not the first time, or the longest. Sobriety, like parenting, is something I'm good at screwing up.

I'd found the Lemur Center position listed in the paper after moving to Virginia to be closer to Leslie. *Calling All Animal Lovers*, it said. *Work with endangered lemurs, aye-ayes, and bush babies.*

Who doesn't love animals? I'd thought. Animals I could do. And I figured that when you worked with animals, especially endangered ones, the focus was on them, not you.

I've come to find that the people at the Lemur Center are good people. People who donate to food banks, adopt incontinent Australian shepherds with epilepsy, bake casseroles for sick coworkers. People whose husbands work jobs they love, rewilding toxic meadows for a paycheck that puts them just above the poverty line.

I figure sooner or later they'll realize I'm not one of them, that I'm not good the way they are. I'm unreliable. I even surprise myself with the shitty things I'm capable of. The only time I took the high road was when I was pregnant with Leslie. I was sober and scared and for the first time I knew I was doing something that mattered.

My doctor had told me that my child was comforted by my voice, could hear everything I said. Your bones are conductors, he'd said. The mother's voice rises above the carpet of sound in utero. When I sang it was often "Edelweiss," sometimes "Rainy Night in Georgia," things my father had sung to me.

My father also taught me to love movies. I loved *National Velvet*, he *Cleopatra*. My father said he liked to lose himself in film. He went to the cinema every weekend, alone if he had to, and was always happier afterward. He spoke about the heroines at the dinner table as if they were real, as if he'd like to have supper with them, give them advice, help them find a happy ending—save them from their heartless husbands or neighborhood racketeers. He'd been working on his own script since college; every few years he sent it off to an agent or studio, but nothing ever came of it. I think its failure to sell was his greatest disappointment.

I liked the starlets in old movies—their neatly nipped waists, thick lipstick, and cherry-pie sopranos. I liked the way they looked when they drank, their red nails on the crystal highball. In old movies, America was beautiful, women could still feign naïveté, men worked one job their entire lives, and everyone could carry a tune. Who didn't want to live in an old movie?

I walk along a worn path to the Lemur Center. The greenway was built in the sixties, and in winter you can see the remains of purple plaster bears—stolen and deposited here by vandals who'd raided a closed Yogi's Fried Chicken in the late seventies.

The icy snow has muted everything except the birds and my footsteps. The pines are crystallized. Tufts of snow blow from the trees into the sheets I'm carrying for the lemurs. I ball up the sheets as much as I can and hunch over to keep them dry.

Walking in the snow, I feel one part home and one part stranger, an exotic escapee. I've read that when separated from native flocks, birds often attempt to join others. There are flocks of red-crowned parrots in Southern California, yellow-chevroned parakeets in San Francisco. There are dogs nursing fawns down the road. Hell—I've seen polar bears in the Bronx Zoo, soot on their white coats.

I hum a Brook Benton tune. My song is my own off-key timbre in the woods, my call.

It occurs to me that sometimes we make homes where we do not belong.

I probably lost Leslie when she was thirteen. It was the year I embraced my alcoholism. My ex-husband, Ryan—Leslie's father—

had moved us to Winston-Salem for a job. I wanted to improve my tennis game, so I spent afternoons at the club. I began interviewing nannies; I wanted someone to be there for Leslie when she got home from school. I also started an outpatient rehab program and Alcoholics Anonymous meetings. Or I almost started.

Rehab was a condition for keeping my marriage together.

You go, Ryan said, and I'll stay.

He was optimistic. I was scared. Ryan was beautiful then. Think Paul Newman in *The Young Philadelphians.*

That first day I was nervous and I sat in my parked car, engine running, outside the Presbyterian church where the AA meetings were held. I was used to drinking when I was nervous, and part of me had already made a mental U-turn for the nearest bar. But I got out, and the first person I saw was a nanny I'd interviewed two days before. She didn't have her teeth in. Her face was drawn, pallid, sad.

Hi, she said. Call me.

Depressed, I went back to the car, drove home, and drank a quarter of a fifth of gin in the bathroom. I hid the rest behind a stack of toilet paper. I'm not sad like *that,* I thought. That's ugly sad.

How was it? Ryan asked that evening. He didn't say what "it" was; Leslie sat between us at the dinner table. She'd put glitter in her hair and was singing a pop song.

Revealing, I said.

I'd microwaved French-cut green beans and baked chicken marinated in lemon. Leslie ate a roll and didn't touch what was on her plate. Our television set was on in the living room: Bogie singing with Chinese orphans in *The Left Hand of God.*

I'm proud of you for going, Ryan said.

Two months more in Winston-Salem and Leslie had found me out. I'd stopped showing up for my tennis lessons at the club. One day she wrote down the tennis pro's message and slipped it to me underneath the bathroom door.

Beneath his number she wrote: *I love you. Please come out.*

I saw the tips of her fingers as she pushed the note underneath the door. I wanted to touch them, but I wasn't good enough for her. I worried something bad would rub off, that she'd adopt my insecurities and quirks as her own.

Mommy will get better, I said. I promise.

I could hear her listening, her face pressed to the door, her breath whistling through the crack. That soft, hot, anxious breath. She wasn't fitting in at school after the move. Like me, she didn't make friends easily. I wanted to hold her tightly, but I knew she'd smell the alcohol on my breath.

Mom's sick, she told her father that night.

I should've told him the truth earlier. I could've told him how afraid I was of aging, how incompetent I felt as a mother. I could have gone to rehab. But if there's one thing I've got, it's a remarkable ability to throw up my hands and self-destruct. Ryan left with Leslie.

I don't call the head of the Lemur Center when I get to the center's gates. I can jump the fence, and I know the code to the aye-aye building. That's the only place I want to go right now, a familiar place. The pressure is getting to me. I can't look at the other lemur houses; some of these things are the last of their kind. They break my heart on an ordinary day—but today, when it feels postapocalyptic outside, when I'm here by myself—I know

I'll see them as they really are, alone. Finished. Hepburn in *On Golden Pond*.

Maybe I'll call the center's director in an hour, find out what she wants me to do. But right now I'm going to a place I know, so that I can stop being nervous and stop wanting a drink. I punch in my code on the keypad and enter the aye-aye house.

Faye Done Away is the resident Lemur Center aye-aye. Even though I've been working with her for a year, we have yet to reach an understanding. She still shirks from my hand when I clean her cage. Four years ago she was found in the back of a pet store after being imported illegally from Madagascar, and the center took her in. She's the size of a raccoon, with blunt features, rounded ears, and a salt-and-pepper coat.

To me, she looks like the love child of a stray cat and an opossum. Her ears are huge. Her head is mostly bald. Her eyes are yellow and piercing. Her tail is a wild pipe cleaner, her fingers nimble and creepy.

As head volunteer of the Feed an Aye-Aye a Raisin program, I show up twice a week to manage a bucket of mealworms and raisins and a line of squirming kids.

Just push it into her mouth, I say, handing them a sickle-shaped worm.

I shudder every time Faye reaches for a grub with her extended middle digit, slender with a plump pad at the tip. She moves in slow motion, leaning forward on her perch toward the food, blinking as parents fire off rapid shots with their cameras. She trembles when excited kids push a worm at her too fast.

Thanks for visiting, I usually say, quickly ushering the gawkers from the aye-aye enclosure.

The older I get, the more I feel like Agnes Moorehead, a typecast grouch. All the good theater work she did overshadowed by *Bewitched*. I'd be pissed, too. But I try to be positive. I try to do the right thing, outpace my past. And I always hope something good is going to rub off on me at the center.

Faye is nocturnal. In order to reverse her sleep-wake cycle and keep her awake for the kids, the center illuminates the space at night. With the power down, the sun is streaming in. I don't see her on the branch, so I figure she is asleep on her nest. The room is cold, so I take one of the pillowcases I've brought with me and drape it over her. She doesn't move—Faye's a deep sleeper.

I sit in the corner of Faye's straw-lined room. There's a large Plexiglas window where kids can watch Faye from the hallway and a long, two-pronged branch that hangs from ceiling chains. The room smells like a compost bin, like damp earth and fermenting fruit. I can't see trees or the snowy lawn outside.

I cover myself with a sheet and fall asleep. I don't know what time it is when I wake up. The sun has disappeared behind clouds and Faye's room is cold and dark. I dig out my phone and try Leslie again.

Mom, she says.

I knew I wanted to call, but I didn't know what I wanted to say.

What are you doing? I ask.

Watching television with Zach, she says. Why are you calling so much?

I picture them in bed together, blank-eyed television zombies.

Look, I say. I think you should come home. Live with me for a while. Go back to school.

I need to go, she says. And I'm not going back to school.

Why? I ask.

Why what? she says. Why anything? It's not worth my time. We have less than a year. . . .

That's a terrible way to live, I say. Thinking the world will end.

You would know, she says.

The line goes dead.

I have a bag of roasted almonds in my coat pocket and I eat them slowly, one by one. Faye has not made a sound since my arrival, so I stand up, brush the hay from my pants, and go over to check on her. I place one hand on her back to feel her body rise and fall with her breath. She's alive.

At the center, they tell us not to handle the animals more than we have to; it stresses them out. But today, I think, is something different, and all rules are off. No one is watching.

I carefully slide one hand underneath Faye's body and lift her, gingerly, as if I am lifting someone else's newborn. Her coat is rough. Her long tail curls around my arm. I take her to my corner of the room. She opens her large eyes, just for a moment, and squirms. I hope she recognizes me. I hope I'm able to comfort her.

I put my back against the wall and slide down, carefully, until I'm sitting with my legs out. I bring my knees up and press Faye against my chest, drawing my coat over half of her body. I can feel her breathing slow, her body warming.

I used to sit like this in my bathroom and smoke cigarettes. I would catch my eyes in the mirror and think: I smoke like Bette Davis. No one could smoke a cigarette sadder than Bette Davis.

I know I should check on the rest of the lemurs. I should call the head of the center. I should distribute blankets and record pulses and press gums and speak soft words of comfort. But here's what I also know—my heart isn't big enough. It never has been. If I look at the rest of them, I will break.

I tell the school kids who visit: In Madagascar, aye-ayes are often destroyed on sight. They're considered an ill omen, death angels. In the wild they are fearless. When their habitat is ruined, they ransack plantations.

The kids say: Why? Why are they deadly?

It's said they can pierce your aorta with their middle finger, I reply.

This is a showstopping lie, one that has been told for centuries by superstitious villagers. Faye treats the hoopla with nonchalance; after her feeding, the alleged killer sleeps in a knot in her nest like a house cat.

When I first met Faye, her yellow eyes reminded me of one thing—my dying father's jaundiced eyes, his liver shot from decades of drinking.

Ryan met my father for the first time the month before we were married. He began to worry about my habits.

You're predisposed, he said, looking at the mountain of beer cans in my father's trash can. We have to be careful.

How is it that a drinking woman is sexy when she's twenty, I said, and an alcoholic in her thirties?

I pretended to have learned something from my father, but I knew I was several miles down our shared road, an ugly biochemical pathway.

Even though I knew I would let Ryan down, I tried. We got married, then pregnant. We were happy, mostly. But I think there is a time in every woman's life, a time in her thirties when she realizes she is past her prime. I'm not talking about the mind. Fuck the mind. The mind grows so sharp that it becomes the *problem*, sees the problem, sees it in men's eyes. I'm talking about the legs, and the breasts, and the smile that used to open doors. I'm talking about the half-drunk swagger that could pluck a man from the bar, any man.

The way my jeans used to fit is what I'm talking about. The way everything smacked of sex, until it didn't.

A year after the divorce, Leslie came to my place for one of her regular weekends. She was fifteen, into Guns N' Roses. She had an older boyfriend, a seventeen-year-old Ryan was trying to chase off.

What's new with you? I asked after Ryan dropped her off and brought her to the front door.

I'm in love, she said, but she said it in a way that was ugly and defiant. She was wearing a skirt that was too short and her nail polish was chipped. Her face was beginning to break out and she'd tried to cover the acne with foundation that was not her shade.

I didn't know how to offer the motherly advice she needed, so I poured a drink. And then another drink.

She was sullen at dinner and afterward she fled to the guest room and played "November Rain" on repeat. For two hours I listened to her play that song.

For chrissake, I said, barging into her room, unable to take it. You'll never be Stephanie Seymour, okay?

I look down at Faye's sleeping body. Her scalp is visible through her coarse hair. Her tail drapes across my knees.

I pull my jacket back and kiss the crown of her head. The wiry white hairs on her neck bristle against my cheek. I hug her close, keep her warm.

I've always had trouble sleeping, and when I see deep sleep my first inclination is to be jealous. That kind of sleep is precious. When she was a toddler, I used to find Leslie dead to the world in the linen closet, a towel wrapped around her bare legs.

It was the kind of peace I could never find.

Sometime during what we call the middle of the night that is really the earliest part of the morning, I tuck Faye deep into my coat and leave the aye-aye house. I take a gravel path to the primary lemur enclosures, a square block of large cages pressed against each other to encourage companionship and play between the primates. There's a roof over the cages, but the front panels are exposed to the elements, though a handful of well-intentioned, snow-logged tarps are draped over a few. It is a cursory inspection; I move fast. Some of the lemurs cling to each other through the adjoining cages for warmth. They are still, but alive.

They do not chatter, or brachiate, or reach for a piece of dried fruit. They only mutter, shift, and resettle.

I'm afraid of interfering, of tipping them toward death. They know best. They must know best.

It feels like lucid dreaming, walking in the snow, an endangered aye-aye in my overcoat. It's like a false start to the morning, the dream you are only one foot out of, a simulation. The kind when you open your mouth but can't talk, when you reach out but can't move.

Please, I'd said to Ryan a few weeks earlier. You've got to talk some sense into Leslie.

It's a stage, he'd said. The more we try to intervene, the more we'll push her away.

I've tried to tell her it's not true, I said. She doesn't believe me. She thinks we're all going to die. Soon.

Ryan was quiet.

What's she going to do when it doesn't come true? I said. When the world is still spinning? What will she have then?

This, Ryan said, is a case of too little too late.

At five in the morning the director of the Lemur Center arrives. She follows my footsteps in the snow to the aye-aye house.

Get out, she says.

Her clothes don't match and her hair isn't brushed and I can tell that these animals are everything to her.

Are the lemurs okay?

I don't know, she says.

She turns her back to me. She's shaking. I can feel her hurt and anger and I knew it was coming all night. Here it is. All for me.

I'm sorry I didn't call, I say.

I deserve every bit of her rage. And maybe I want it. Maybe I want to wear her scorn, bear its weight, feel its teeth.

I'm as bad as you think, I want to say. Worse, maybe.

She flips the light switch; the power is back on. My eyes sting. She stomps out of the aye-aye house.

Faye is stiff with sleep and cold. I stuff her into my overcoat and begin the walk home.

I tell myself: *This is not a big deal.*

The early sun is already melting the snow and the trail home is dark and muddy. I cradle Faye with one arm. Her nails dig into my skin and her tail hangs out from beneath my coat. If we pass anyone, they will think I am holding a cat, or perhaps a raccoon.

I reach my apartment complex and notice the power is back on; I can see my downstairs neighbor's television through the window. He's watching Turner Classic Movies—overacted movies in muted colors. Like me, I think, he's still holding out hope that the best days aren't gone, that the best times weren't the years when Elizabeth Taylor and Richard Burton were together in Technicolor bliss.

I trudge up one flight of stairs. I'm tired. It's as if I have a morning hangover; the sun is too bright, the day too fast for my eyes.

People are walking dogs, brushing off cars, returning to normalcy.

What is it about an unseasonably warm day that makes me think of my childhood? I can smell the bread and taste the chicken casserole and poached pears my mother used to make. I can feel grass underneath my thighs. I can picture my father sitting in his car alone, parked in the driveway, rereading his movie script, the paper stacked against his steering wheel. I can picture Leslie playing in the sandbox, turning to me for a hug before she knew how to hold a grudge.

I can always tell when I've done something wrong. It's a feeling I've known every day of my life.

I know I'll pour myself a drink when I walk inside. I don't want to do it, but I will. I have a half pint of bourbon in a box in the back of my closet that I can finish off neatly. It's the perfect amount. And if I'm going to do it, I might as well enjoy it. Maybe I won't drink in the bathroom, which I do sometimes even now, living alone. Maybe I'll sit Faye on the ottoman, give the drink the glass it deserves, a cut-crystal highball. Ice.

But I don't drink. I enter my apartment and make a nest for Faye in my walk-in closet and return to my book about yearling moose. I promise myself that I'll travel to Maine in the spring, find the yearlings, show them how to keep clear of the road, remind them of water holes nearby.

Every five minutes I crack open the closet door to look at Faye, who is sleeping. I fill a ramekin with dried cranberries and half of an old banana and place it next to her. I turn up the thermostat.

When I return to the living room, I'm conscious of Faye's absence, the loss of her warmth against my body. It reminds me that she will not live forever.

I make myself some tea and wait for the phone call, or the knock on my door. They will notice she is gone. Maybe I have a night, or a few hours.

I want to call Leslie again. I want to call her and tell her about the night I saved an aye-aye, slept with a death angel pressed against my warm breast. I want to call her and tell her I'm sorry, that I understand, that the world will not end. I want to call her and tell her that she will be safe from everything, that it's not too late to be Stephanie Seymour, that she's too good for the life she has now. I want to exaggerate, extol, explain, atone. I want to tell her about the endangered prosimian in my closet. I want to call and tell her I love her; I want to tell her another story she won't believe.

The Urban Coop

Pay no attention to the soot on the buttercrunch, I told my new assistant.

We were looking at a row of lettuces in Mac's Urban Garden.

You wash those, right? she asked.

I didn't tell her how often I'd caught the homeless harvesting team urinating near the zucchinis. Saint Charles with his cowboy hat and soiled cargo pants. Tiny Hanson with her high-heeled boots and cut-up snowsuit. The Neil Diamond look-alike in his black trench coat.

Sam didn't know it, but I had plans for her. I wanted her to take over the garden.

Produce to the people! she'd said in her phone interview, and I was sold.

Now Sam knelt in front of the budding kale and Swiss chard in her expensive windbreaker. Her luxury hybrid was poorly parked outside the garden entrance. Bangs hung in front of her eyes. A half hour into her tutorial and she was already clutching her back.

Two types of people came to Mac's—those who were hungry, and those who wanted to feel good about themselves. But I'd learned feeling good about yourself could be hard work, backbreaking even.

That's tatsoi, I said to Sam, pointing to the plants with delicate spoonlike leaves next to the kale. Good with mustard, so tell the boys and girls that free packets of mustard from McDonald's work just fine if they need to stretch a meal.

I'm late for a therapy appointment, I said. Think you can do some weeding for an hour until I'm back?

Sam shrugged. She seemed unsure about the new job.

I was one month into the worst guilt of my life, and after I explained to Sam the danger of cabbage loopers and flea beetles, I went to my car. I cranked the ignition and began to cry.

My dog, Zydo, sat next to me in the passenger seat. I rolled down his window, and he thrust his head out and wagged his tail, as if I had never done him wrong.

I didn't deserve Zydo. In fact, I didn't know anyone good enough for a dog like him. Loyal to the point of self-destruction.

Mac and I had a boat—the Excitecat 810. On weekends we left the community garden to volunteers and drove to Beaufort, where we anchored and partied with friends. Zydo always came along. A lab mix, he loved the water. He'd pace the length of the boat and bark at passing crafts. His shaggy blond ears crimped in the humidity. His nails scratched the deck when he walked.

Mornings on the boat, I'd make instant coffee, Zydo at my feet. We'd climb quietly onto the deck, careful not to wake Mac, and listen to the birds. Zydo would sun himself with his chin on my legs until Mac was awake, and then we'd motor over to Shackleford Banks to let Zydo kick sand and chase gulls. Once, we saw two deer swimming past the boat toward land; Zydo had quivered with excitement but stayed by my side, obedient.

Aside from a touch of separation anxiety, Zydo was the perfect dog.

Then, one Saturday afternoon, our friends came by in an inflatable dinghy.

Let's hit the Dockhouse for live music, they said. Climb in.

Room for Zydo? I asked.

I worry about his nails, someone said. We're drunk, and if the boat sinks . . .

The crowded boat had burst into laughter. The sky was still blue, but we could see the moon. The water made a soft slapping sound against the side of the dinghy.

He'll be fine on board, Mac said, handing me a fresh beer. There's nowhere he can go.

The cool aluminum can between my fingers, the reggae our friends played from a portable radio—these things made me believe in okay, in *just fine,* in letting go.

We'd never left Zydo alone on the boat, and as the dinghy pulled away he lifted his chin to the sky and whined. Some cord in my chest pulled tight. I looked away.

When we returned that night, singing, smelling of beer and sunburned skin, he was gone.

What do you want? my therapist asked.

A baby, I said. I want a baby.

She folded her manicured hands and nodded. It struck me as a learned nod. I'd once heard that women nod their heads to build rapport—even when they don't agree.

I'd started therapy after Zydo's accident. My guilt had consumed me. I needed direction. My therapist plumbed me like a well, pulling out fistfuls of trouble, messy tangles of fear and longing.

What prevents you from having a baby? my therapist said.

I'm getting old, I said. My partner *is* old. And if I can't take care of my dog, I don't deserve a baby.

Silence the inner critic, she said. How old are you?

Thirty-nine and a half, I said, but Mac is in his fifties. And I think he's lukewarm on the idea. He's not *trying* very hard.

A few months earlier I'd said to Mac, Wouldn't it be fun if we had a full house?

You want another dog? Mac had asked. More chickens?

Mac was a good person, a visionary. We'd met at a bar in Duck, discussed our love of dogs, open water, and community agriculture. Our relationship was simple. We kept separate bank accounts. We didn't fight.

Three years ago, Mac and I had driven into Raleigh towing a yellow '74 Volkswagen bug that had silkie bantam hens roosting in the backseat and two goats hanging their whiskered chins out the windows. Mac had taken a job as a professor of agriculture at the state college. We settled in a historic neighborhood one block from the prison. A year later, Mac got a government grant to build a community vegetable garden on a plot downtown. It was *his* dream, but someone had to manage things while he taught, and that person was me.

I like my simple life, Mac often said. I don't need anything more than what I've got.

In vitro might be a possibility, my therapist said.

Yeah, I thought. A ten-thousand-dollar, pain-in-the-ass possibility.

When I returned from my appointment, I found Sam baffled by the tool sign-out sheet and food records. She tossed her bangs aside as she scanned the clipboard.

Skinny Meatloaf? she asked. One-Eyed Gloria Gaynor?

When the customers won't give you a name, we name them after musicians they resemble, I said. There is One-Armed Snoop Dogg, Phil Collins with a Mustache, and so on.

Sam wrinkled her nose and brushed soil from her jeans.

It's pretty obvious who's who, I said.

I don't know, Sam said, rubbing her lower back.

I worried she was looking for a way out. Assistants never lasted long at Mac's. From what I could tell, they liked talking about the job more than working it.

It isn't meant as a sign of disrespect, I said. It's just our way of tracking assets.

I signed out a hoe to Neil Diamond. The strawberry patch could use weeding, I told him.

I had to remind myself I was dealing with people, not characters. Our Neil Diamond really looked like Neil Diamond, wily eyebrows, thin lips, and all—but there was no swagger in his comb-over. Tiny Hanson told me Neil Diamond had a daughter in town who wouldn't see him, that he paced her neighborhood on weekends, hoping to catch her on the way to her car.

Wife left him long time ago, Tiny said. Girl probably ain't even his.

I turned to Sam.

By the way, I said. There are brown spiders that scare the bejeezus out of me in the strawberry patch. Jumpers. Wear gloves over there.

This isn't . . . she said, wrinkling her nose in disgust. *Ugh.*

Sam stared at her hands and began to clean beneath her nails.

Waste of time, I said, hoping I wasn't scaring her off.

The soil had burrowed into the lines of my hands the first year of the garden. When Mac and I went out to a nice dinner, I painted my nails deep red to hide the black earth.

Sam's hair was shiny and her skin was smooth. I found myself thinking about her ripe ovaries. What are you, twenty-five? I thought. A hundred and thirty pounds? You'd be easy to knock up. You have all this *time.*

I wanted to borrow her body for the weekend.

A handful of customers, or as the head of the neighboring condominium home owners' association called them, "vay-grints," had gathered for work and scattered themselves across the four garden quadrants. Buildings that weren't quite skyscrapers cast shadows across the plants. The bus station spilled over with people on their way to work. Two blocks away, Not Grandmaster Flash played the *Love Boat* theme on trumpet.

Saint Charles tugged at my sleeve.

I been vomicking again, he said.

I dug into my purse and fished out Tums. Sam stood next to me, eyes on the compost.

Don't eat out of the trash if you don't have to, I told Charles.

He crushed the tablets with his teeth and sauntered off to tend the kale.

When we got the grant money, this place was covered in cigarette butts, I said to Sam. And now . . .

I surveyed the garden. The roots of old, knotted oaks bulged underneath the cement sidewalk. The trees' shade was a godsend when the summer heat began to bear down. The early crops looked healthy and Tiny had done a good job picking up the Styrofoam cups and cigarettes that littered the place each morning. Mac had fashioned cone-shaped trellises out of driftwood for the newly planted peas. A clump of azaleas lined the Blount Street entrance.

This isn't what I expected, Sam said.

I lied. It will be if you give it time, I said. Hard work can turn any old dump into a fertile paradise.

Two fishermen had found Zydo just before nightfall, disoriented, paddling out to the horizon. At first, they said, they could not believe what they saw.

We thought it was a porpoise, one said.

Zydo had been dehydrated and confused. He'd snapped when they lifted him into their boat.

Desperate and lonely, he had swum a mile into the open sea.

That evening I returned home from the garden with a headache and a bag of early cucumbers.

I don't think Sam is going to work out, I said.

Mac slid his reading glasses down on his nose and laid the newspaper on the kitchen table.

I sat cross-legged on the kitchen floor and scratched Zydo's stomach. His back legs twitched when my nails found a good spot.

Pregnancy test was negative this morning, I said.

I felt my bottom lip begin to quiver.

Don't cry, Mac said.

It's karmic, you know, I told Mac. We've done this really bad thing with Zydo, and now . . .

You're paranoid, he said, rising to rub my shoulders. And superstitious.

He began washing the cucumbers. I pressed my face into Zydo's coat.

I wondered who knew me better—my partner or my dog, who sat up and shoved his nose into the crook of my neck, resting his chin on my collarbone, as if to say *There, there, there.*

At six a.m. Zydo touched his cold nose to my shoulder, a leather lead in his mouth. I put overalls over my nightgown and grabbed a cup of feed from the garage.

I kept an urban coop in the backyard stocked with silkie bantams. An ornamental breed, they produced tiny eggs and paraded around the coop like *Solid Gold* dancers, their legs ensconced in black feathered pantaloons, heads topped with Afro-shaped tufts. The hens were gentle and broody, good mothers who'd go so far as to raise eggs that weren't their own.

Zydo and I fed the silkies each morning. We walked out to their fenced-in coop, crouching down inches away from the gate. The ladies sprinted from their henhouse down the wooden ramp, lunging at the ground in fevered hunger.

The first time I saw a chicken run to food, I was inspired. A full-on sprint, stride like a split. That's how you get what you want, I thought. Go all out or give up.

The morning was cool. I could see the barbed wire atop the tall prison fence a block away. I stretched from side to side, trying to warm up my body. These days I woke feeling stiff, mechanical. Old.

As my hens clucked and the lone rooster postured, I imagined a baby's lips tugging at my breast. Hot breath on my skin, innocent eyes.

I'm sorry I eat your children before they hatch, I said to the hens.

One of the perks, I told Sam later that morning, is that you can take home produce every day.

I was going for the hard sell.

Tiny Hanson sat on the sidewalk with her feet spread out in front of her. The cuffs of her snowsuit pinched her swollen ankles. There was gum on the bottom of her scuffed leather pumps. Tiny took one off and rubbed her heel. She trailed Sam with suspicious eyes.

I don't know if I like kale, Sam said.

You learn to love it, I said.

The truth was, every year I reached a point where I couldn't look at another leaf of kale, another fanned-out collard the size of my face. Hot sauce, garlic, and brown sugar be damned—by the end of the summer I only had eyes for ice cream.

Last September, while pounds of kale and chard wilted in the back of my sweltering truck, I sucked down a milkshake at the Dairy Barn and let Zydo lick the cup when I was done. I lay down on a picnic table and looked up at the sky, one hand on Zydo's belly.

Waste not, want not, I had lied to myself.

The sound of children laughing, the sight of their ice-creamed faces had made my body cramp with need. I wanted to lay my hands on their sun-kissed cheeks, comb their soft hair with my fingers.

While Sam weeded, Tiny approached me, shoved her bad breath and broken teeth in my face.

What, she said. I'm not enough help? You don't love me no more?

I love you just fine, I said, stepping back. Sam's just here to learn.

Ain't no love gon' fix me now anyway, Tiny said, scratching her neck.

Let me see that, I said, peering at the scaly rash underneath her chin.

I'll bring calamine lotion Monday, I said. Don't scratch. You might spread it.

I cupped the back of Tiny's head.

You're going to be okay, I said.

Sam came up to us. She had dirt on her forehead and a million questions behind her eyes.

How do we feed everyone? Sam asked. You can't eat an uncooked potato.

Tiny sauntered off, muttering: And who's the prized whore now?

We don't have to worry about potatoes until June, I said. But there's a stack of black stockpots in the shed. If I'm not around, just start a fire in the pit, put the grate down, and boil the potatoes.

The boys and girls will bring their own ketchup packets, duck sauce, salt. Smashed peas aren't bad for flavor.

A fire? Sam said.

The tomatoes are what you have to worry about in the summer—they go fast, I said. The customers won't riot, but they get grabby. No one but Tiny really likes turnips—you can leave those in a grocery bag for her.

I don't think I can do this, Sam said. I thought I was just volunteering to water plants.

Just stay on until Monday, I said. Please. Mac and I are out on the boat this weekend. Managing the garden's not as hard as it sounds—just different.

Sam rubbed the back of her neck and raised her eyebrows.

I *need* this weekend, I pleaded.

She fiddled with the Velcro on the outside of her glove.

Maybe you could be a surrogate mother, I thought, looking at Sam's unlined face and strong legs.

I think I'd be better off doing advocacy work, Sam said.

When the sun is setting and you've got ten or so customers sitting on the sidewalk, quiet as can be with their mouths full, you'll see, I said. They'll drift away, and you'll find yourself alone in the garden, kale to your knees, feeling good. I always sit for a moment in the center, eating strawberries, and watch the sun disappear.

I don't want to be here alone, Sam said.

Tiny will help you, I said. Tiny always helps.

Sam was quiet.

I'll pay you under the table, I said. Whatever it takes.

I went home to pack for the boat trip. I groped for my travel toothbrush in a drawer full of ovulation indicators, my digital basal thermometer, and an ovulation chart. I was my own science fair project.

Zydo was on his back in our bed, rooting through the pillows, dirt from his nails marking the sheets. I didn't care. I'd let him do anything. Lick my cereal bowl, chase the chickens. I would atone forever.

I thumbed through old clothes, clothes I thought I should give to Tiny. Frayed sweatshirts, grass-stained shorts.

Mac and I had promised each other we'd stay out of the customers' personal lives, but I had made exceptions. Recently, I'd purchased bedroom slippers for Tiny so she could rest her feet at night. I slipped anti-inflammatories and Tums to Saint Charles to soothe his stomach.

Without realizing it, I had let Mac's Urban Garden become more mine than his. These days, I might not know myself without it. My therapist said I had a garden full of orphans.

It's too much, I'd told her, and yet not enough.

I spied my negative pregnancy test in the trash can.

Piss on it, I said.

Driving to Beaufort, Mac pointed out his family farm, the old farmhouse now a hay barn for someone's heifers.

There are pieces of me everywhere down east, he said. An uncle here, a cousin there. Most with no teeth to speak of.

All the reason to make more pieces, I said. Better pieces.

Sam called as Mac and I were settling in on the boat. Mac whisked two bags of groceries into the galley. I figured he was disappearing on purpose. He was more concerned with future projects—a weekly farmer's market in the poor area of town, an environmentally friendly fishmonger on Blount.

Jesus Christ, Sam said, panting into the phone. Saint Charles took a disproportionate share of collards. Phil Collins with a Mustache is selling our zucchini flowers for a profit at the farmer's market on Blount Street.

That's okay, I said. I wish Phil had asked, but we don't use the flowers.

Not Grandmaster Flash bit into an onion like an apple, Sam said. Tiny tied prayer flags into the pea fencing.

Not all bad, I said.

But that's not the worst, Sam said. This morning Our Neil Diamond pulled his penis out and danced around the cantaloupe patch, screaming, "Impotent melons! Impotent melons!"

What's important, I said, is that you keep the shears and the hoe close to you, and cultivate a sense of authority.

I quit, she said.

The day we retrieved Zydo from Animal Control, he was limp with exhaustion and had just come off intravenous fluids. He thumped his tail once or twice upon seeing us.

I did not say it, but I blamed Mac, whom I could hardly speak to after seeing Zydo's weak body. Mac was too easygoing. He did not play worst-case scenario. Next time I would listen to my gut.

I held Zydo in the backseat of the car as we drove down the pine-lined highway toward Raleigh. I spooned his tired back, rubbed his ears. I massaged the muscles weary from the Big Swim. My fingers ached from planting, but I did not stop stroking Zydo. My heart was subterraneous, a root crop, damp, hiding from the sun in shame.

It could be simple, I thought to myself. I could tell Mac how much I want a baby. I could tell him that I think we can do more, that I need his enthusiasm.

I went to find him. Zydo trailed me.

Mac sat next to the motor with his feet in the water. He was smoking a cigar and looked satisfied with life.

Sam quit, I said. And I want a baby. I'm willing to do anything. Things that cost money.

Looking pensive, Mac nodded and blew smoke toward the clouds. He wasn't the type of man to respond quickly; he liked to have processing time. He lay back on the deck, hands behind his head. It had taken me years to find comfort in his silence.

I peeled off my T-shirt and jumped into the ocean. Zydo followed.

I closed my eyes and felt the water rush over my head. If Mac left me, I could take up agility training with Zydo. We could walk the halls of hospitals. We could corral errant geese at airports. We could find a sperm donor.

But what if it was me who didn't work? What if I was rusted inside, imperfect, past my prime? Cursed?

Zydo and I paddled around near the boat. I let him swim to me, felt his claws on my arms and chest. I didn't mind the welts, not now. I inhaled the smell of his wet fur. In a moment, we would both be tired enough for land.

Stay with me, I said to him, and I will make it up to you. Again and again.

Treading water, I turned to look at the fading sun. There was something appealing about an uninterrupted horizon.

I imagined Zydo swimming out into the open water. Sometimes you didn't know what you were after, I thought. Maybe there was a speck on the horizon and you followed it, hoping for the best.

I pictured Sam leaving the garden, knocking off her boots before driving away in her expensive car. Tiny would sleep there, watch out for things until I was back. She'd shoo Phil away from the early cucumbers, keep Saint Charles from eating too many strawberries. I never asked, but I knew she'd do it anyway.

Tiny with her tired feet and cavernous mouth. Tiny with her varicose veins and dirty snowsuit. Tiny discarded by her family. Tiny with her whispered threats and kind actions.

Mac helped Zydo and me back onto the boat. I kissed his forehead and went to shower. As I stood underneath the sliver of water, I panicked. I needed to know that Zydo was safe. I ran out onto the boat deck, towel halfheartedly tucked between my breasts. Zydo and Mac were napping on the bow, a bottle of beer in Mac's hand.

Trust me, Mac said, both eyes closed, fingers tangled in Zydo's ears. Just trust me.

He opened his eyes and removed my towel with one hand, led me to the cabin with the other.

After making love, Mac peeled himself off of me and offered me the towel.

I shook my head.

Zydo put one paw on the side of the bed.

Do you ever get tired of begging? I asked Zydo, though I was happy to have what he wanted.

Mac left the room to pour us drinks.

No rocks for me, I said.

Ice on the boat was made from frozen seawater. To me, it filled bourbon with the taste of crustaceans, shells, salt, soft-bodied mollusks—the building blocks of living things.

Raise your hips, I'd read, let gravity help the sperm make its way to your eggs. I gripped my hip bones and thrust my pelvis into the air.

Just days before, Tiny had lifted up her shirt and showed me her sagging breasts, the jagged white stretch marks surrounding her areolas.

My babies done sucked me dry and moved on, she'd said.

The boat rocked with Mac's shifting weight. Zydo paced the hallway, keeping one eye on me and one eye on Mac. Though my chances were ugly and greatly diminished, I put my legs up on the wall to hold them all inside.

The Right Company

The month after I found out my husband, Nate, slept with a woman who rode dressage, I rented a run-down cottage on Abbet's Cove with sloping pine floors and a large front porch that caught the sound-side breeze. The Realtor dropped a marble and it rolled from the front door to the back. I'd always wanted to live in an old house, but Nate had preferred new construction. Perfect, I said to the Realtor. I'll take it.

I attached an oil painting of the Virgin Mother to my headboard with a Chip Clip. She was street-vendor beautiful and reminded me of Donna Reed, draped in a blue bedsheet, lipstick and rouge faultlessly applied. That night I almost slept, the faint smell of Fritos above my pillow.

Dear Mary, I prayed, let me be celibate and rational. Let me, for once, forget about men and be happy.

Lights off, I lay in bed, no one but Mary listening, remembering all the men I'd slept with, the boys I'd wanted who hadn't wanted me back, and how it had ruined parts of my life. The love letters I'd left in a locker for the star pitcher in high school—he hadn't read them. The beers I'd bought for the guitarist six years my junior—he'd blushed. The husband I'd loved—he'd strayed. Maybe I hadn't tried hard enough. Better not to try at all, I figured. Better to cut out the complexity and admit that I never really believed in marriage, the power of a vow between flawed people.

Mother Mary, I said. How can I find peace after this year?

Have faith, she said.

You always say that, I said. Everyone does.

Two cats were already living in the house when I moved in. I let them stay. I let them sleep in the bed.

When I couldn't sleep—I've had insomnia for years—I walked through my new neighborhood and gazed into other people's living room windows. Televisions lit rooms like squad cars. I saw the backs of people's heads, arms around shoulders, the moments when a family has relaxed into itself, into the couch, faces unwatched and watching.

Sometimes I sat outside and watched the silhouette of my new neighbor on his ham radio, his tin-sided shed lit up at night. From the porch swing I could hear the anarchist funk band practicing in the abandoned barbershop, the metallic sound of the doughnut shop stacking trays in trucks for the morning delivery.

I was a runaway from a husband who had cheated but felt bad about it—bad enough to want me back. I just wasn't brave enough to go. I was onto something about myself. Even if my heart was broken, maybe this was my chance to live the way I wanted to live, and where. Sure I'd be lonely. Sure I'd crave companionship. But the idea of real freedom was seductive.

Within two months, I'd made one new friend in town—Al Hastings. Al was a food writer who frequented the mom-and-pop restaurants of Eastern North Carolina. He talked about vanishing Americana, red-eyed gravy, the genericized Southern vernacular. He was fat and harmless, and we shared a love of comfort food. Five mornings a week at eight o'clock, Al and I ate breakfast at Ella's, a brick diner a few blocks from the harbor. He only had eyes for food, but he was company. I didn't have to sleep with him to earn a conversation over breakfast. Though we spent a lot of time together, we never held hands, or even hugged for that matter. I'd only seen him look at Mae's plates with lust, never my décolletage or tanned legs. I didn't want to sleep with him, but I wanted him to want me all the same.

My husband once said attraction is accidental, that bodies decide on each other. Al and I seemed to have bodies that ignored each other, bodies more focused on what hip, cheap meal lay ahead.

In Abbet's Cove, I found comfort in routine—in scratch biscuits and Sanka, in the company of a man who loved to lick grease from his fingers. Sometimes Al ordered things I couldn't watch him eat, like brains and eggs. When he placed his order, his accent was thick, like he was trying to get in good with the waitress.

One morning, five months into our breakfast routine, I slid into the booth next to him just as the waitress was handing him a menu. He smiled at me and did not waste time placing his order.

Fried chicken and hotcakes, he said. Thank you, ma'am.

Try and write a review without the words *tender* and *crispy*, I said. Can you do it?

Ella's had six booths and a lunch counter. Al liked to watch the fishermen, fresh off the morning's boats, order biscuits and gravy. The booth stuck to the undersides of our thighs. The linoleum floor peeled underneath the chair legs. An air-conditioning unit hummed and dripped in the corner window. There was a display of Lance snack foods next to the counter that no one ever touched, though the honey-bun package said *bakery fresh!* Ella was long dead, her skillet bronzed and mounted on the wall. The short-order chefs, former marines from the nearby base, were large and sweaty and peered through the window behind the counter. The menu was listed on a ribbed plastic board that hung next to Ella's skillet. Underneath were stacks of newspapers and a gum and cigarette machine.

I liked eating at Ella's because it was sacred to a few loyal customers but otherwise seemed forgotten. It was a quiet place, a time warp that reminded me of growing up in the South, going out to lunch with my father after his golf game, or eating with my mother during a shopping trip. At Ella's I didn't feel like anyone's wife; I felt like my old self.

Did you know they have three types of ham here? Al asked. Country, city, and Virginia country. I've never counted before, he said.

Each morning went like this. Margie, the waitress, fussed over Al's hair, smoked as she topped off his mug. After ordering, we'd watch Mussolini, the small Italian man who owned the market across the street, open up his shop. Mussolini stocked sauce, cheese, wine, and pasta. He arrived each morning with his large white dog, who rode in the front seat of his van.

For weeks I'd been feeling sorry for Mussolini. He looked like a tragic character, balding and stooped, and his shop didn't seem to do a lot of business. He lived nearby and kept his dog outside his house at night, chained to an oak tree. I'd seen the dog on my insomnia-fueled walks.

Look at him, I said. A sad man. Weighed down by his name.

Do you want cheese grits, Cajun grits, or plain? Al asked.

I'm feeling downright humble, I said. Plain with butter, please, sir.

Al's book *Eating the Americana Way* was under contract, and we were planning a party at Ella's to celebrate. It was a good distraction for me. I needed something to take my mind off of my husband. Last year I'd found a note I did not write in Nate's pocket: *Imagine what I can do with my entire body.*

Nate and I still talked on Fridays. He was always the one to make the call. Never me.

Every time we spoke, he said he wanted me back, even after the months I'd spent here in bed with two cats.

I don't really need a man in my life right now, I'd tell him. You gave me an out.

Nate was an animal behaviorist from California who'd come to North Carolina for further training at the state veterinary school. He'd started off as a condor nesting specialist, then turned to academia. I'd studied politics but began catering weddings after college. I wanted to go to law school but was afraid to take out the loans.

We *are* married, he told me. It's the same pot.

I want to pull my weight, I said. Not take three years out of working and acquire six figures of debt.

During our relationship, I'd often complained of feeling trained. I rejected bouquets and chocolates as positive feedback. How's this any different from rabbit meat? I'd ask, picturing myself a hooded bird clutching his arm in anticipation of a reward.

Don't be so principled, he'd say. Let me spoil you. Let me feel necessary.

But even when we were together I kept my own bank account and a separate group of friends I could go out with when he worked late. I liked to have a contingency plan—people died, spouses cheated. My father had left my mother for a family friend when she was fifty-three, and I'd seen the damage it had done. Before he left, my mother had never lived alone or worked. She shut down afterward, only going to church and running the occasional errand. I wanted to keep my independence tangible, not be forced to find it late in life.

There were things about Nate I didn't like. One, he wasn't a dog lover and refused to let me keep one in the house. What kind of man didn't like dogs? He also was addicted to exercise and hated cooking, sometimes choosing to slice fresh bananas over instant oatmeal for breakfast and dinner instead of eating the meals I'd prepared. He cringed when I made pies. All that butter, he said.

When we talked after my move, Nate closed each conversation with a question: Are you happy?

I always lied. Each day in Abbet's Cove felt like an audition. I was learning the layout of the grocery store, how to walk the hot sidewalks in my bare feet. Aside from Al, I had not made friends. The locals had cancered faces, sun-white hair, and scratched boats. They wore gold-rope jewelry and boat shoes and drank beer in the morning on the boardwalk. I wondered if you could love a town despite its people.

I had one friend, Rhea, who called every week and wanted to visit. She thought I'd made a rash decision. I'm concerned, she said. Rhea worked the late shift at an animal shelter in the town an hour west of where I'd lived with Nate. She cared for incontinent cats. Rhea was outdated, her hair permed and jeans cuffed. She talked like a bus driver. I'd known her since I was five.

She came by one afternoon after my breakfast with Al, bursting into the house, smacking her gum. I like this place more than I thought I would, she said. It fits you. Needs more furniture, though.

I followed Rhea through the house as she wandered down the hallway and peered in each room. She stopped in my bedroom and walked toward the bed.

Wash your hands before you sit down, I said.

Already washed, she said, showing me her palms and sitting down on my coverlet, which was covered with cat hair. How are you?

I'm okay, I said. I'm thinking of getting some catering gigs going down here.

How's Al? she asked. Are you sleeping together yet?

He's fat, I said. Which means we can focus on other things.

Rhea kneeled on my bed and touched Mary's face. One of my nameless cats straddled the headboard like a tree branch and sniffed at Rhea's hands, agitated, tail flicking.

What's this bullshit? Rhea asked, pointing at Mary. You've never been religious.

I talk to her about men, I said. Haven't I told you? I'm giving them up.

Rhea suggested that as the Christchile's mother—and she said it like that—Mary probably had an entourage of hair and makeup professionals who followed her around the Holy Land in case she had her portrait painted.

It's easy to be beautiful, Rhea said, when you have an entourage.

I stroked the cat's chin.

What do you think Mary's going to do for you? Rhea said.

Have you ever thought about what it would be like, I said, if sex wasn't important? If it didn't matter? If you could just go on about life as a happy, single person? Why don't more people do that?

I think you're getting weird here, Rhea said, blowing a bubble with her gum.

A doctor I'd once seen for my insomnia had explicit instructions: "Use the bed only for sleeping and sex." I asked Rhea to put out or get off the bed. She hugged me and went home to her husband and kids, to the place where she belonged.

I left Nate the night I found the note in his pocket. I dropped my wedding ring in the gravel lot of the Abbet's Cove Piggly Wiggly, where I'd stopped to buy a twelve-pack of anything. I left it there.

My parents had taken me to Abbet's Cove for a week when I was ten. We stayed at the Shady Lake Motel, which boasted a fifteen-foot plaster woman in a bikini out front. Back then there were canoes and a diving board, and you could cross the road to the beach. Everyone was barefoot that summer except for the proprietor, who dragged her oxygen tank around the parking lot while the families cooked on the grills and watched fireworks launched from the base. My mother had worried the proprietor was flammable and shooed her away.

We lay on the beach for hours that first full day, my mother covering my father's back in sunscreen, passing him the occasional beer or sandwich. Sand crabs scurried from one hole to another. I put my feet in the ocean and watched tiny bivalves bury themselves in the sand around my toes. During high tide, small fish came in with the waves and swam the expanse of shallow water. I was fascinated by the lives I saw, so when it came to eating what my father had caught for dinner, I went hungry—I couldn't bring myself to consume the creatures I'd watched all day. I cringed as my father sucked down raw oysters. I've been a vegetarian ever since.

The night I left Nate, the first place I thought of was the Shady Lake. It was the last place I could remember seeing my parents genuinely happy together, and it was close by. I drove up and down Highway 301, saw the plaster woman was gone, and so was the lake. Instead, I found an unnamed vinyl-sided motel run by two Indian women. The sign said only: *Free HBO*. I stayed there anyway. I wasn't planning on sleeping.

I took the Bible out of the bedside table drawer for inspiration or comfort. It didn't help, and neither did free HBO, which in the early hours of the morning seemed to show nothing but soft porn.

One program showed a woman in a purple nightie straddling a motorcycle and pleasuring a man with her manicured hands.

You know you really just want him to take you to dinner, I said to the screen, and tell you how pretty you are. That you're smart. That you don't have crow's-feet.

The day after Rhea's visit, at breakfast with Al, I worried about Mussolini's dog. It was warm out, perhaps ninety, and Mussolini had left the dog in the van.

Al! Margie called out from the kitchen, holler at me when y'alls ready to order.

I picked at the laminated specials list.

Fried-egg sandwich? Al asked, scanning the menu he must've known by heart.

Biscuits and honey, I said. Remind me to ask Mae for Country Crock in the little packets so I can take some home for the cats.

Mussolini stood in the doorway of his shop, hosing down his sidewalk. He scowled. The last of his hair whipped across his forehead. He wore his khaki pants high and his white-collared shirt tucked in. I tapped on the window. Your dog, I mouthed. It's hot.

Shhhh, Al said, nodding toward three blue-hairs in the booth next to ours. Those old ladies are sharing recipes for pimento cheese.

Al craned his neck as if that would help him hear better. He flipped to a clean page in his notebook. Beads of sweat ran down his nose. I wondered how much longer he would last with all that lard in his arteries.

Just write down mayonnaise and be done with it, I said, miffed he wasn't paying me enough attention.

A few minutes later one of the ladies, her white hair curled and translucent, said: And hell or high water I was gonna get married! Won't no one gonna call me off Daniel. I'm sure y'all was the same way.

Their laughter made me think for a moment that it was a good idea to live in the same town all your life, but I knew better. When your husband cheats on you in a small town, everyone knows, and then you have to move away to hold your head up and stop being the person everyone hugs.

I don't want people feeling sorry for me, I'd told Rhea when I decided to stay in Abbet's Cove. I hate that look.

I want my release party to be chic but humble, Al said. I want to remind folks about how good life used to be when people ate butter.

I reminded him these were the same people that pushed tobacco and voted for Jesse Helms. You can't romanticize the Dixiecrat palette, I said. It's not good for anybody.

Mussolini tacked up new signs for cannoli and prosciutto. He sat in a folding chair outside and smoked a cigarette as if he was daring customers to come in.

Later, with grits in his mouth, Al imagined talking to Mussolini: Your mozzarella is fantastic, but who wants to buy cheese from a fascist?

Al reminded me of some greasy Buddha, grinning and full, elbows on the table, both chins resting in his hands.

So, I said. Are we seeing a movie tonight?

Sorry, Al said. Dinner with my mother.

Drinks at my place afterward? I said.

Early to bed for this guy, he said, shaking his head.

Wasn't there a small part of him, I wondered, that wanted to know me better? Undress me?

I pictured Mother Mary, then, and let her clean up the corners of my mind, which had landed in the gutter, wondering just how bad Al looked without clothes on.

Two months ago I had broken my celibacy vows and called Nate. We'd met at Free HBO. There was sand in the sheets. We ripped each other's clothes off. I slapped his face and bit his shoulder. Afterward, he held onto my hip as we lay silent on the bed, watching a fly on the wood-paneled wall. The fly moved left, left, up, right in logical squares of movement.

I hated myself for giving in.

Every fly, every gnat, is driven by algorithms, Nate said.

You just want me to believe that you couldn't help it, I said, pulling away.

The fly has more faith in his gods than we do, he said.

You've said that before, I said, putting on my pants. Probably about a condor. Math is not a good enough reason to sleep with someone else.

Do you plan on coming home to pick up the rest of your stuff? Your winter socks or your guitar? Nate asked. He swung his long legs out of the twin bed. I just need to know when to expect you.

I no longer expect anything, I said. Not winter or love or the way soy scrapple might make my stomach feel. This year, I'm letting those things sneak up on me, if that's all right with you.

You don't know what you want, he said. That's the problem.

Nate's divorce papers arrived the day before Al's party. Seeing the documents made me realize the finality of the situation. I called him.

I have to move on, he said. His voice was soft and serious. I know I'm the one who did wrong here, but I can't keep waiting.

There's someone else? I said. The one who rides dressage?

You can keep the silver, he said. And the dining room set. Anything, really.

I don't care, I said. That stuff only matters to women who need men.

I'm moving back to California, he said. I'll give you my new number.

I won't call, I said.

I knew I wouldn't, but I knew I'd be tempted to. I was over being Nate's wife, but I grieved the loss of his attention. I enjoyed that part, feeling wanted, feeling like the thing that got away.

I hung up the phone and called Al. I wanted to distract myself.

Margie called to let me know the peach ice cream turned out beautifully, he said. She also mentioned that she saw Mussolini kicking his dog in the street this morning—a real shame.

Someone should intervene, I said.

I know, Al told me, breathing hard into the phone. But this is going to be a fun party. Did I mention I'm gonna hand out my grandmother's hoecake recipe as a party favor?

You can't bring hoecake back, I said. People got rickety down here when they ate all that corn.

Have you been crying? he asked.

I'm fine, I said, suddenly eager to hang up the phone.

I went walking that night. I itemized my old furniture in my head to the drowned sound of acoustic guitar on the boardwalk. The soft putter of a catamaran motoring into a slip for the night. Someone washing dishes with the alley door open. On the sidewalk, I passed gas streetlights, shadows of old buildings. The empty bank, the map store, fishing nets in the shop windows. Gulls balanced on pier posts, their loose down caught on the jagged wood. The organist in the old church practiced for Sunday's service.

My mother once told me: Never underestimate avoidance as an effective coping mechanism.

I'd heard of a woman who only had use of her right brain after a stroke. She lost her ego, left it like a suitcase in another country. This was how she found bliss.

My bedroom in the new cottage was still full of suitcases, bags stuffed with old blouses and ceramic animals. Boxes of books lay underneath the bed. I hadn't unpacked; I was still deciding, still searching for the right company.

I made my way home. My cottage was small and dark and the roof sagged. Yellow paint peeled from the front door. I let myself in and turned on the lights. The cats scattered.

I am vulnerable but not scared, I thought, getting in bed. I'm alone, but in charge of my life.

I opened up one of the Country Crock containers I kept in the drawer of my bedside table. I let the cats lick my fingers, then the packet. I fell asleep, but like many other nights I woke up after a few hours, my mind racing. I pulled on shorts, grabbed twine for a makeshift leash, and walked out the front door. The sound of the key turning in the lock seemed to echo down the street. The park was quiet, the gutter punks had gone, and the organist was satisfied.

I walked to Mussolini's house, a small brick ranch painted white and surrounded by a chain-link fence. The streetlights hummed overhead. I leaned over the fence, pressed my finger to my lips, and said to the white dog: I have a bed you can sleep in.

The dog did not want to leave. Free of his chain, he went back to the tree and lay down, curling his body into a sickle shape, fanning his tail over his nose.

You can have better, I told him, backing away. This is your chance.

I walked back to the harbor side of town. I took my sandals off, sat on the dock, put my feet into the dark water, laid my forehead against the cool metal railing.

When I was younger, I would put my ears, then my mouth, against the glass walls of aquariums. I would speak to the sharks, the turtles, the translucent squid. *Remember me.*

But this year, I might eat whatever someone put in front of me.

Rhea called early the next morning.

I heard from Nate, she said. About things being final. Are you okay?

Me? I said. I'm okay.

I want to tell you about this blind cat, she said. The star of the shelter.

He's all white, she said. Useless eyes. Ulysses, we call him. And every night I watch him jump from the floor to a perch, four feet in the air. He never misses.

Is this to keep me from feeling sorry for myself? I asked. Or does he need a home?

It's about faith, Rhea said. You're going to be okay.

On Sunday mornings, a gospel choir would walk by my cottage in their robes, singing *Oh shout it out!* The first time I heard them, I ran to the front porch in my bathrobe and started crying. They pulled children in wagons, their voices visible in the cool air. Every Sunday I waited for this.

All I needed of religion, I realized, was the beautiful sound of someone else's faith.

After Rhea's call, I walked the neighborhood. Only the very old and very young were awake. The retirees read their papers; it was early enough to wear a bathrobe on the porch. A mother nursed her baby on a porch swing. Her hair blew wild in the wind, which had begun to pick up as a morning thunderstorm rolled in.

I came home and picked out a low-cut dress for Al's party. I hung it on the top of the bedroom door.

If only I had an entourage, I said to Mary. People to smooth my hair, brush eye shadow on my lids, promote my miracles on billboards.

I returned to my bed at eight. Mary hung crooked, but I left her that way, beautiful and imperfect. She hovered over me with the grace of a drunk. The wind stirred the walnut tree next door; shells pelted the siding of my house like gunfire.

I turned on the television and watched from my bed. The morning news footage showed coast guard helicopters searching fruitlessly for a young girl sucked into the sea on a riptide. The weatherman issued a small-craft advisory.

My sheets were cold. I slid my legs to one side. Once, unable to sleep and walking at sunrise, I'd seen a blue heron circle the rooftops downtown, its legs limp, trailing. I pictured it now, gray and archaic, searching for a place to land. In towns like these, I thought, there are no perfect rescues. You go down with your own ship.

Night Hunting

Every year we went to a holiday party at Mr. Simons's, where a haggard orange tabby held court on a chair with broken caning and an apricot poodle wove between guests' legs. Mom and I always came back to Pawlet for the holidays to be with my grandparents—they were usually staples at the party. This year they were in Florida on a senior cruise, but Mom and I promised we'd attend in their place, especially since we'd just moved back to Pawlet for good.

Pawlet was a small town in southern Vermont, the kind of place where you couldn't count on cable or phone reception. We'd been used to living in wild places, quiet towns that sat on the verge of nothing, towns that bordered vast deserts or thousand-acre tracts owned by paper companies. Six months ago we'd moved to Pawlet to be near my grandparents, taking a rental next to their house. Mom was sick. Every night, every family dinner, there were unspoken words in her mouth: *When I die*.

Our life in Pawlet was a contrast to the solitary existence we otherwise led; we went to basketball games at the high school, pancake breakfasts at the community center. In her last months Mom wanted to be around people, to feel the warmth of connection, for both of our sakes.

Mr. Simons's driveway was iced over and Mom and I shuffled our way from the dirt road to the front door in the country dark. The house glowed, and the silhouettes of neighbors filled the windows. The floodlights revealed the breath of the horses grazing in the side pen, the slick spots ahead of us.

That's coyote scat, I said, pointing at a pile in the driveway.

Dog, Mom said, trying to hurry me inside with a palm on the back of my neck.

Similar but different and I know when I'm right, I said, standing over it. You can always tell by the hair. And the oval prints.

Mom was afraid of coyotes, and for good reason. Back in Utah, one sank its teeth into her leg as she defended her favorite dog, a terrier named Aida. Round about fall, people in Pawlet started talking about a seventy-pound albino coyote in the woods behind our house. I'd noticed Mom stayed out of the backyard. I hated to see her scared.

Lightning can't strike twice, I'd said, but then we'd both thought about the return of her cancer. The theory was shit.

Mr. Simons's slate steps were slick with ice. The soft roar of the party enveloped us as we opened the door. Mom scanned the overburdened coatrack. I stuffed my mittens into the pockets of her jacket for safekeeping. I was notorious for losing things.

Remember, Mom whispered, squeezing my hand, gripping a bottle of wine in the other, be polite.

Marvelous! Mr. Simons cried, walking toward Mom and me. He kissed us each on the cheek. So glad you're here.

Where are your folks? he asked Mom.

Florida, she said. I *made* them go. They never travel, you know. They deserve it.

Mom had begged them to leave; they hadn't wanted to. I think Mom saw the cruise as a premature thank-you for taking care of me, a chance for them to rest before the cancer worsened and she needed more help.

The party crowd was old, dignified, their un-made-up faces welcoming in the low light. Bakers, lawyers, farmers, quilters, retired teachers. They wore heavy knit sweaters to keep out the Vermont wind, long velvet skirts, artisan earrings. The kitchen and dining room tables were crowded with potluck fare. Masking tape marked the plastic trays and wooden bowls: *Daniels Family. Griffin. Please return to Bob C.*

Pepsi, please, I said to the sullen man behind the card table bar. Maker's on ice for my mom. Stir in a little orange juice to make it healthy.

Point to your mother, the bartender said.

Mom waved.

Mom had one breast and a habit of moving towns when she got bored, dating men who could never hold her interest. She liked it that way. But now her cancer was back and she was weak. She held on to the kitchen counter as she greeted friends, mostly people my grandparents knew. She smiled, but I could see the dark circles around her eyes, her hollowed-out cheeks and thinning hair. I memorized her body, her voice. Everything she did felt like the last time. Everything she said felt like the last word.

Last summer Mom and I had lived in a single-wide in Moab. We'd patrolled a stretch of the Colorado River in a rubber boat, Mom's dog, Aida, running from end to end. Every night we heated a simple dinner, usually scrambled eggs with black beans and diced peppers, and held court over a splintered picnic table next to the trailer. Mom drank warm wine and read romance novels, Aida safe on her lap. At sunset, a lone coyote would come to drink at the river, the water between us like a moving fence.

What will it be tonight, I always asked him. Chicken? Rabbit?

At night I imagined the coyote coming to me like a dog, resting his head on my knee as I groomed his coat with my fingers, leaving tufts of hair on the dry ground.

Watch out for a pack, Mom had warned me. You're bite-sized.

By December I had already tired of the gray Vermont winter and found myself wanting to return to red-rocked Moab, the dusty bike trails and wide-mouthed sky. I loved to run and in Utah I could go for miles without ever seeing another person. But Pawlet was the right place for Mom to be.

One of Mr. Simons's poodles, Fauna, forced her head underneath my dangling fingers and leaned against my thigh. Her coat was sculpted perfectly, a living, breathing, manicured hedge.

Hey, lady, I said to her. Nice 'fro.

Aren't they marvelous, Mr. Simons was saying across the room, pointing to his moccasins. Millie made these for me when I was in college.

Thirty-six years ago, Millie said, adjusting the tortoiseshell comb at the nape of her neck.

Millie Banks was a hundred years old. She was slight and

stooped, and wore her white hair in a loose bun on her crown. Brown leather boots peeked out from underneath her plaid flannel skirt. When Millie spoke, no one interrupted. We looked at her as if a centenarian were another species. I followed her as she walked down the hall to the living room.

Every year Millie played the violin and led the string trio in carols at Mr. Simons's party, and every year I stood at the back of the room pretending to sing, watching her face. She was legendary. When she was seventeen she'd fought off a cougar in the woods behind her father's dairy. Talked it down for half an hour in a calm voice, I'd heard, then poked its eyes out with her thumbs when it finally lunged. People often asked to see the claw marks on her calf; they knew she'd oblige. It was her story, part of her myth.

Millie lived alone, drove her own tractor until she was ninety-two. Split her own wood. She and Mom had much in common—except their longevity. They were independent outdoorswomen, native Vermonters.

I wanted to be near her, siphon off a handful of her years and give them to Mom.

Millie turned the corner just as Erik Sanderson caught my arm.

Hannah! he said, popping a shrimp tail into his mouth.

Erik was in his early thirties, good-looking but strange. He lived down the road from the place we were renting and was interesting as hell, but I'd have to find a way out of the conversation. Even though I wanted to talk to him, I couldn't stand to make Mom worry any more than she already did—she'd think I was flirting.

Don't take up with someone like that, she'd said recently, referring to Erik. I heard words she didn't add: *when I'm gone.*

Pawlet was the kind of place where young girls fell in with older men and got pregnant; slim pickings led to cross-generational romance. Mom was insistent that I stay single and go to college.

Erik means well, I'd said.

I'd recently found myself thinking of Erik at night. He was robust and competent, a survivalist who wasted nothing. He lived in a tricked-out shed with a woodstove and a composting toilet. I liked his wild eyes, the gray hairs in his beard. I liked the way he looked at me; he didn't talk to just anyone. He was the kind of man who made you feel safe.

He'd suck the joy out of a young girl's life, Mom said. He's always waiting for a financial meltdown, the apocalypse—Lord knows what he's got stashed in those outbuildings.

Hear the coyotes these last few nights? he asked, standing close enough for me to smell the wood smoke in his sweater.

I nodded. I had, only because our dogs woke us at weird hours, howling responses through the windowpanes into the dark night.

They make Mom nervous, I said. She's keeping the horses in the front pasture, under the lights.

Erik speared a sauced-up minifrank with his toothpick.

Coyotes, he said, got my friend's beagle down the road. One drew him into the field and the others converged from the tree line. Brutal. I saw . . .

Is this a ship in a bottle? I asked him, pointing toward the mantelpiece. I couldn't stomach any stories about death.

More of a Plexiglas box, Erik said. You can cut a custom box with any old band saw.

You could always draw Erik onto the next thing as long as you talked how-to's. How to transplant a raspberry patch. How to keep foxes out of the henhouse.

Erik had been learning Chinese and stockpiling reading glasses, scrap metal, and tampons. I'll be rich in the next barter economy, he claimed.

I found a jacket that might fit you in the church lost and found, Erik was saying. Kid's down jacket, I think.

People began filtering in from the kitchen to cluster near the piano where the string trio had assembled. I caught Mom's eye across the room.

Erik tugged his ear and looked at the threadbare Oriental rug.

Mr. Simons tapped his wineglass with his fork.

Time for carols, Erik said. He nodded at me and moved toward two French doors that opened onto a patio. Mom left the kitchen and stood behind me, held me by the shoulders.

The house became silent as Millie tuned up, resting and readjusting her wrinkled chin on the violin. Guests thumbed through the lyric bulletins with the righteous glow of people who are about to SING.

I found myself dreading the carols. This year, something inside of me was too sad, too tired to hit the notes.

Erik rested his forehead against the back door. I imagined he was used to colder rooms and was coming up for air in the corner by himself. He wore a leather vest over his sweater, chewed a toothpick.

Just as Millie lifted her bow, Fauna shot out of the doggie door into the backyard. Fauna! Mr. Simons yelled, running toward the door. Erik looked at me, then bolted outside. As Millie's bow began to smart the strings of her violin, I watched him disappear behind the tree line, iced grasses knee-high and strangling his legs. The carol was anemic, though a few continued with the song, unconcerned. Dogs will be dogs, someone said. Through the window I could see Mr. Simons pacing the back patio. I wondered how fast Erik could run.

Make peace with the food chain, Mom had told me out West one night when we were looking at the neighbor's chicken coop. Do it now, before it breaks your heart.

Last week I'd seen a hawk fly onto a branch, wings massive and gray, and snatch a squirrel from a maple. I'd watched, helpless, as the yellow-eyed bird sank his claws into the writhing gray body, brought it to the frozen ground. The squirrel had made a sound that stayed in my ears for days. The bird had concentrated on his kill, eyes wide as if he were straining to get the job done. I yelled and charged him, but he would not be moved. He flew when satisfied, carried the squirrel's limp body across the field and into the trees.

The best predators, I realized, had no empathy.

People finished singing and Millie put down her bow. The rest of her trio followed suit; the pianist folded his hands into his lap.

Millie, someone said. Show us your scars.

Millie stood up and handed the pianist her violin. She made a motion for him to scoot to the edge of the bench. One hand hiking her skirt, she used the other to roll down her hose.

There, on Millie's pale leg, were three deep scratch marks, raised, the color of dark wine.

I felt Mom stiffen beside me. She had her own scars. Bite marks on her calf. Her right breast now folded into itself, the nipple gone, a purple ridge across her chest.

I can still *feel* them, Millie said to the room.

Suddenly Erik burst through the back door, Fauna in his arms, blood on his leather vest.

They took her down, he said, chest heaving. But I beat them off with a branch. The white coyote was there. It's a bitch, too. A bitch coyote, with some wild dog in it. Pups to feed and mean as hell.

Fauna's neck was bleeding. Erik wrapped it tightly in an old T-shirt and helped Mr. Simons take her out to the car.

I apologize, Mr. Simons said to the room as he was leaving, but the party's over. Linger if you need to—

Call the vet at home, Erik said. Long driveway off of Route 30. He'll meet you at the barn when it's a real emergency.

After Mr. Simons drove off, people began to say their goodbyes—kissing each other on the cheek warmly, shaking hands. I took another long look at Millie. Every year I thought I'd never see her again.

Mom and I walked slowly to the truck. On the ride home I cracked the windows to feel the cold sleet on my face.

What are you thinking about? Mom said.

The right answer would have been this: blood. How all my fear, all the looking over my shoulder added up to nothing—what I really wanted was a fight. To come out the other side, wiser.

At the side of the road, I could see our headlights pool in the eyes of a smattering of deer in the apple trees. A herd of five, they rooted in the snow for fallen apples.

The coyotes are coming for you, I said.

Don't be dramatic, Mom said. I've told you about being dramatic.

Mom exhaled. Her breath hit the window.

I thought: *This is the last time her breath will hit the window.*

The night Mom found out her cancer had returned, I'd slept by the doorway to her bedroom, just in case she needed me. I wanted to be close to her.

The night of Mr. Simons's party, Mom went to bed in her clothes.

I'm tired, she said. Can you check to make sure the horses' water isn't frozen?

I went out to the pasture and kicked snow from a crate of crab apples. There were ice crystals like webs on the horses' hocks, trails of hoofprints in the snow. We'd come home too late to lock the hens in and they'd gone up into the trees. A few clucked and cooed as I walked past.

Mom had always taught me that a horse would sense danger first. If your horse won't go, she'd say, don't go. Snakes, bears, coyotes—the horse's instincts about them are better than yours.

So, I asked the horses. What's in the woods tonight?

Half asleep, they stomped and stared and prodded my clenched fists for food. Their breath hung in the air like small clouds.

It's all about apples with you, I said.

That night, before falling asleep, I thought of the famed fourteen-year-old Texas boy who'd killed hundreds of wild hogs by leaping onto their backs and slitting their throats with a butcher knife. My grandfather had told me that one way to hunt was to make a sound like a dying cat and then lie in wait.

I mean really wail, he'd said. Cry like a baby if you have to. Sound like something worth eating.

At two a.m., the rooster crowed. Roosters are dumb as shit. They're so brave they're stupid, or they're so stupid they're brave. I'm not sure which. Regardless, they'll fight anything.

I couldn't fall back to sleep, so I walked down the hallway to Mom's room. I pushed open her door and watched her. Her sleep was deep and fitful and God knows how many painkillers she had to take to shut up all of the worries and hurt.

Years ago, Mom had studied to be a dental hygienist. She'd always liked teeth. She swore to me she'd cut my baby teeth by pressing the back of a silver spoon against my gums. She would clean my teeth herself, using her old equipment, which she doused in mouthwash. Sometimes, when I was talking, she'd slip a finger into my mouth and pull down my lip to check for tartar. She'd done it just the other day and I'd thought: *This may be the last time Mom checks my teeth.* Her finger felt rough on my gums. I could hear her jagged breath, see the yellow in the whites of her eyes.

The dogs were all sleeping in her room now, as if they knew something. I slipped down the hall to the front door, careful not to wake them. I pulled on Mom's coveralls and the sweatshirt that she kept on hooks in the garage. I cuffed the legs so they wouldn't get soaked when I went outside.

It was snowing just a little and the air was cold enough to freeze the inside of my nose. The horses were still and the rooster was quiet and the old silo in our backyard shone underneath the moon. The silo was full of bats and busted rakes and looked like a grounded spaceship. The moon was a waxing gibbous, almost full, bright enough to get around in.

The snow wasn't deep. The ground crunched as I walked through our back fields. I kept walking. Whatever made me love running made me love moving, distance, an open field. My fingers were cold; I should have worn gloves. I reached the old orchard and put one leg over the barbed-wire fence. The apples weren't good enough for whoever owned them, so they rotted, fed bears.

Hundreds of trees bore fruit in the fall. Now the apples were black and the trees without leaves. There were cattle out here—heifers and calves. I could hear them at night, especially when they were in heat. Soon they'd take the calves from the mothers and sell them for meat. Dark hulking shapes; I could feel the warmth of their bodies and smell their fermented breath as I moved past.

I knew that if I followed the ATV path through the orchard, I'd come to the back of Erik's fields. The moon caught the ice on the branches. I concentrated on the sound of my boots in the frozen snow.

I came to a barbed-wire fence Erik had thrown up over one of the old stone walls. My grandfather told me once that at the turn of the century Vermont had been near bald, all the trees stripped to make pasture for sheep and dairy cows.

Nearby, I heard branches breaking. Probably a spooked deer, I told myself.

I wondered if Erik was up at this hour, but I knew a high school girl had no business knocking on a grown man's window in the middle of the night. Still, I imagined slipping into his bed, moonlight streaming through the window, the surprised look on his face, the tender way he'd remove my clothes and drape himself over me.

If he was smart, he wouldn't do it. I knew that. He'd get into trouble; I was too young. But I liked the idea, the heat it generated in my body.

I pushed on. The skin on my face was so cold that it moved in slow motion. My boots weren't waterproof and my feet were starting to feel damp and numb. Erik once told me never to come into the woods without a leather belt, that with a belt you could do anything.

When under attack, he'd said, hold it in front of you for the animal to bite, then strangle the bastard.

I felt my waist. Bare.

A few hundred yards and I'd be near the Wells's old dairy, the yard where Millie had fought off the cougar with her bare hands and soft voice. So this was Vermont in the dead of night—wild, beautiful.

A snow plow seemed to appear out of nowhere on the road nearby, metal against ice. The sound sent something flying through the woods on my right.

I stood, motionless. I had to remind myself to breathe.

I thought of Mom then. How brave she'd been this year. I thought of the night she'd come sprinting back to the trailer in Utah, sobbing, her pant leg soaked in blood, saying: Aida, Aida. I thought of the way the painkillers took something out of her, put a crazy look in her eyes, the way she gripped the backs of chairs and stood with her teeth clenched while the tumors inside of her grew.

The rustling stopped. It seemed as if the snow had muted everything around me—the birds, the road, the wind. I saw thin strips of smoke rising on the hill, wood fires dying as people slept beneath their thick winter quilts.

I knew I couldn't stay in one place for long with my feet this cold. I stumbled through the pasture, backtracking. I paused and listened. Nothing. I went on. I paused again. I was convinced I heard the soft shuffling of feet in fresh snow. I groped around in Mom's pockets and found her penknife. I switched open the blade and began to run.

For maybe half a second, it occurred to me that I could die, maybe from the cold, maybe from something worse, and that if

I did, I wouldn't have to live through my own mother's death. But then I pictured her face, how tired she was, and I knew I couldn't let it happen. I'd been looking for a fight, and maybe I'd found one.

I stopped at the creek that branched down the hillside and into the valley. In the dead of winter it would be frozen over, the ice blue and warped by rocks. But for now it was moving too fast to freeze and I could hear it, full from the snow and late-fall rains. I stood on a slick rock in the middle of the creek, trying to regroup. The cold adrenaline made my body feel electric.

I heard the coyote huffing, sucking in air and releasing a series of small yips. Large, white, and graceful, she trotted past me, circled back, and stood on one side of the creek. Her three pups followed. She curled her lip. She was close; it would take nothing for her to lunge at me. I didn't know whether the water would stop her.

I could see her eyes shining gold. My stomach plummeted; my mind and heart began to race.

Get the fuck out of here! I tried to shout, but my voice was small and scared.

I put the knife in my mouth and without breaking eye contact I stooped to pick up a large rock. My fingers went numb in the water.

I'd always hated my grandfather's hunting. I'd never understood how he could kill another living being, not until this night, when, for the first time, I realized I might do anything to survive.

The coyote paced the bank and came close enough for me to strike. We were both desperate. Her eyes locked on to my body. I was sure she wasn't going to let me pass, and still I hesitated. I didn't want to hurt her. She came closer. Her lip curled.

I thought, then, of Mom coming into the trailer in Utah, her leg covered in blood. I thought about the way she avoided the backyard after twilight now, sick and lacking the strength to face down her fear.

I hurled the rock and hit the coyote on the right side of the head. She went down. She'd begun to pull herself back up when I took off. She was plenty big, but smaller than people said she'd be.

I ran with her eyes at my back. I ran for ten minutes, tripping over rocks and roots. I didn't find the ATV trails. I bushwhacked, prickers dragging across my pants. I was breathing hard. My extremities began to warm. Blood began to seep from my right hand.

Without realizing it, I had clamped down on the open switch-blade.

As I ran, I thought of the bare skin on the underside of a dog, the vulnerable patch of naked flesh on the torso and hind legs. I pictured the coyote bitch rolled on her side, her pups curling against her body, taking the last of her warmth. She would give it to them; she would give them everything.

I broke through the woods and spotted our house, a white farmhouse, faintly lit from within. The woodstove chimney sent up a sad stream of smoke, the fire nothing but cinders by now. My fear was beginning to turn to grief, my thoughts to the wounded coyote whose pups wouldn't make it through the winter. I thought of my mother in bed and hoped she was still asleep. I thought of the wild cells ravaging her body without pause.

The dogs sensed me coming through the woods; I could hear their muffled barks, and, as I neared, their claws digging at the front door.

I stripped down and left Mom's coveralls on the floor. I

wrapped a washcloth around my hand to stop the bleeding. Shivering, I opened Mom's bedroom door. She was sitting up in bed, still in her faded party clothes, her arms outstretched. I went to her. She pulled me against her body, as she had done when I was a child, and held me there, in the cave of her chest, in the place of everything that was missing.

Every Vein a Tooth

He left when Salli, the one-eared retriever, ate one-third of his leaf collection.

She has separation anxiety, I said, pleading her case and mine. She was abandoned, attacked by a pack of dogs and left for dead.

What kind of house is this? he asked.

The technical answer: A Victorian Queen Anne with stick detailing in the gable. A spindled gingerbread in disrepair.

Gray was referring to the three golden retrievers in various states of decline—Salli with her missing ear and lumps of scar tissue, paralyzed Prince dragging his cart down the hallway, toothless and epileptic Sam dreaming wild on the kitchen floor. Or, it might have been the declawed raccoon marauding in the living room. The one-eyed chinchilla nesting in cedar chips in what could have been the nursery. I didn't count the feral cats—they lived underneath the sofa, largely out of sight.

Before he left, we had spent a day at Lake Mattamuskeet, collecting what Gray called "complete leaves"—leaves undamaged by frost or insect.

Ideally, he had said, we want the entire leaf, a small part of the twig, and a terminal bud.

Mattamuskeet was a mosquito-filled wetlands depression surrounded by flat farmland and hunting clubs. Just deep as a swan's neck, Gray had said.

I tried not to think of the hidden predators—red wolves behind the tree line, alligators in the marshlands, as I stood next to Gray in a patch of wild millet.

Don't get me wrong, I told Gray, I love predators. I'm just intimidated by teeth.

You should think about getting rid of that chinchilla, he said, waving a bandaged finger at me. What good is a snap-happy, one-eyed chinchilla?

Gray reached for the triangular toothed leaf of an eastern cottonwood with his pocketknife shears. In the distance I could see a great blue heron standing awkwardly in the water. A cormorant floated by, and I wondered what it would be like to be aerodynamic, to shoot through the water like a bullet.

Hand me the magazine, Gray said, looking down at me from his portable ladder.

Cat Fanciers' Almanac or *Guns & Ammo*? I asked, handing him both.

You won't be getting this one back, he warned me, holding the magazine fronted by a sleek Japanese bobtail.

I don't have much love for hobby breeders, I said. Put it to good use.

And this? he asked, holding the camouflaged cover of *Guns & Ammo*.

Compliments of the local hunters' association, I said, after the press covered the shelter's protest on Sunday hunting.

Don't tell me, he said, shaking his head.

The cormorant made a quick exit from the water and perched at the top of a bald cypress, drying his wings in the winter sun.

Gray carefully inserted the cottonwood leaf into the pages of *Cat Fanciers'*. With the toe of his boot he nudged an open sleeve of Laffy Taffy and a condom wrapper that lay in the grass.

There's a story here, he said, raising an eyebrow.

We cast off in the canoe with a bag of peanut butter sandwiches and a small cooler of beer. Deep as a swan's neck or not, the water was opaque and choppy.

I looked for the yellow eyes of alligators.

I always count the geese, Gray said, eyes to the clouds. If they aren't an even flock, something's wrong. Someone's been left behind.

One thing I do not understand are sentimental hunters.

Did you scoop the litter before leaving? I asked, already thinking about my house full of pets, the chaos of dinner.

Nope, Gray said, taking a bite of his sandwich.

He'd been mad at me since I'd brought home the last feral cat. I considered his negligence of the litter box just one in a string of rebellious acts.

Gray stared at the sky, inspecting a skein of Canadian geese.

Two, four, six, eight . . . all's well, he said, his words tangled in peanut butter.

When we got home, the cats had marked on the couch. Prince had pulled cereal boxes from the recycling bin. Salli had gnawed through two of Gray's leaf albums, spread the pages and specimens from one end of the living room to the other.

Gray grabbed a fistful of his hair in frustration and knelt next to his chewed albums.

Unacceptable, he said.

I tried to keep the house clean. I kept the closet door closed. I bought a special vacuum cleaner for pet hair. I lit fragrant candles. I wrapped the couch in plastic sheeting. But there were some things I could not control. I said nothing and went to the kitchen for a beer.

As Gray packed, I sat on the living room carpet with my chin on my knees and listened to the sound of him leaving me. He cleared his throat. Walked to and from the closet. Splashed water on his face. Riffled through the junk drawer. Zipped the duffel bag.

Maybe if you can get your life together, he said, pausing at the door.

I accepted his assessment. My mother had felt the same way. Not everyone could live with tumbleweeds of dog hair on the steps, the night sounds of feral cats exploring the house, the raccoon rattling his cage door at two in the morning.

The retrievers came to me, stuck their cold noses on my cheek. Aged and humbled, they looked like orangutans, their cinnamon-and-honey-colored coats matted, their eyes framed in white.

When Gray left, the cats came out of hiding long enough for me to name them.

Two weeks after Gray moved in with his mother, the head of the shelter called.

They finally busted him, Emory said. The suburban shepherd.

I'll be there in fifteen, I said.

Bring your mask and gloves, she said. It's worse than we thought.

I hung up the phone and took the retrievers outside, topped off the various water bowls around the house, and caged the raccoon. I'd learned early there was no such thing as a raccoon-proof home. I had a hole in my mattress to prove it.

The suburban shepherd lived in a termite-eaten farmhouse on the edge of town. His porch sagged and the paint peeled. A weather-beaten American flag flew from a piece of PVC pipe. There were a handful of small businesses and a chicken joint across the street. A new school was being built nearby. It was an increasingly gentrified area in a good location; the people around him had fixed up their homes and petitioned to have him investigated. There were pens outside, but everyone knew he was also hoarding sheep inside of his house. You could smell them in the heat of the day, see them in the windows at night, strange silhouettes standing on the couch.

I arrived at the suburban shepherd's house in the late afternoon. Three television news vans were parked out front. The shelter had pulled their mobile unit around back. Two police cars blocked the driveway.

I'm with the shelter, I said to the cop.

He didn't question me further—my car must have said enough. Most of us shelter folks drove pickups or wagons with the paint nearly invisible under layers of stickers. *I Love My Mutt. Woof. Give Wildlife a Break. My Cat Adopted Me at the Hoke County Shelter.* The back of my wagon was stuffed with crates and ramps for my special-needs retrievers.

You won't believe it, Emory said, grabbing my arm and leading me into the house. She was a heavy woman, breathing hard. Her dye job had grown out and her clothes were covered in white cat hair. Emory smelled like cigarette smoke and wet dog, but she was beautiful to me. Powerful. Her voice was loud and her passion was evident. Her eyes flashed when she was interviewed on television. People always say "It takes a special person to do that job." That person was Emory. She was tireless. She could stabilize an emaciated horse in the morning, trim a goat's overgrown hooves before lunch, attend a court hearing in the afternoon, and still be home to feed all of the animals she kept herself.

We were the purveyors of the downtrodden and hard to love, the Quaker parrot with a swearing habit, the incontinent Chihuahua, the tetraparetic Pekingese, the Tennessee scare goat with skin allergies.

And now, sheep. Seventy of them. But Emory could find anything a home.

Show me, I said.

I first met Gray at a Ducks Unlimited banquet. I was disguised as a waitress. Black jeans, black shoes, white button-up.

Emory had a knack for PR. She knew how to get herself on television.

When they turn the music down and cue the mics, that's when I'll run to the front, she had said. I know someone in catering who knows someone in event planning, and they'll give me a signal.

What do you need us to do? I asked.

Bail me out of jail, she said, and winked.

Emory had requested that four shelter workers sign on as temporary waitstaff for the event. We'd been interviewed over the phone by someone who had asked if we were on drugs or had a critical record.

You mean criminal, I had said.

Whatever, she said. You're slinging plates of microwaved chicken cordon bleu. Can you handle that?

I went to the banquet filled with nervous energy. Here I was, part of a plot that would piss off a hundred semiwoodsy men, some possessing sniper-level accuracy, some already drunk on boxed wine.

As dessert was served, Emory received the signal. She refilled the speaker's sweet tea and then turned to command the mic.

How can ducks be unlimited if you shoot them? Emory asked the audience. You conserve so you can kill them? So your children can kill them?

She cleared her throat. The screech of feedback from the microphone ricocheted off the walls.

You talk about how to save them, she said. Then you talk about how to *hunt* them.

An embarrassed man in a bow tie tugged her down from the podium and escorted her out of the room by the elbow.

I finished serving flourless chocolate cakes to a roomful of disgruntled hunters and businessmen, and when the catering staff moved into the dining room for cleanup, I took an extra cake and snuck out the side exit.

Golf carts lined one end of the parking lot, which was filled with expensive SUVs and luxury sedans.

Gray was sitting on the curb outside the door, legs outstretched, smoking a cigarette and drinking whisky from a flask.

The spring night held a chill. Gray offered his sport coat.

You want to share some of that cake? he asked.

I sat down next to him and handed him the ramekin.

Dig in, I said. Fingers are fine.

Gray was tall and lean and kept his long hair pulled back in a ponytail. He was wearing what looked to be a pair of wing tips.

He saw me looking at his feet.

An old pair of golf shoes I took the cleats out of, he said, shoveling chocolate into his mouth.

Whenever I dine at country clubs, I said, which isn't often, I only eat dinner rolls and dessert.

I know what you mean, Gray said. They think they can slap nuked cafeteria food on nice china and fool us all.

Why are you here? I asked.

I'm a bow hunter, he said.

I pictured him in a loincloth, jogging through the forest with a handmade bow and feathered arrow.

We passed the flask of whisky back and forth until both of us were drunk.

A friend once told me there were two kinds of urban naturalists. The McDonald's-eating semihoarder animal activist, and the armchair conservationist with bloodlust.

I have to tell you something, I said.

He bent down close as if he was going to kiss me.

You're the enemy, I said, laughing.

Maybe not, he had said. We want the same thing, right? Ducks?

We made out behind the bushes. I felt like a traitor.

Emory led me by the forearm to the basement of the suburban shepherd's farmhouse. The brick walls were lined with skulls.

We stood in silence, taking it in. There were at least fifty sheep skulls with open sockets, worn molars, and gently curved mandibles stacked in neat rows.

The smell was too much.

I need to go outside, I said, pushing open the basement door.

The bright sun made my eyes water. There were sheep tightly packed in the small backyard pen. Some dragged themselves across the grass, their hooves so destroyed they were forced to walk on their knees. You could count ribs on each of them like the bars of a birdcage.

The ground was littered with Styrofoam and paper bags from the fast-food joints across the street.

My first reaction was to throw up, my second to cry. I pictured the slow torture of the suburban shepherd in his own basement.

Two malnourished lambs licked each other's coats in the fence corner.

These are things we need to see, Emory said, wiping her eyes. To remind us.

Show me someone who can explain her first love, my mother once said.

I tried to explain Gray to myself. Here I was, in love with someone who killed animals for sport. We were like people of opposing religions, but I wanted it to work.

He was passionate about his hobbies. He spoke beautifully of his love for rare tree species, his need to see a Lost Franklinia and protect the Carolina silverbell. I was with Gray the afternoon he saw his first mountain camellia. It was like watching a man find God.

Gray was competent—he could cook with nothing but a multitool at his disposal, start fires, do taxes, hang pictures. He cleaned his aging mother's house, made her lasagna and eggplant parmesan, let me buy junk food and keep it on a shelf only he could reach. Gray knew what days I needed chocolate biscotti doled out.

He had a fascinating collection of stolen bowling shoes and golf cleats, and tolerated my fear of predator cats, alligators, bears. He was an alpha presence in the house, an armed companion in the woods, a voice of reason in my chaotic life. Bottom line: Gray made me feel safe in a way I never had, and I did not want to give that up.

I'm asking you to dinner, Gray said when he called that night.

Even after I'd showered, I felt as if I smelled of sheep.

Gray was waiting for me at the bar, his wing-tipped, cleatless golf shoes propped on the stool rung.

I kissed him on the cheek.

How are you? he asked.

I burst into tears. I could not decide if it was because of the sheep or my empty bed at home.

I let Gray jump to conclusions.

Come here, he said, bringing me close. We can work this out.

He gave me his glass of wine and ordered another.

After dessert, Gray walked with me to my car and got in the passenger side.

Are you sure? I asked.

I drove home with his hand on my knee, then up my skirt. The neighborhood was quiet—it seemed as if everyone else knew something we didn't, that there was a reason to be in bed with the lights off after dinner.

When we entered the front door, the dogs greeted Gray with gusto, rubbing their muzzles on his thigh, leaning into his legs, whining.

I missed you, too, he said, crouching down to let them kiss his face.

The feral cats remained hidden. I imagined them still as garden statues underneath the couch, ears clipped, nails carved into the wooden floor.

We went to bed with the door closed. Gray undressed me, rubbed my shoulders.

I want to come back, he said.

Prince began whining at the door.

Gray moved his hands lower, began kissing my neck.

Prince paced the hallway. His cart had a squeaky wheel. The sound was impossible to ignore.

Gray pulled away. I can't, he said in frustration.

He flipped over on his side and put a pillow over his head.

Lying back, I noticed I had wet dog food underneath my fingernails. I'd heard from friends what infants did to your sex life. I imagined disabled dogs did the same.

Prince barked and rattled the doorknob with his nose.

I'm coming, I said.

When she was alive, my mother had a compulsive need to exhibit porcelain Christmas villages year-round. When I would visit on Sundays she'd make hot tea and show me the new figurines she'd acquired. Over time she placed cider stands in front of city hall;

frosted fir trees, stray dogs, and hobos by the train station. I hated them all—houses with glowing windows, children with cherub cheeks, plastic geese on the frozen pond, men in top hats gazing sentimentally at petite wives.

When she passed away, she willed them to me. All ten thousand dollars' worth. As if she was saying to me: *Live like this.*

I sold them immediately and used the money for a down payment on a new house—I needed more room. I knew it was wrong, using her money that way, funding a lifestyle she did not condone.

You'd give those dogs your own bed, she'd once said, not realizing it was true.

Mom had her villages, Gray his leaves. The dogs, the raccoon, the chinchilla, the feral cats—these were mine.

When I was younger I grieved for birds nesting in the sickly dogwoods outside McDonald's, the wet deer carcasses left to rot on the side of the road. I thought twice about killing bugs in the house, opting instead to usher them out the door on sheets of paper.

One afternoon after we first met, Emory hit a bird with her car and called me.

Talk me through this, she said.

Can it be saved? I asked.

No, she said. It's suffering.

She was standing over it in a parking lot, her car running.

Run over it again, I said. You have to.

She gunned her engine.

We cried together, hysterically. I had finally found someone who understood me.

If I come back, Gray said on the phone, the raccoon, the chinchilla, and the cats have to go. The dogs can sleep downstairs.

I'll have to think about it, I said. I can't make promises.

At the shelter we stared coolly at people dropping off dogs, had no sympathy for those who didn't trust cats around the baby or whose boyfriends were allergic to dogs.

But I missed Gray. I missed his shoe collection in the closet. I missed watching him brush his hair, as if I was seeing something I shouldn't. He said he felt effeminate styling his hair in front of me, pulling it back into a slick ponytail. I missed his body in the bed, the way he slept with one arm tossed across my back.

But when I lay in bed at night I saw the deep abscesses on the chests of the sheep, dragging themselves to food and water across a rock-strewn lawn. The scared eyes of the feral cats underneath the sofa. I felt the warm bodies of the retrievers next to me, the kind of limitless love other people dreamed of and I had—all to myself.

Procter and Gamble arrived in the backseat of Emory's jeep, freshly castrated.

At first we could not coax them from the car. I pulled dog treats from my jean pockets and offered them in my hand. They stared at me with slivered eyes and split lips. Both sheep were chestnut brown with black spots.

Grazers, Emory said. Probably not interested in faux bacon.

For a minute I thought it best if they stayed in Emory's car, cowering in the backseat. It might save me from what I was about to do.

You're going to keep these guys in the dog run out back? Emory asked.

Sure, I said.

Emory and I pushed and pulled the sheep into the backyard.

Two things you've got to do, she said after we'd gotten them into the pen. First, you've got to deworm these babies. You put the pill in the back of the throat like this.

Emory deftly pried Gamble's mouth open and shoved the pill in.

You want to bypass their first stomach and get the pill directly into their second stomach, she said.

Fine, I said.

I wanted to act as if I were not intimidated, as if this were not the first time I was learning of multiple-stomach scenarios, of pilling sheep.

Second, she said, you'll need to trim their hooves regularly.

With what? I asked.

Trimming shears, she said. Hold the foot by the ankle in your left hand, the shears in the right.

Emory flipped Gamble upside down to demonstrate. His stomach was the color of oatmeal.

Good ram, I said.

A castrated male is a wether, Emory said. Gamble hasn't been a ram in a week, have you, Gamble?

His body was rigid, inflexible. He did not respond to her voice.

These guys will take your yard in two days, Emory said. Then they go bipedal on you, standing on their back hooves and eating the leaves off your trees. I'd recommend getting some hay. You don't have a neighborhood association, do you? she asked.

Not one with any bite, I said.

As the sun went down I found myself afraid to leave the sheep untended in the backyard. They huddled together in the dog run. I peeked at them through the blinds every ten minutes.

That night, while I was watching *Mr. Ed* reruns, the raccoon crept onto the back of the couch and grabbed my necklace, snapping my head backward.

Rodent! I said.

Later, I found the retrievers licking plates in the open dishwasher.

Get! I said. Get out!

I was embarrassed by the desperate, angry sound of my voice.

Sam lowered his head, then raised his large brown eyes.

We are just being dogs, he seemed to say.

One of the feral cats brought a rubber band to my chest during the night. A gift I consciously mistook as gratitude.

Gray and I had a tradition when it came to rashes. We named them after members of the Jackson Five. Gray once had a patch of poison ivy named Tito. I had ringworm named Jermaine.

A new ringworm had appeared on my elbow. The doctor said I had gotten it from Procter and Gamble. Emory said I had washed them too much, removed natural lanolin that protects them from the worm.

I broke with convention and named it La Toya.

I thought of the pristine sheep in my mother's Christmas village, their white coats like fine cashmere, led down cobblestone streets by fungus-free children.

Gray and I had started home-improvement projects before he left, painting the front door pale blue, planting bulbs, laying sod. It had taken Procter and Gamble a day and a half to work over the back lawn after I'd let them out of the dog run and into the fenced yard for a change of scenery. We'd planted a melon patch in the side yard that was beginning to come up. I figured the sheep would get that, too, given time.

In my mother's Christmas village there was a cottage garden overgrown with ivy and wisteria. A woman with golden ringlets sat on the stone steps, a baby in one arm, a cup of tea beside her.

Live like this.

Even at two in the morning, my house felt alive. I could hear the raccoon chittering at the cats, Sam dreaming, the chinchilla knocking his head against his water dish. Salli had taken Gray's spot in the bed, her legs outstretched, head on the pillow.

I was outnumbered, outmaneuvered. There was no one to do the dirty work for me. The dirty work wasn't lifting hair balls from the living room carpet. It wasn't mashing Sam's dog food with water and fish oil tablets. It was discipline.

I did two strange things that week. I began sleeping with Gray's flannel shirt underneath my pillow. Then I took a volume of his leaf collection—the one with the pressed, waxy leaves of the mountain camellia—and hid it in the drawer of my bedside table.

When he came back for the remainder of his things, these I would keep.

Gray called me at home the following week to see if I'd had a change of heart. Have you thought about us? Gray asked. Are you ready to make some adjustments? Ditch the chinchilla?

I'd love to have you here, I said. But you know I can't get rid of the animals.

I'm not asking you to get rid of *all* of them, he said.

You know I can't, I said. Not any.

I'm looking at a job in Texas.

I understand, I said.

You could go with me, he said.

I couldn't.

I'll call before I leave, he said, and hung up the phone.

For my birthday Gray had given me an antique display case lined in white canvas that held a mounted Amazonian parrot wing, emerald green with flecks of blue and yellow. Pinned below was the skin of a small marsupial, then two leaves that looked like lace.

It's beautiful, I told him, lying. He beamed. I knew it was an expensive gift, something he thought represented the convergence of our interests. Something we might pass down to our children.

A conversation piece, he said.

I was too embarrassed to display it, worried Emory would see the remnants of animals pinned like trophies behind glass when she came to the house.

That night I took it out of the china cabinet and opened the glass lid. I stroked the soft wing and marsupial pelt, then touched the leaves. They crumbled like dust.

Recipes began appearing in my mailbox, compliments of neighbors. Braised lamb shanks with rice. Curried lamb stew. Lamb kebabs. Tandoori-spiced leg of lamb.

You should move farther out, Emory advised. Get into the country.

For an animal activist, moving to the country meant moving across the line from hobby rescue to sanctuary. I was not ready for that.

I'm happy where I am, I said.

How are the sheep? Emory asked.

Sheeplike, I said.

Procter and Gamble reminded me of garden gnomes, frozen when I was outside yet surprisingly destructive when unwatched. They stiffened when the retrievers sniffed their tails, flattened their ears like Yoda.

Remember, Emory said. Dogs have double lives. They can kill the sheep when you're not looking.

One of my dogs has no teeth, I said. One is bound to a cart. The other has one ear and fear issues.

Over fifty percent of sheep attacks are launched by domestic dogs, Emory said.

There are other things I'm losing sleep over, I said.

To Emory, all living things were in danger. It made her feel like a hero.

I spent the afternoon laying stones for the sheep, hoping the friction would help wear their hooves down. The spring sun was warm. I drank lemonade and vodka and let the dogs loose in the backyard.

Sam found a rabbit in the ivy patch. He gummed the rabbit by the neck, brought him to me.

The rabbit was half dead, but not because of Sam. He had silvery blisters in his ears. He was mite-ridden, missing an eye. Soon, he'd be caught by a cat or a hawk. He shook in my arms.

Gray would tell me to snap its neck. He'd shown me once with a squirrel he'd run over in the driveway.

I placed the rabbit underneath the porch with water and food.

I was the shepherd of a strange flock.

You are looking for things to put between us, Gray had said when I told him about the sheep.

Maybe it was true.

Was there room for me in the porcelain village? My run-down house, my dogs, my sheep? Would my figurine be coated in hair?

The sheep huddled in the corner of the yard, leaned into each other, suspicious of my stones, Salli's strange gait, Prince's squeaking cart.

I went inside to top off my vodka and lemonade. I thought of Gray's leaves in the drawer of my bedside table and went upstairs to retrieve them. The raccoon had nested in my pillow. He looked so gentle, so asleep, that I did not shoo him away. I took the album outside and sat on the back steps—the one-eyed rabbit underneath me, the dogs beside me, the sheep watching me with their slivered eyes.

People always say: Don't give up so easily on things you love.

But you can, and I did.

I ripped the leaves from the album's pages and threw them into the air like confetti.

Feast, I said to the sheep.

And eventually, they did.

The Artificial Heart

2050

My father was ninety-one and senile but insisted he could still look for love. The dating service paired him with Susan—an octogenarian feminist who listed skee ball and container gardening as her primary hobbies. She was in the early stages of Alzheimer's and chewed nicotine gum when she talked. They'd been dating a month, and when he was lucid, Dad was smitten.

Companionship of any kind is important, the dating service director assured me on the eve of their first date. The couple comes to the Senior Center and we serve them a steak dinner followed by tea and cheesecake on the center terrace. Love keeps them in the present; a relationship is a tether to the future.

Help appealed to me; keeping Dad in the present was a lot of work for one person. It meant constantly exercising his memory—note cards, photographs, detailed answers to his repeated questions. Each month I could feel him slipping further into dementia; our conversations were his life raft. I quizzed him over meals, moving from our shared history to details from the morning: *What did you have for breakfast today? Who won the US Open this week? What was the name of my first dog? Explain to me the design of your homemade water filter, the one you patented in 2025.*

Dad muddled through explanations but always excelled at questions directed at his earlier years—it was the last ten years he couldn't hold on to. I worried he'd become proficient at duping me with general expressions, clichéd answers, pronouns instead of proper names. He was often too proud to admit his failing faculties and limited short-term memory. He always ordered "the special" at restaurants because he couldn't read the menu, and he'd suffer through rich bisques or adventurous pastas when what he really wanted was a burger or chicken sandwich.

Dad had never been one for romance, but watching him with Susan was heartening. I'd observed their third date. Susan and Dad held hands throughout dinner, and he'd offered her his dinner jacket to keep warm.

It's Florida, she said, waving him off with one hand. It's always hot. And I have my own sweater. But thank you.

I like your eyes, he said. They're so blue.

I have cataracts, she said. Are you Jim?

I'm Stu, he said.

He seemed to forgive her missteps and poor temper. In all honesty, I'm not sure he was in love with anything except the idea of her company.

They'd moved onto dessert served on a terrace surrounded by potted tomato plants and fruit trees. Susan wiped the cheesecake from Dad's chin. He appeared to relish the simple pleasure of being touched. When we got home, he asked me to write her name on a piece of paper, which he kept by his bedside. That way, he said, when I wake up I can think of Susan.

I didn't mind helping him remember to love her.

I'd become one of many cash-strapped caregivers with no children of my own—just the responsibility of an aging parent modern medicine had turned into an invincible robot, a robot puttering around outmoded and diapered, trying to make sense of tangled strings of thought. We lived in my father's oceanfront house in Key West, Florida. Residing on an island had enabled Dad and me to live an almost antiquated life in a small neighborhood between resorts. People come here to escape real life, he'd once said. We live somewhere between real life and respite, a sunny kind of purgatory.

My partner, Link, lived with me in my father's house, but Dad was so old, so near death, that we'd begun calling it *my* house in private. Dad lived in a suite we'd made for him out of his old bedroom, the one he'd shared with my mother for seventy-three years. He'd had an artificial heart installed fifteen years ago, a blood-compatible, synthetic ticker that pushed his body beyond its intended mortal means.

The doctor, prior to inserting the heart, regaled us with stories of a calf who'd lived hundreds of days on an early model of the heart. But now the doctors referred to Dad's as a jalopy of hearts and told us of newer, more infallible models. Not interested, Dad would say. When I was a boy, if you died, you were dead. Why keep a bunch of zombies my age running around anyway?

The morning of his latest date with Susan, Dad got going about storm-water collection. He moved in and out of lucidity, inhabiting the present for only moments at a time.

Rest up, Dad, I said. Big plans tonight.

The war for water begins, Dad said, launching one of his demented rants. I belted him into his recliner and set him up with lukewarm coffee and a large print projection of real-time news. His body hinged over the black safety harness, leering, eyes bulging, ready to reel off a dated tirade that would probably include references to the Symbionese Liberation Army, farm subsidies, Nixon, and, if he was really getting after us, Beyoncé.

Don't get yourself worked up, I said, touching his forehead with the back of my hand. You'll spill your coffee. And talking like that might scare Susan. Remember to ask about her kids.

I've been worked up for sixty years, he said. It started with Reagan . . . what was it he said about common sense and acid rain? If Michael Jackson hadn't endorsed Pepsi, things would be different now, wouldn't they? Endorsements change the course of the universe. It's always about stuff. Electric sedans and petri-dish livers. You can buy anything. Who's Susan?

Susan, I said, is your girlfriend. Silver hair in a bun, floral blouses, khaki pants. Smart as a whip when she remembers what she's talking about.

I wrote Susan's name down on Dad's notepad in large print, showed him a picture of her. He claimed he could remember things better that way. We had a whole series of captioned photographs to help his recall stay fresh.

I want to buy her something, he said.

Do you want your shoes on or off? I asked.

I want to take her somewhere, he said. Do something I'm good at. Fishing, maybe. Link can bait the hooks.

I'd have to call and ask permission, I said.

I'm ninety-one, he said. Why do I need permission for anything except dying? Can Link take us to the beach? I'm tired of dinner at the Senior Center.

Link was Dad's ideal avatar, the sentient being he sent out into the world to accomplish the things his aged body couldn't. Dad admired Link's rational approach to life, his tool-savvy, survivalist ways. Whenever we argued over the thermostat, the dying ocean, theocracies, or how to best grill sausages, Dad wanted to know: *What does Link suggest? Ask Link what he wants to do*. It was hard to see Dad embrace the role of a beta male when he'd been the alpha figure for most of my life.

Dad fingered the raised bump of flesh on his chest where his heart had been installed.

Hurts today, he said.

Rest, I said, and remember to stay out of the kitchen. Too much exposure to machines is bad for your heart.

This damn thing is invincible, Dad said, pounding it with his fist.

Dad had once requested that we help him commit suicide on his hundredth birthday. Link can figure out how to stop my heart, Dad said. Because we felt sure he'd never make it that long, we indulged him. Of course, Link said. I could wrap a lump of raw magnets around your chest, or sneak you into the hospital and jam your heart with radiation. Excellent, Dad said.

I'm so tired of being alive, Dad had begun telling me some nights, his voice a whisper of its former strength. His back hurt; he stooped like a shrimp when he walked. He wore soft caps over his melanoma-ridden bald head and refused new clothes, intent on wearing old fishing T-shirts and a reliable pair of baggy Levis that chafed his sensitive legs. His toenails were yellow, chalky, and coiled, his feet swollen and calloused. I hated to touch his feet; they were the saddest thing about him and, next to his mind, heart, and lungs, the things he needed most. He still walked on his own—though no more than two blocks—and until recently had fished once a day, standing up from his frayed lounge chair to reel in anything that tugged his line—a small tarpon, a fetid mound of seafaring trash.

I gingerly removed Dad's fleece-lined moccasins so his feet could breathe. He ran them across the carpet like a child.

I want to get out later, he said. I want to take Susan fishing.

Dinner's at four, I said. I'll call the center and Susan's son to see if a fishing date is possible beforehand.

Are my clothes clean? he asked. Do I have the heart of a pig? I saw a special this morning about putting pig hearts in men.

I'll be on the roof, I said, patting his hand. We're gonna use your design for the rain barrels. We're taking precautions—Link wants to maintain our own water supply. When did you write the book?

Nineteen ninety-eight, he said, though I worked on chapters in the eighties.

Correct, I said.

I walked outside and grabbed the extension ladder—already hot to the touch—which Link had propped against the side of the house. I found him on the roof, shucking off sheets of historic Spanish tile in the morning sun. He hunched shirtless over the tile, cutting fasteners with a hacksaw. He was one of the few people I knew who still managed to work in the sun; most laborers worked by night under artificial light. Link's skin was the color of eggplant, except for his butt and midsection, which, when uncovered, appeared white and phosphorescent in contrast to his deeply tanned legs, arms, and back.

Cover up, I said. You'll burn.

He stood up, sweat sliding down his body in sheets. Just another half hour and I'll go in for a break, he said. Almost done removing this patch of tile.

Using a design from Dad's *Living Rogue* manual, Link was connecting our barrels to a gray water system with which we'd trap the Key West rains. He held plastic tubing up for inspection.

Gray water might be passé, Link said, duct taping the tubing to a black plastic barrel, but it's genius.

Is that why we can't understand it? I said, leafing through pages of numbered diagrams.

Living Rogue was an old book that had been handed down to me like a silver tea set. Link revered every word. My father had written *Living Rogue* in 1999 when he thought the millennium would bring Chinese rule, a barter economy, and rationed power supplies—none of which had happened. Regardless, I grew up knowing how to fish for sustenance, maintain potable water, and commit a painless suicide in the face of nuclear warfare. Link, whom I'd met in high school, liked to say that I was the only cheerleader who knew how to fire an Uzi and field dress a deer—fictional ideas that I swear turned him on.

When I was younger, I suspected that Dad had *wanted* his doomsday predictions to come true. Maybe he thought socio-political turmoil would increase his relevance to society; maybe he wanted to hang on to the physical world he understood. He'd always pictured himself a sort of blue-collar genius, but he wasn't, and I think deep down he knew it as much as anyone else. Now Dad lorded the past over us with nonlinear rants and lauded the superiority of simpler times, though I'm not sure he ever enjoyed living through them. But when he was with Susan, he smiled easily and his face softened in a way I'd never seen.

I worry about the structural soundness of this design, Link said, thumping the tubing.

If you have questions, I said, I'm sure Dad would love to hold forth on water collection and home wind power.

Your dad was high on painkillers when he wrote that chapter, Link said. He told me so. It's a Percocet-fueled manifesto.

I threw up my hands. Your time to waste, I said. I'm sure there are better methods now.

Link and I had been sleeping together on and off for twenty years. We were partners, not spouses. Friends one year, lovers the next two. No merged bank accounts, no children, no rules, no problems. Dad had raised me to be independent.

Dad wants to go fishing with Susan, I said.

She's hot stuff, he said, for an eighty-year-old.

Stop teasing, I said. You know she has a crush on you.

Susan always lit up when Link and I came to fetch Dad from the date. She referred to Link as "the handsome son" and reached out to lovingly pat his hand and kiss him on the cheek when it was time to go. I found her flirtations harmless and flattering.

Would you be willing to take them fishing if the center agrees to it? I asked.

Sure, Link said. He went back to work, looking at the book, then the barrels.

We had a great view of the ocean from Dad's roof. I looked out at the gray expanse of water. It smelled different this year, like warm vegetable soup, or leftovers forgotten in the trunk of the car. The sea wasn't stagnant—the tide was negligible but present, and waves broke on the dead reef miles out, sending timid ripples to lap against the rocky shore of the island. But experts said little to nothing but bacteria could survive in the ocean now; the water was warm and nearly oxygen-depleted. Anoxic, they called it. Two weeks after the big die-off, talking heads were still trying to assign blame, but I had stopped listening. Anyone with a brain knew it was everyone and everything, inevitable and awful, the beginning of the ugly end.

Hold this for me, Link said, handing me the torch he was using to solder the tubes.

His resolute industriousness was something to love and hate about Link. He had an affinity for projects. In a town of burned-out drunks, he was a doer, a prolific odd-jobber. Link was animated but hard to anger and had a sense of humor about everything. He'd once laughed at his own dislocated shoulder during a flag football match. But even he wasn't taking the dying ocean well. I found him teary-eyed on the beach after the die-off. I think I'm ashamed to be human, he'd said, looking out at the water.

Thanks to Dad, I've lived my whole life waiting for apocalyptic events, environmental tragedies of epic proportions. The sun could explode, he'd say, and the world would still be looking at geriatric Madonna in a leotard. But now that a catastrophic event was happening Dad was oblivious, and I felt we'd irrevocably tipped our fortunes in the wrong direction, that my bones would, in millions of years, be like those of a velociraptor or trilobite. Soon, I told Link, we'll be fossils, ripe for misinterpretation. I was sure some well-intentioned extraterrestrial would re-create my body, a hypothetical figure complete with unflattering body hair, and pose me participating in a drum circle on a fake beach in an oxygenated museum.

If I can't convince you to come down and get out of the sun, I said, I'm going inside to call the Senior Center.

Make sure he has enough water, Link said. And tell him I'll need him up on the roof later to supervise.

Fat chance, I said, unless you rig a harness with a sunshade.

Link smiled.

I know, I said. You can. But don't.

I poked my head into the living room to look at Dad. He was blank-eyed, his favorite game show on full volume. He liked to watch shows where competitors used their wits to survive or complete daring physical tasks—drinking raw ostrich eggs from a glass, rappelling down skyscrapers, escaping from Plexiglas cages underwater. He liked to see fear, mainly because he still thought he was the kind of man who could avoid it; he'd maneuver his way through adversity with ex–Navy Seal cleverness.

I phoned the Senior Center.

My father would like to take Susan fishing, I said.

We can't allow that, the director said. There are no unsanctioned visits. The liabilities . . .

I'll supervise, I said. What's the big deal? They've been together for a month. They need to switch up the routine, keep things fresh.

I can't give you permission, the director said. Plus, what's there to fish for anymore?

I called Susan's son.

What do you think about Susan fishing with my dad this afternoon? I said. A change of pace. My partner and I will take them out. You'll just have to drive Susan to Higgins Beach.

I don't know, he said. Susan's son was an antiques dealer who had always struck me as squeamish, but my judgment of men was harsh—the curse of being raised by a survivalist father.

It would really mean something to Dad, I said. He enjoys fishing so much; he'd like to share it with her.

Do they even know the difference between the Senior Center living room and the beach? he asked.

On a good day, I said.

A half hour, he said. Mom can't take much sun time. I'll send her with an umbrella and a pound cake.

I hung up and found Dad awake and hungry in the living room. He was a foulmouthed infant, needy and irritable.

It's hot, he said.

Stay hydrated, I said.

I don't want to waste the water, he said.

Drink it then, I said, pushing his cup toward him.

Paul McCartney, Dad said, advocated vegetarianism, but I don't see how that helps the workingman, the man bolting up one of them cars in Detroit.

Men haven't made cars in years, Dad, I said. And Paul McCartney is really dead this time.

What we all need, he said, is a little self-sufficiency, less flatulence. Fuel ourselves. Remember LeBron James? He's giving schoolkids the old razzle-dazzle, trying to sell us the Chinaman's leather shoes.

LeBron is almost seventy. You need a nap, I said, escorting him to his bedroom, where again I strapped him into bed to keep him from falling and breaking another hip. Getting him settled was an exhausting process for both of us, one that sometimes confused and hurt him. Why are you trapping me? he'd ask. Why am I tied into my own bed? Sometimes he would pull off his diaper, or lie with his blank eyes fixated on the ceiling, making me lean down into his face to check his breath like a new mother, assure myself that he was still alive.

Stay here with me for a minute, he said, gripping my upper arm.

I paused and held his hand, half loving, half impatient.

Can we go fishing when I wake up? he said.

Yes, I said. With Susan.

Who's Susan? he said.

Your girlfriend, I said.

Do I love her? he said.

You tell me, I said.

Yes, he said. I'm taking her fishing today. Link will help me set up the rods, won't he?

Of course, I said. We'll meet Susan at the beach at four.

Link and I roused Dad at three and assembled our gear. It took us less than ten minutes to walk to Higgins Beach. Link ran ahead to set things up while I walked with Dad, holding him by the arm. He was moving more slowly than usual.

Your feet hurting? I asked.

Hmm? he said. He didn't hear well, despite the cochlear implant.

Are your feet hurting? I asked, louder.

Everything hurts, he said. And then he laughed, but it was not a funny laugh, it was a sad laugh, the kind of tired laugh an old person uttered for lack of anything better to say. A laugh that said *I pretend living is better than dying, but I'm never sure; I can't think straight anymore. I can't engage with your conversation. Where are we going? I'll take the special.*

Our neighborhood street was lined with palms, cinnecord and spider lily. Heat-stricken cats draped themselves across front porches; a skinny rooster crossed the road in front of us like a bad joke, then disappeared behind the tire of a parked truck to crow boldly. The tips of stucco resorts crowded the horizon. A bright orange tractor careened around old palms and trolled the length of the beach, its metal plow raking up dead fish and putrid sea grass. Rubber gloves, beer cans, cigarette butts, and dog shit littered the sand, which wasn't natural sand—it was trucked in annually from a gravel pit. Dad once said Key Westers will stick a palm tree and a bar in any old dump and call it a resort.

Lately I'd found myself pausing on the public beach to watch the ocean, drawn to the dirty mass that, with its steady shore-slapping rhythm, deposited mounds of grasslike seaweed on the rocky coastline. Perhaps I was grieving it, the miles of water that had surrounded me my entire life, fed me, half drowned me as a child. To Dad, the ocean was the survivalist's answer to everything—starvation, escape, autonomy. You ever find yourself in trouble, he'd say, you take one of them old houseboats from the marina out at night, paint over the name, and fish for a few weeks over one of the reefs or old wrecks. Call me, of course. I'll be waiting. I'll know.

Dad, I'd said. I don't plan on getting into trouble.

No one ever does, he said. But live a little, sweetheart.

Sometimes I thought it would have pleased Dad if I'd amped up my inner butch a little more, tattooed my forearm to match a Harley, ran immigrants ninety miles from Havana to the Keys in the blue morning. Instead, I bought storefront space and served homemade crepes and Cuban coffee to tourists and read books in the off-season, dutifully cared for my father, sat with him for hours as he fished in the afternoons.

For years the ocean had been in decline—overfished, polluted, diseased—sea species genetically weakened and unable to thrive. But every so often Dad could pull out a fish or two—nothing you'd be wild about eating—or you'd hear of someone finding a school in the deepest pockets of water.

When I was a child, Dad had read the fish report aloud every morning, carefully reviewing water temperatures, tarpon migration patterns, anecdotes about how wrecks and reefs were fishing. He'd trail plain ballyhoo from the back of his johnboat for dolphin and sailfish. He liked old-school fishing. If he pulled up anything under sixty pounds, he'd bludgeon it with his beer bottle the way his father had taught him. Whenever I was in the boat I tried not to let him see me cry as I watched the fish struggle to survive. It's a strange thing to see a man kill something he loves with a blank face, beating the life out of another being. But every few months we got a real fighter in the boat, a fish that flopped and tossed violently until it launched itself overboard, and I silently cheered it on as it swam away into the vast ocean and my father swore like the part-time sailor he was.

Susan's son stood clutching his mother under an umbrella. Her face was covered in sunscreen; he hadn't done a good job rubbing it into her skin. Her khaki pants were cuffed and her pedicured feet were bare. Her hair was pulled into a small ponytail at the nape of her neck. A visor covered her eyes. Her red lips were vibrant succulents between liver-spotted cheeks.

My father smiled and dropped my arm. He began to breathe faster. He moved toward her with as much energy and youth as he could muster.

Link! Susan exclaimed, pointing at my partner, who was plunging PVC pipes into the sand so that Dad and Susan would not be entirely responsible for the weight of their fishing rods.

You're here to see *Stu,* Mother, Susan's son said. He pointed at my father.

I know who I'm here to see, she said, and sulkily crossed her arms. Link! she shouted. Come give me a kiss.

Dad stopped in his tracks. She had not yet acknowledged him. His clothes were already damp with sweat.

Link waved from the beach and jogged over. He was shirtless and bent down to kiss her cheek. He was in his fifties but carried only a slight amount of extra weight around his waistline. A small patch of hair spread across his chest.

You smell delicious, she said.

I most certainly do not, he said. Are you ready for your date?

Dad was stoic. His mouth was set in a determined line.

Susan nodded.

Susan's son and I stood back, giving the group space. He talked about his antiques business, some bureaus he was moving to New England, but I didn't listen. I watched my father with concern but didn't intervene, even though I thought some small talk might ease the tension. When possible I tried to let Dad exert control over his life, especially on a date.

Can I escort you to your chair? Link asked.

Of course, Susan said, clutching and patting his arm as they moved toward the two chairs Link had set up at the water's edge.

I offered Dad my hand, but he didn't take it. He trudged through the sand, pausing to wipe his brow with a handkerchief before sitting down. I told myself that my father regarded Link as a son and was not threatened.

Susan, he said. You look beautiful today.

Hello, she said, looking him over like a stranger. I worried that it was not a good day for either of them, that the heat was not doing their faculties any favors.

Link baited their rods with cubes of cheese and rattailed maggots.

My custom lure, he said. He cast the line for each of them and placed the rods in their hands. Dad gripped the rod's shaft with surprisingly sure and nimble hands.

You can take mine back, Susan said, thrusting the unwanted rod at Link. Link placed her rod in the PVC pipe at her feet. She pushed the sand into piles with her toes. Clearly, Susan did not like to fish.

Would you like a drink? Link said, playing host. He handed Susan a beer. Dad stared out at the ocean and the small waves rolling onto the rocks.

How are your kids? Dad asked. I smiled. He'd remembered my advice.

That one over there, Susan said, pointing at her son, is a leech.

Tell me more, Dad said.

I grabbed Link by the hand and pulled him a ways behind the chairs. Let's give them space, I said.

He uses my checkbook, she said. He buys bad art with it. I've never seen such a lousy—

Dad stood up from his chair, knocking it over. I've got one, he said. Something's tugging on the line.

Impossible, Link said.

It seemed to take Dad a painfully long time to reel in his line, but Link let him do it alone, and sure enough there was a small fish, hooked through the cheek. It curved its body in fight, nearly touching its tail to its head, an angry silver arch.

Link! Susan said. Come get this thing.

I've got it, Dad said.

Disgusting, Susan said, wincing, cupping her chin with her hands.

Throw it back, Dad, I said. It's a shallow hook; the fish could live.

I couldn't help but root for this fish, a survivor in an oxygen-depleted ocean.

Dad acted as if he didn't hear me. He wiggled the hook out of the fish's face with brute force and threw the fish onto the back of his overturned chair. He grabbed Susan's beer bottle and began to club the fish.

Damn it, he said, hitting the fish's head with the bottom of the bottle. Beer ran down his wrists. He struck over and over again. *Damn it, damn it, damn it,* he said.

Dad, I said. *Stop*. I grabbed his arm. He shook free and struck the fish savagely again, this time across the gills. The fish thrashed and fell onto the sand, eyes open.

Susan ran to Link and threw her arms around his waist. Take me home, she said. Take me home. She started to cry.

You know what else you can do for me? Dad said, turning to Link. Sleep with her. Take her to bed while you're out playing hero.

I pulled Dad away; he was a ball of confusion and hurt on the inside, bursting open in public. I glanced back and saw Link pause to pick up the fish by the tail and hurl it back into the sea. A hopeful act.

I turned to apologize to Susan, but her son was already escorting her toward his car. He flashed an angry look of disapproval over his shoulder.

Dad was sweating and had clearly overexerted himself. I knew we couldn't walk back to the house. I stood on the side of the road and tried to flag down a car, hoping for a neighbor. I felt like a disappointed parent. His failings were now my own. I felt Dad's pain acutely, but part of me wished my responsibilities were over. I was tired. The feeling reminded me of the look I'd seen in a friend's eyes as she repeatedly corrected her special-needs child, who bit the other kids in his playgroup—embarrassment, love, determination, fatigue.

We could help him die, I realized. Link knew ways to stop his heart. We could move on, sell the house, relocate even. I felt guilty, selfish, calculating.

I never wanted to be this way, Dad said. A practical man living an impractical life.

I was too mad to answer. I knew my grip on his arm was too rough; I wanted him to know I was disappointed. But there were multiple emotions colliding inside of me. I had to take some responsibility. What was I thinking, pushing love on my father at his age? What could be expected between two people with half their brains carved out by time?

A cop car pulled over. The officer rolled down his window. He was thin and deeply tanned, and worked a toothpick between his teeth.

Get into some trouble there? the officer asked. Old man okay? Wandered off on you?

We could really use a ride home, I said.

Close by? the officer asked, looking me in the eye, critical, as if he was onto my thoughts. I nodded.

Mind dusting the sand off your feet and drying the old man off? the officer said. I try to keep the car clean. He fetched a towel from his trunk and handed it to me. I gave it to Dad, who stared at the neatly folded towel in his hands as if he did not know what it was for. Chivalrous to the end, he tried to hand it back to me; I shook my head.

The officer helped us into the car and pulled away from the curb.

Where to? he asked.

Eight blocks down, I said, leaning over the front seat. Shore side.

Why am I wet? Dad said, looking at his beer- and sweat-soaked shirt.

You went swimming, I said, teeth clenched.

Why are we in a cop car? Dad asked.

We're on our way home, I said. Stop asking questions.

We passed familiar houses, pink stucco facades, white clapboards with green hurricane shutters. The people on the streets—we knew them all, though not their names. The cop's radio scratched and buzzed. Dad looked nervous. He didn't know where he was or why he was here.

Are you in trouble? Dad whispered. Take one of those house-boats from the marina and paint over the name. Drag a block of frozen chum off the side near the reef and you'll eat well. I'll send someone for you.

For a moment, I was speechless. His eyes were certain and his words authoritative.

I know you will, I said, realizing that Dad might lose his short-term memory, but not his pride, his sense of dutiful fatherhood.

A wreck or rock pile will work, too, he said. You'll find snap-per and mutton.

There are no more snapper and mutton, I said. Everything is changing—

Why am I angry? Dad asked, a hand over his heart. I feel—

You fought with Susan, I said.

Who's Susan? he said.

I thought for a minute that I might tell him the truth, fight to keep him in the present, refresh his memory. But my feelings for him were beginning to warm and I reached for his hand, the blued knuckles that had, moments ago, held a bottle like a crude mallet.

No one special, I said.

Why am I wet? Dad asked. His shirt hung from his collarbones, clung to his thin skin.

A fish pulled you in, I said. One with a lot of fight.

Cruise ship comes in this afternoon, the officer said. I'm expecting a long night.

I ignored him the way my father had taught me. Only acknowledge authority when it's earned, he'd said.

Perhaps it was only his body, not his ideas that were outmoded. I was surprised that our small, personal tragedy felt sharper than the broken ocean, that this man's one overextended life troubled me more, in this moment, than the epic loss of life underwater. I was surprised at the lengths I'd gone to protect his life, enrich it, prolong it. Moments after murdering him in my imagination, I again felt as though I'd do anything for his comfort, his temporary happiness.

Did I get it? Dad whispered. The fish?

I draped the towel over his bony shoulders and pulled the ends together across his chest, where I could feel his artificial heart thumping like a piston, impossible to stop, impossible to break.

Of course you did, I said. But in the end you let it go.

The Two-Thousand-Dollar Sock

Vito was lethargic, curled up in his fleece bed with sad eyes. He wasn't eating. I touched his distended abdomen and he recoiled as if it was sore.

Six times he'd eaten a sock. Five times it had come out the other side, worse for the wear, composted. But not this time.

It was the sixth sock that did not pass. Not Poppy's baby sock, or Russ's wool hiker, but *my* sock. An old sock. A sock that had been with me longer than my husband. A sock with a cotton ball on the back like a rabbit tail. A *cute* sock. A sock that blocked my shepherd's intestines.

Anything, I said to the vet. I'll do *anything*.

It was that kind of week. The kind where I put face wash in my hair, ran out of milk, bruised my shin on the bed frame in the night. The kind where my infant daughter discovered she preferred my husband to me, turned to him with the cry of a kitten, cooed at his touch.

It was the kind of week where a black bear discovered my honey stash, rifled through two hives in the backyard. It was a character-building week, a week that thinned my hair, put circles underneath my eyes.

Once bears taste honey, a neighboring keeper told me, they'll stop at nothing to have it. I've seen them take shock after shock from an electric fence just to shove that sweet stuff into their mouths.

They're gentle, he said, but determined. First they sniff out the honey. Then they go bipedal, ripping the top from your apiary, pushing the hive to the ground.

Put away bird feeders and buy a bear-proof garbage can, we were told.

A fed bear is a dead bear, my neighbor said.

We didn't listen.

Russ taught Poppy the pilot's alphabet.

Alpha, Bravo, Charlie, he said. Victor, Whisky, X-ray.

I liked the way the *s* in whisky rasped through Russ's missing teeth.

Poppy grinned an empty grin, her teeth only beginning to bud. It was hard to tell if she absorbed his words, or if she just liked the sound and attention.

So P is for Papa and M is for Mike? I said. What gives?

Russ smiled his fighter's smile. Where's Poppy's Bink?

Bink was Poppy's comfort toy. Bink had the head of a bear and the body of a soft blanket, rimmed in lavender silk. I pulled him from her diaper bag and handed her the toy.

Poppy brought Bink to her mouth and looked up at me with shy eyes. Her eyelashes were long and thick.

You eat that bear! I said, tweaking her nose. Eat him!

Russ was an amateur boxer. A former college wrestler, he scrapped for fun, for money, for pride. He boxed in gyms, back-alley rings, parking lots if the mood was right.

Lower death rate than horse racing, he told me.

We'd met working out at the gym, Russ pummeling the punching bag. Me sparring with my father, who'd learned sword fighting in Thailand. Dad thought I was good enough to get acting work.

Maybe you could be a stunt double, he said. For that Xena chick. A warrior princess.

The problem, Pop, I said, is that I don't look like a movie star.

Get porcelain veneers, he said, pushing his dentures forward.

I want a family, I said.

Dream bigger, he said.

Dad and I had just moved to Massachusetts from North Carolina. He'd inherited a house from his uncle. It was a free house, but the move disconnected Dad from his past. We kept training and looking for work. The best gig I got was fighting a team of actor ninjas with a trick sword on the stage of a thumping private nightclub in the city where the guests were too coked to notice.

But Russ found the sword skills sexy and let me hang a Taiwanese sword with a beveled edge over the bed, a fencing foil over the couch.

Dragon slayer, he said, kissing my neck.

When he wasn't fighting, Russ was a pilot for hire. He'd flown F-15Es in the first Gulf War and then got a commercial license, but work was scarce in western Massachusetts. I'd worked as a receptionist at a trucking company until my third trimester. When I quit, we lost our benefits. We rented a house from Russ's mother, down a dirt road, on the edge of a national forest. There were heirloom currants in the backyard, rusted-out tractors and stone-pile fencing behind the trees. The vinyl siding was dirty from hard winters. A stone fawn curled up between two boxwoods near the front door. All that land, staring us in the face.

The thing about an old house, I'd said, is that you have to pick up where someone else left off.

A transitional period, Russ called it.

I took Vito to the veterinarian's office while Russ idled a jet at the airport for some CEO.

I'll keep him here for observation in case he passes the sock. We could do an exploratory, the vet said. See if we can locate the foreign body.

You'll let me know before you operate? I said.

Of course, the vet said.

I couldn't look at Vito when it was time to leave. I *said* we'd do anything, but I was worried we couldn't afford to treat him. I knew his eyes would convince me to mortgage the house, become a one-car family, eat ramen noodles five days a week. I heard the cage close.

I could sense Poppy's hunger as I signed a form at the check-out counter. She began thrusting her head into my chest, rooting for my nipple.

No, honey, I said, readjusting her.

By the time we reached the car she was sobbing, her lips pursed like the beak of a small bird, wanting.

I mixed a scoop of formula and water into a bottle and sank into the sun-warmed passenger seat to feed her. I stroked the short fuzz of new hair on her head.

I looked at Poppy the way I would look at my own heart—with confusion and gratitude. There were days when I burped her too hard, prayed for her to fall asleep. There were nights I couldn't put her down, her fresh face burrowed into my body, hand around my finger.

Mommy's here, I said, though I felt like a fraud.

Before Poppy was born, we'd discussed ways to make money.

We could distribute the census, I said.

Become freelance property managers, Russ said.

Or keep bees, I said.

We received our first mail-order queen in March. She'd arrived with four worker bees in a candied box.

I'm not doing this to fit in, I told Russ. I'm doing it to sell honey. A work-from-home operation that will pay for itself.

I bought a smoker secondhand, sealed an old jacket and leather gloves with duct tape. I used my fencing mask for a veil.

I'm glad you found *something*, Russ said.

I was eight months pregnant, thirty pounds heavier, and desperate to be happy.

There were days when I could ride my bicycle without a helmet and smoke a cigarette at the same time, I said. I was once practiced in the art of fire breathing. Give me a bottle of vodka and a lighter and I could show you.

Russ grinned and pinched the seat of my maternity jeans.

I've still *got it,* you know, I said.

When we returned home from the vet, I propped Poppy on my left hip and took a walk around the property. The sunflowers were budding. The corn was calf-high. The barn swallows swooped over us like stunt pilots.

Vito usually took the walk with us, his back sloped and hips low, nose to the ground. I missed his lithe body weaving through the grass, brushing against my legs. I missed watching him charge the moles and chipmunks that lived beneath the brush pile, sprint after the garbage trucks that used our driveway for a turnaround. He was a runner, a stalker, a too-fast-to-call-off dog.

We loved his gusto, the way he ran at things he wanted with what my dad would call a devil-may-care sprint, saliva streaming from his mouth, his bear-sized feet tearing up the earth.

That morning, Russ and I had talked about him as if he were already gone.

Remember how he used to dive underneath his bed in winter and wear it like a turtle shell? Russ said.

How about the time we took him to the Christmas-tree farm? I said. He was small enough to fit inside your coat.

He raised his leg on a tree, Russ said. That's the one we took home.

But now Poppy and I walked down the slope of our backyard alone. We paused to refill bird feeders with sunflower seed and grease poles with Vaseline to keep squirrels away.

The pediatrician told me: Narrate your life to encourage language. Speak in the third person.

Mommy and Poppy are walking through the green grass, I said. Mommy and Poppy are outside. See the blue sky? See the white clouds?

Poppy's chin glistened with drool. Her wide eyes scanned the ground.

Bear scat during berry season is unmistakable—seedy, fragrant, copious. We passed two piles near the blackberry brambles.

Big bears make big piles, I said.

One apiary lid was pried open.

I got chills as I scanned the tree line behind our house, knowing the bear was likely within a square mile, likely to make another go at our honey stash. Once bears find your apiary, they return night after night.

Bad bear, I said, shaking my finger. I felt the unmistakable flash of adrenaline.

I had very little experience with bears. Eastern black bears, Russ promised, are like big dogs.

I'd fed them once behind a shopping mall in western North Carolina on a road trip with a group of friends. We tossed boiled peanuts into their mouths. The bears were jesters—fat and gluttonous—and leaned back on their haunches like begging pets.

I knew I was more likely to die of a lightning strike, hypothermia, or even bee stings than from a bear attack. But bears can spread their claws nearly ten inches wide, run thirty-five miles per hour. At their worst, they can eat you alive.

Big, bad bear, I said again.

Poppy laughed and buried her head into my armpit, her sticky fingers curled into my open mouth.

After Poppy was born, I couldn't breast-feed. I spent a week and a half trying. We ended up on the floor most nights, Poppy failing to latch and screaming with hunger, me crying in frustration as Russ stroked my hair and shushed her.

She's losing too much weight, the pediatrician said, so I expressed milk for her, hooking myself up to a pump that tugged my milk down into plastic vials. Every two hours I woke to pump and feed her, rousing myself from a feverish sleep, breasts full and hot.

In the white noise of the breast pump, I heard: *Kim Jong Il's noodles. Kim Jong Il's noodles. Kim Jong Il's noodles.*

Heavy components, I said to Russ one morning at three o'clock.

We're switching to formula, he said. You stopped making sense a week ago.

I put my head underneath the pillow and bit my lip.

Relax, he said, stroking my back. This is not a failure.

I just want what's best for Poppy, I said.

Take cats, he said. Excellent mothers. Let little ones fend for themselves occasionally.

If I carried Poppy in my mouth by the nape of her neck, I said, child services . . .

I want to take the night shifts, he said. For a while.

In the winter we left wine to chill in the snow. In the summers we kept a supply in the outdoor fridge next to the refrigerator pickles and spare zucchini.

The first night Russ left the bed for Poppy, I got up for a glass that turned into a bottle.

Russ was not well. He'd scrapped with an off-duty air traffic control guy in the back of a cargo hangar and come home with a busted lip and a screaming headache.

What does vertigo feel like? he asked. He cracked open a beer, took two long sips, and reached for Poppy.

I made him a peanut butter and honey sandwich. He slid potato chips into the center.

I like to hear them crunch, he said.

He fell asleep on the couch with Poppy on his chest. Her mouth left a puddle of drool on his softening pecs.

I touched his cauliflower ears, the ridges of cartilage broken and scarred over from high school wrestling. I kissed both of them on the forehead and found myself loving them so much—their long eyelashes, the fat of their cheeks—that I could not move.

The evening light gave our house a dreamlike quality. The carpet was warm on my bare feet. The curling wallpaper and inherited furniture were reassuring. The upholstery smelled of old chicken suppers and cigarette smoke. Instinctively, I looked for Vito, patted the loveseat as an invitation. Then I thought of him alone in his cage at the vet clinic.

I lifted Poppy from Russ's chest and took her upstairs to her crib. She rolled onto her side and began to suck her fist.

Poppy's skin made everyone else's look old. Her hands and cheeks were milk white, downy. My hands were sun-stained, wrinkled, rough.

Maybe I *was* old.

At night I looked at my naked body in the shower. Once it had been something to look at. Now it was covered in jagged red stretch marks, soft skin. Now I made love with a shirt on.

Back in the living room, I climbed on top of Russ, rubbed

his chest with the heels of my hands, massaged his temples. His eyes opened to small slits, then closed. The corners of his mouth turned upward, a slight smile. I squeezed him with my thighs.

Don't knife me in my sleep, he said.

His naked chest was warm from the late sun streaming through the window, and I slept there until midnight, one hand cupping his jaw.

I dreamed I was standing over Russ's bed with Poppy, teaching him to talk.

His dark eyes were hidden in pockets of swollen flesh. His head was shaved, his forehead was raw, his lip split. I held Poppy in the crook of my left arm, stroked Russ's hand with my right.

Poppy recited the pilot's alphabet.

Lima, Mike, she said. Oscar, Papa.

I woke up and walked out into the yard. The grass was cool. The birds were quiet. I could smell wild dill in the fields. Next to the moon, Jupiter was the brightest thing in the sky. I sensed the bear in the forest behind our house. I pictured myself in his eyes, my body a small shadow on his horizon.

My milk was drying up now and my breasts stung. I clutched my chest and returned to the house, pausing to look over my shoulder before opening the door.

It occurred to me that I did not yet know the sound of Poppy's voice. What it would sound like when she spoke for the first time, called for me.

Russ was still on the couch, missing work.

The light hurts my eyes, he said. And my body—my body just feels like shit.

I called a friend of a friend who would write prescriptions for us without an appointment.

Let me jog over to the pharmacy, I said to Russ. I'll pick something up for you.

I watched the lumpy shadow my body made on the hillside, my torso backlit by the sun, my rump a shadow on the grass. I hoped my silhouette was a liar.

What happened to the beautiful woman I always meant to become?

First Russ was a body. A big, rippled body, ripe and stone strong. Sweat beading on his skin as a fight wore on, blood slick across his teeth. A strange smile in anticipation of the next punch, a resilient swagger.

Watching him fight was a high. I gripped my thighs, tugged my hair, screamed at his opponent. The light shone on his wet skin. I could hear his breathing, see him planning his next move from my ringside seat.

The first time I went home with him after a night at the gym, he was still in his black silk training shorts. He took his clothes off and walked to the bed as if giving me a minute to take him in.

I had never been attracted to muscular types, but Russ was different. He used his body. It had a function.

Now, married, we slept on a borrowed bed and linens from our grandmothers. I'd learned to appreciate the impoverished elegance of heirlooms, but somehow felt that our own bodies had aged less beautifully.

The next morning we went to the veterinary clinic as a family. It was a split-level house converted into an office. Split-level houses always depressed me.

Given Vito hasn't passed the sock, an exploratory surgery is our best option, the vet said. The cost of foreign-body removal is two thousand dollars.

We can't afford that, I said.

I ran my hand down Vito's body, paused to scratch the base of his tail. He lifted his black nose, then lowered it to his front paws.

Poverty, Russ liked to say, is a state of mind.

Is there a chance he could still pass the sock? I asked.

A small chance, the vet said.

But there *is* a chance, I said.

He may well pass the sock, the vet said.

I had a feeling he was trying to make it easier on us.

Heart of a fighter, Russ said, patting Vito's head.

How do you step into the ring, I asked Russ on the way home, knowing how bad it's going to hurt?

It's like labor, I guess, he said. You anticipate the pain. It's productive. Makes me feel alive.

Maybe that's why, the next day, he head-butted a marine behind the DMV and came back smiling with a broken rib.

This is how Alive looked: dried blood on the corner of

its mouth, bald head perspiring, a ripped T-shirt, shit-eating grin.

Months before, my father helped me move into the new house. His mind was slipping, but we didn't talk about that.

I'm worried about you, he said.

He drove me down the dirt road to the new house. Dog-eared barns and sagging fences hugged the rough-and-tumble road. The truck he'd borrowed from a friend churned up gravel. I laced my fingers over my pregnant belly. You know, he said, motherhood is hard. Marriage is harder. I never pictured you living in a place like this.

He could've said anything and left a bruise.

I know what I want, I said. I can take care of myself.

Give up the illusion of control, my father said. Now.

Six weeks later, we used the same truck to move him into the veterans' home, a place where he had to record his bowel movements, ask permission to smoke.

The hummingbird feeder's empty, Russ said. You can't just stop feeding them. They might die.

He had an old towel tied around his torso to hold two ice packs to his side and back. He never went to the doctor—not for noses, ribs, or wrists. He let them heal on their own.

I whisked sugar into boiling water for the homemade nectar.

I think I've got a loose tooth, he said. He held on to his eyetooth with dirt-stained fingers.

If you didn't before, I said, you will now.

He curled up on the floor beside Vito, who slept on a pile of towels.

Think he'll last the day? I asked.

I think he'll last the year, Russ said.

Vito did not move. His breathing was labored and shallow.

I picked Poppy up from her play mat. She sucked on my collarbone.

Have you been down to the hives? Russ asked.

I will, I said. Soon.

The truth was, I was afraid to go.

Just big dogs, I thought.

That night I decided to sleep on the screened-in porch with my sword.

See you in bed, Russ said, raising his eyebrows.

I'll scare him off, is all, I said.

I could tell he thought I was being ridiculous, and I was relieved he didn't say more. I made a bed for Vito next to me on the porch, set a bowl of leftover rice near his head.

Anything you want, boy, I said, massaging his ears.

I thought of my father as the night wore on, as the cicadas tuned up and night sounds drowned out the washing machine.

If you must cede ground to your opponent, he'd say, break rhythm. Change the tempo. Remember—nature is mercurial.

Vito growled low and long. I sat up from my sleeping bag and saw the silhouette of a bear, illuminated by the porch light, just a screen between us.

I could not move. My mouth watered. My chest tightened. A small sound came from my lips.

Years later, when I told this story at parties, people imagined me defiantly raising the sword above my head. But I was paralyzed. My hands never touched the sword.

Vito growled again, and the bear tumbled down the steps, his musky coat gleaming in the floodlights.

He could smell the rice, Russ said later.

I heard Poppy crying upstairs, awake for a night feeding, or perhaps from the commotion.

I ran up the stairs, past Russ making a bottle. Poppy whimpered in her crib. I didn't bother to turn on the light and crashed into the bed frame with my shin. I reached for her, brought her to my chest, wanting her skin against mine. She put her lips around my breast, but I was dry.

Russ went to the doctor the next morning. He was worried that the vision in his left eye was failing.

How did it go? I asked after he came home. Everything okay?

I'll live, he said.

Sometimes, I wondered if that was true.

It seemed like the harder I tried to manage my life and the people in it, the more it fell apart. The more I fell apart. Now the woman I meant to become was on vacation, on the other line, otherwise engaged. She'd eloped with my free time, taken my figure, seized my sense of control.

Every time I thought I was unhappy I looked at Poppy's face, studied her. Once I watched her, standing where she could not see me. She stirred in her crib, tried to calm herself with steady breathing. Her eyes searched the doorway. Her arms stretched outward—*come back for me*.

Russ was watching a fight on television.

Turn that off, I said. It's not the same.

The television went dark.

Russ got up from the couch and limped over to me. I pictured my body as a salve, ran my hands the length of his back. We held each other without words until Poppy woke from her evening nap and Russ went to her.

I could hear her melodic sobs, Russ trying to placate her with Rolling Stones songs.

Later, Vito and I made our beds on the porch. I had rehearsed my moves. The idea was to scare and not to kill. I placed another plate of rice in front of Vito.

I lay down next to him. I lifted his lip as I had seen the veterinarian do and pressed my finger into his gums. They were pale. His breathing was shallow.

Vito heard the bear first.

I've read stories of mothers who found strength from nowhere, lifting cars to free their children. Vito's sprint was no less remarkable. He opened the screen door with his muzzle, sailed like lightning down the porch steps and into the night.

I could not stop him. I could not bring him back.

Russ would tell me later of his retinal detachment, the early tremors of Parkinson's the doctor had found, the fact that he was done flying.

But that night he was a warm chest. He squeezed the back of my neck.

Be brave, he said.

The next morning Vito's black and tan coat was covered with dew. His side was still. Unscratched and beautiful he lay, all of him spent.

We buried him out back, next to a rusted steel till and a swath of wild honeysuckle.

There was an unsigned check in my wallet. I had written it on the way to the vet, thought of passing it to him when Russ was not looking. An empty promise.

I knew there would be lips to suture, ribs to mend, mouths to feed, socks to buy.

I like to think of it—the way Vito ran that night. Fast. On point. Nose to the ground. Fearless.

There is no need to explain to our daughter the death of her first dog. Poppy, better than any of us, understands the urge to have what you must have. She can still wring what she wants from the world. It has listened to her cries and delivered. She still trusts the raw pull of desire. One day it will tear her away from us, take her down a dirt road to a place she does not recognize, and there she will make her home. Away from everything she understands, and close to everything she wants.

Acknowledgments

I'm grateful to the teachers I've had who have offered advice, edits, and inspiration. George Singleton, you were first, and reeled in a girl who was, initially, just as enthusiastic about the Furman cafeteria French fries as your writing workshop. I'm thankful for my instructors at Bennington, all of whom helped turn raw ideas into publishable work, particularly the dog-friendly and skillful trio of Amy Hempel, Bret Anthony Johnston, and Nick Montemarano.

These stories were further shaped by the generous editors and journals that published them. My sincere thanks to: Karen Seligman and Hannah Tinti at *One Story*, Carol Ann Fitzgerald and Marc Smirnoff at *Oxford American*, Tom Jenks and Mimi Kusch at *Narrative*, David H. Lynn and Tyler Meier at the *Kenyon Review*, Ian Stansel at *Gulf Coast*, James May at *New South*, Jim Clark at the *Greensboro Review*, Cara Blue Adams at the *Southern*

Review, and R. T. Smith and Lynn Leech at *Shenandoah*. I'd like to thank Ladette Randolph at *Ploughshares,* and also guest editor Jim Shepard, who works magic.

My sincere appreciation to the editors who included my work in recent anthologies: Geraldine Brooks, Heidi Pitlor, and Houghton Mifflin Harcourt for *The Best American Short Stories 2011;* and Amy Hempel, Kathy Pories, and Algonquin for the 2010 edition of *New Stories from the South*.

Next, I'd like to thank the wonderful team at Scribner for taking me on, particularly Kara Watson and my editor, Samantha Martin. Sam, you are kind and brilliant. Thank you for making my work better and understanding my intentions.

I'm also deeply indebted to my agent, Julie Barer, of Barer Literary, who, despite her charming urban savvy, takes the time to understand and do right by my rural musings.

Rhombus, Dad, and Emily: You are good readers and patient believers. And even though I moved to New England, you'll always have that Fort Macon video to remind me where I came from; don't use it unless you have to.

To the Dogtor and Wumpus: Before you, I had nothing to write about. Dogtor, you enable, inspire, and help me write intelligently about urinary wall tumors and cows with mastitis. I am undeniably lucky with you in my life.

Wumpus, you are the most beautiful of muses. You cried and cracked the world wide open.

Please turn the page for an excerpt from Megan Mayhew Bergman's new book

ALMOST FAMOUS WOMEN

Now available from Scribner

Praise for *Almost Famous Women*

"Lovely and heartbreaking."

—Anjelica Huston, author of *Watch Me*

"Megan Mayhew Bergman breathes life into lives that men and history have cast aside. It is rare that an author is as fearless as her characters. Bergman is, and *Almost Famous Women* is a stunning feat of great daring."

—Lily King, author of *Euphoria*

"Megan Mayhew Bergman is a tremendous writer—compassionate and intelligent, generous and funny—and *Almost Famous Women* is a collection filled with empathy, insight, and extraordinary psychological precision. Mayhew Bergman has made the women who inhabit this beautiful book come fully to life—I won't ever forget them."

—Molly Antopol, author of *The UnAmericans*

"*Almost Famous Women* is sharp, compassionate, and strong, just like the women depicted in its pages. Megan Mayhew Bergman writes with such precision that we should all quake in her presence. This book only looks like it's made of paper—you are holding priceless diamonds in your hand."

—Emma Straub, author of *The Vacationers*

"Megan Mayhew Bergman writes with an astonishing force of empathy, a compassion as bright and illuminating as a klieg light. The reader of *Almost Famous Women* can't help but be seduced by these eccentric, subversive, passionate women who lived their lives with their entire souls and who were furiously unapologetic for doing so."

—LAUREN GROFF, AUTHOR OF
THE MONSTERS OF TEMPLETON AND *ARCADIA*

"Every one of these stories is as vibrant, as urgent, as surprising as the women therein. What a thrill to listen as they cohere into a chorus of powerful, affecting and often hilarious voices, each unforgettable, together undeniable. Another stunning collection from the brilliant Megan Mayhew Bergman."

—CLAIRE VAYE WATKINS, AUTHOR OF *BATTLEBORN*

THE SIEGE AT WHALE CAY

Georgie woke up in bed alone. She slipped into a swimsuit and wandered out to a soft stretch of white sand Joe called Femme Beach. The Caribbean sky was cloudless, the air already hot. Georgie waded into the ocean and as soon as the clear water reached her knees she dove into a small wave with expert form.

She scanned the balcony of the pink stucco mansion for the familiar silhouette, the muscular woman in a monogrammed polo shirt chewing a cigar. Joe liked to drink her morning coffee and watch Georgie swim.

But not today.

Curious, Georgie toweled off, tossed a sundress over her suit, and walked the dirt path toward the general store, sand coating her ankles, shells crackling underneath her bare feet. A lush, leafy overhang covered the path, which stopped in front of a cinderblock building with a thatched roof.

Georgie looked through the leaves at the sun overhead. She lost track of time on the island. Time didn't matter on Whale Cay. You did what Joe wanted to do, when Joe wanted to do it. That was all.

She heard laughter and found the villagers preparing a conch stew. They were dancing, drinking dark rum and home-brewed beer from chipped porcelain jugs and tin cans. Some turned to nod at her, stepping over skinny chickens and children to refill their cans. The women threw chopped onions, potatoes, and hunks of raw fish into the steaming cauldron, the inside of which was yellowed with spices. Joe's lead servant, Hannah, was frying johnnycakes on a pan over a fire, popping pigeon peas into her mouth. Everything smelled of fried fish, blistered peppers, and garlic.

"You're making a big show," Georgie said.

"We always make a big show when Marlene comes," Hannah said in her low, hoarse voice. Her white hair was wrapped. She spoke matter-of-factly, slapping the johnnycakes between the palms of her hands.

"Who's Marlene?" Georgie asked, leaning over to stick a finger in the stew. Hannah swatted her away and nodded toward a section of the island invisible through the dense brush, where a usually empty stone house covered in hot pink blossoms stood. Joe had never explained the house. Now Georgie knew why.

She felt an unmistakable pang of jealousy, cut short by the roar of Joe pulling up behind them on her motorcycle. As Joe worked the brakes, the bike fishtailed in the sand, and the women were enveloped in a cloud of white dust. Georgie turned to find Joe grinning, a cigar gripped between her teeth. She wore a salmon-pink short-sleeved silk blouse, and denim cutoffs. Her copper-colored hair was cropped short, her forearms covered in crude, indigo-colored tattoos. "When the fastest woman on water has a six-hundred-horsepower engine to test out, she does," she'd explained to Georgie. "And then she gets roaring drunk with her mechanic in Havana and comes home with stars and dragons on her arms."

"I've never had that kind of night," Georgie had said.

"You will," Joe had said, laughing. "I'm a terrible influence."

Joe planted her black-and-white saddle shoes firmly on the dirt path to steady herself as she cut the engine and dismounted.

"Didn't mean to get sand in your stew," Joe said, smiling at Hannah.

"Guess it's your stew anyway," Hannah said flatly.

Joe slung an arm around Georgie's shoulders and kissed her hard on the cheek. "Think they'll get too drunk?" she asked, nodding toward the islanders. "Is a fifty-five-gallon drum of wine too much?"

"You only make rules when you're bored," Georgie said, her lithe body becoming tense under Joe's arm. "Or trying to show off."

"Don't be smart, love," Joe said, popping her bathing suit strap. The elastic snapped across Georgie's shoulder.

"Hannah," Joe shouted, walking backward, tugging Georgie toward the bike with one hand. "Make some of those conch fritters too. And get the music going about four, or when you see the boat dock at the pier, okay? Like we talked about. Loud. Festive."

Georgie could smell butter burning in Hannah's pan. She wrapped her arms around Joe's waist and rested her chin on her shoulder, resigned. It was like this with Joe. Her authority on the island was absolute. She would always do what she wanted to do; that was the idea behind owning Whale Cay. You could go along for the ride or go home.

Hannah nodded at Joe, her wrinkled skin closing in around her eyes as she smiled what Georgie thought was a false smile. She waved them off with floured fingers.

"Four p.m.," Joe said, twisting the bike's throttle. "Don't forget."

At quarter to five, from the balcony of her suite, Joe and Georgie watched the *Mise-en-scène*, an eighty-eight-foot yacht with white paneling and wood siding, dock. Georgie felt a sense of dread as the boat glided to a stop against the wooden pier and lines were tossed to waiting villagers. The wind rustled the palms and the visitors on the boat deck clutched their hats with one hand and waved with the other.

Every few weeks there was another boatload of beautiful, rich people, actresses and politicians, piling onto Joe's yacht in Fort Lauderdale, eager to escape wartime America for Whale Cay, and willing to cross a hundred and fifty miles of U-boat-infested waters to do it. "Eight hundred and fifty acres, the shape of a whale's tail," Joe had said as she brought Georgie to the island. "And it's all mine."

Georgie scanned the deck for Marlene and did not see her. She felt defensive and childish, but also starstruck. She'd seen at least ten of Marlene's movies, and had always liked the actress. She seemed gritty and in control. That was fine on-screen. But in person—who in their right mind wanted to compete with a movie star? Not Georgie. It wasn't that she wasn't competitive; she was. Back in Florida she'd swum against the boys in pools and open water. But a good competitor always knows when she's outmatched, and that's how Georgie felt, watching the beautiful people in their beautiful clothes squinting in the sun onboard the *Mise-en-scène*.

Joe stayed on the balcony, waving madly. Georgie flopped across the bed. Her tanned body was stark against the white sheets.

"Let's send a round of cocktails to the boat," Joe said, coming into the room, a large, tiled bedroom with enormous windows, a hand-carved king bed sheathed in a mosquito net. Long curtains made of bleached muslin framed the doors and windows, which were nearly always open, letting the hot air and lizards in.

"I'm going to shower first," Georgie said, annoyed by Joe's enthusiasm.

Joe ducked into the bathroom before heading down and Georgie could see her through the door, greasing up her arms and décolletage with baby oil.

"Preening?" she asked.

"Don't be jealous," Joe said, never taking her eyes off herself in the mirror. "It's a waste of time and you're above it."

Georgie rolled over onto her back and stretched her legs, pointing her painted toes to the ceiling. She could feel the slight sting of sunburn on her nose and shoulders.

"My advice," Joe called from the bathroom, "is to slip on a dress, grab a stiff drink, and slap a smile on that sour face of yours."

Georgie blew Joe a kiss and rolled over in bed. It wasn't clear to her if they were joking or serious, but Georgie knew it was one of those nights when Joe would be loud and boastful, hard on the servants. Maybe even hard on her.

The yacht's horn blew. Joe flew down the stairs, saddle shoes slapping the Spanish tile. Hannah must have given the signal to the village, Georgie thought, because the steel drums started, sounding like the plink plink of hard rain on a tin roof. It was hard to tell if it was a real party or not. Joe liked to control the atmosphere. She liked theatrics.

"Hot damn," she heard Joe call out as she jogged toward the boat. "You all look *beautiful*. Welcome to Whale Cay. Have a drink, already! Have two."

Georgie finally caught sight of Marlene, as Joe helped her onto the dock. She wore all white and a wide-brimmed straw hat. Even from yards away, she was breathtaking.

My family wouldn't believe this, Georgie thought, realizing that she could never share the details of this experience, that it was hers alone to process. Her God-fearing parents thought she was teaching swimming lessons on a private island. They didn't know she'd spent the last three months shacked up with a forty-year-old womanizing heiress who stalked around her own private island wearing a machete across her chest, chasing shrimp cocktails with magnums of champagne every night. A woman who entered into a sham marriage to secure her inheritance, annulling it shortly thereafter. A woman who raced expensive boats, who kept a cache of weapons and maps from the First World War in her own private museum, a cylindrical tower on the east side of the island.

"They'd disown me if they knew," Georgie told Joe when she first came to Whale Cay.

"My parents are dead and I didn't like them when they were alive," Joe said, shrugging. "Worrying about parents is a waste of time. It's your life. Let's have a martini."

As she listened to the sounds of guests downstairs fawning over the mansion, Georgie had trouble choosing a dress. Joe had ordered two custom dresses and a tailored suit for her when she realized Georgie's duffel bag was full of bathing suits. Georgie chose the light blue tea-length dress that Joe said would complement her eyes; the silk crepe felt crisp against her skin. She pulled her hair up using two tortoiseshell combs she'd found in the closet and ran bright Tangee lipstick across her mouth, all leftovers from other girlfriends, whose pictures were pinned to a corkboard in Joe's closet. Georgie stared at them sometimes, glossy black-and-white photographs of beautiful women. Horsewomen straddling Thoroughbreds, actresses in leopard-print scarves and fur coats, writers hunched artfully over typewriters, maybe daughters of rich men who did nothing at all. She couldn't help but compare herself to them, and always felt as if she came up short.

"What I like about you," Joe had told her on their first date, over lobster, "is that you're just so *American*. You're cherry pie and lemonade. You're a ticker tape parade."

Georgie loved the way Joe's lavish attention made her feel—exceptional. And she'd pretty much felt that way until Marlene put one well-heeled foot onto the island.

Georgie wandered into Joe's closet and looked at the pictures of Joe's old girlfriends, their perfect teeth and coiffed hair, looping inky signatures. *For Darling Joe, Love Forever*. How did they do their hair? How big did they smile?

And did it matter? Life with Joe never lasts, she thought, scanning the corkboard. The realization filled her with both sadness and relief.

On the way downstairs to meet Marlene, Georgie realized the lipstick was a mistake. Too much. She wiped it off with the back of her hand as she descended the stairs, then bolted past Joe and into the kitchen, squeezing in among the servants to wash it off. Everyone was sweating, yelling. The scent of cut onions made Georgie's eyes well up. Outside the door she could hear Joe and Marlene talking.

"Another one of your girls, darling? Where's she from? What does she do?"

"I plucked her from a mermaid tank in Sarasota."

"That's too much."

"She's a helluva swimmer," Joe said. "And does catalog work."

"Catalog work, you say? Isn't that dear."

Georgie pressed her hands to the kitchen door, waiting for the blush to drain from her face before walking out. She took her seat next to Joe, who clapped her heartily on the back.

The dining room was simply but elegantly furnished—white-washed walls and heavy Indonesian teak furniture. The lighting was low, and the flicker of tea lights and large votives caught on the well-shined silver. The air smelled of freshly baked rolls and warm butter. Nothing, Georgie knew, was ever an accident at Joe's dinner table—not the color of the wine, the temperature of the meat, and certainly not the seating arrangement.

She'd been placed on Joe's right at the center of the table. Marlene, dressed in white slacks and a blue linen shirt unbuttoned low enough to catch attention, was across from Joe. Marlene slid a candle aside.

"I want to see your face, darling," she said, settling her eyes on Joe's. Georgie thought of the ways she'd heard Marlene's eyes described in magazines: *Dreamy. Smoldering. Bedroom eyes.*

Joe snorted, but Georgie knew she liked the attention. Joe was incredibly vain; though she didn't wear makeup, she spent time carefully crafting her appearance. She liked anything that made her look tough: bowie knives, tattoos, a necklace made of shark's teeth.

"This is Marlene," Joe said, introducing Georgie.

"Pleased to make your acquaintance," Georgie said softly, nodding her head.

"I'm sure," Marlene purred. "I just love the way she talks," she said to Joe, laughing as if Georgie wasn't at the table. "I learned to talk like that once, for a movie."

Georgie silently fumed. But what good was starting a scene? If I'm patient, she thought, I'll have Joe to myself in a matter of days.

"I'm sure Joe mentioned this," Marlene said, leaning forward, "but I ask for no photographs or reports to the press."

"She has to keep a little mystery," Joe explained, turning to Georgie.

"Is that what you call it?" Marlene asked, exhaling. "I might say sanity."

"I respect your privacy," Georgie said, annoyed at the reverence she could hear in her own voice.

"To reinvention," Joe said, tilting her glass toward Marlene.

"It's exhausting," Marlene said, finishing her glass.

Aside from Marlene, there were eight other guests at dinner—including Phillip, the priest Joe kept on the island, a Yale-educated drunk, the only other white full-time inhabitant of the island. There were also the others from the boat: Clark, a flamboyant director and friend of Marlene's; two financiers and their well-dressed wives, who spoke only to each other; Richard, a married state senator from California; and Miguel, Richard's much younger, mustachioed companion of Cuban descent. Georgie noticed immediately that no one spoke directly to her or Miguel.

They think I don't have anything worth saying, she thought. She turned the napkin over and over in her hands, as if wringing it out.

Before Joe, she'd never been around people with money. Back home, money was the local doctor or dentist, someone who could afford to send a child to private school.

Hannah, dressed in a simple black uniform, brought out fish chowder and stuffed lobster tail. The guests smoked between courses. Occasionally, Joe got up and made the rounds with the wine, topping off the long-stemmed crystal glasses she'd imported from France. After the entrées had been served, Hannah set rounds of roasted pineapple in front of each guest.

"How many people live here?" Clark asked Joe, mouth open, juice running down his chin.

"About two hundred and fifty," she said, leaning back in her chair, an imperial grin on her face. "But they're always reproducing, no matter how many condoms I hand out. There's one due to give birth any day now. What's her name, Hannah?"

"Celia."

"Will she go to the hospital?" Clark asked.

"I run a free clinic," Joe said.

"You have a doctor here?"

"I'm the doctor," Joe said, grinning. "I'm the doctor and the king and the sheriff. I'm the factory boss, the mechanic too. I'm the everything here. I give out mosquito nets and I sell rum. I sell more rum than anything."

"Well, more rum then!" Clark said, laughing.

Joe stood up, grabbed an etched decanter full of amber-colored liquor, unscrewed the top, and took a swig. She passed it down the table, and everyone but the financiers' wives did the same. Georgie kept her eyes on Marlene, who seemed unimpressed, distracted. She removed a compact mirror from her bag and ran her pointer finger along her forehead, as if rubbing out the faint wrinkles.

When she wasn't speaking, Marlene let her cigarette dangle out of one side of her mouth, or held it with her hand at her forehead, resting on her wrist as if she was tired of the world. She smoked Lucky Strikes, Joe said, because the company sent them to her by the cartonful for free.

"How does she do it?" Georgie whispered to Joe, hoping for a laugh. "How does her cigarette never go out?"

Joe ignored her, leaning instead to Marlene. "Tell me about your next film," she said, drumming her fingers on the white tablecloth.

"We'll start filming in the Soviet Occupation Zone," Marlene said, exhaling.

"No Western?"

"Soon. You like girls with guns, don't you, Joe?"

"And your part?" Joe asked.

"A cabaret girl," Marlene said. "But the cold-hearted kind. My character is a Nazi collaborator."

Joe raised her eyebrows.

"Despicable," Marlene said in her husky voice, "isn't it? Compelling, though, I promise."

"You always are," Joe said.

Georgie sighed and stabbed a piece of pineapple with her fork. The rum came to Marlene and she turned the bottle up with one manicured hand. She even knew how to drink beautifully, Georgie thought.

Joe moved her fingers to Georgie's thigh and squeezed. It was almost a fatherly gesture, Georgie felt. A we-will-talk-about-this-later gesture. When the last sip of rum came to Georgie, she finished it off, coughing a little as the liquor burned her throat.

"More rum?" Joe asked the table, glancing at the empty decanter.

"Champagne if you have it," Marlene said.

"Of course," Joe said. She pushed her chair back and went to discuss the order with a servant in the kitchen.

Georgie shifted uncomfortably in her chair, anxious at the thought of being left alone with Marlene. Next to her she could see Miguel stroking the senator's hand underneath the table while the senator carried on a conversation about the war with the financiers.

"And you," Marlene said to Georgie. "Do you plan on returning to Florida soon? Pick up where you left off with that mermaid act?"

Georgie felt herself blushing even though she willed her body not to betray her.

"It's no picture show," Georgie said, smiling sweetly. "But I suppose I'll go back one of these days."

"I suppose you will," Marlene said, staring hard at her for a minute. Then she flicked the ashes from her cigarette onto the side of her saucer and stood up, her plate of food untouched. Georgie watched her walk across the room. Marlene had a confident walk, her hips thrust forward and her shoulders held back as if she knew everyone was watching, and from what Georgie could tell, scanning the table, they were.

Marlene slipped into the kitchen. Georgie imagined her arms around Joe, a bottle of champagne on the counter. Bedroom eyes.

Georgie took what was left in Joe's wineglass and decided to get drunk, very drunk. The stem of the glass felt like something she could break, and the chardonnay tasted like vinegar in her mouth.

When Joe and Marlene didn't return after a half hour, Georgie excused herself, embarrassed. She climbed the long staircase to her room, took off her dress, and stood on the balcony, the hot air on her skin, watching the dark ocean meet the night sky, listening to the water crash gently onto the island.

Some days it scared her to be on the small island. When storms blew in you could watch them approaching for miles, and when they came down it felt as if the ocean could wash right over Whale Cay.

I could always leave, Georgie thought. I could always go back home when I've had enough, and maybe I've had enough.

She sat down at Joe's desk, an antique secretary still full of pencils and rubber bands Joe had collected as a child, and began to write a letter home. Then she realized she had nothing to say.

She pictured her house, a small, white-sided square her father had built with the help of his brothers within walking distance of the natural springs. Alligators often sunned themselves on the lawn or found the shade of her mother's forsythia. Down the road there were boys running glass-bottom boats in the springs and girls with frosted hair and bronzed legs just waiting to be discovered or, if that didn't work, married.

And could she go back to it now? Georgie wondered. The bucktoothed boys pressing their faces up against the aquarium glass to get a better look at her legs and breasts? The harsh plastic of the fake mermaid tail? Her mother's biscuits and her father's old car and egg salad on Sundays?

She knew she couldn't stay at Whale Cay forever. But she sure as hell didn't want to go home.

In the early hours of morning, just as the sun was casting an orange wedge of light across the water, Joe climbed into bed, reeking of alcohol and cigarette smoke. She put her arms around Georgie and whispered, "I'm sorry."

Georgie didn't answer, and although she hadn't planned on responding, began to cry, with Joe's rough arms across her heaving chest. They fell asleep.

She dreamed of Sarasota.

There was the cinder-block changing room that smelled of bleach and brine. On the door hung a gold star, as if to suggest that the showgirls could claim such status. A bucket of lipsticks sat on the counter, soon to be whisked away to the refrigerator to keep them from melting.

Georgie pulled on her mermaid tail and slipped into the tank, letting herself fall through the brackish water, down, down to the performance arena. She smiled through the green, salty water and pretended to take a sip of Coca-Cola as customers pressed their noses to the glass walls of the tank. She flipped her rubber fish tail and sucked air from a plastic hose as elegantly as she could, filling her lungs with oxygen until they hurt. A few minnows flitted by, glinting in the hot Florida sun that hung over the water, warming the show tank like a pot of soup.

Letting the hose drift for just a moment, Georgie executed a series of graceful flips, arching her taut swimmer's body until it made a circle. She could see the audience clapping and decided she had enough air to flip again. Breathing through the tricks was hard, but a few months into the season, muscle memory took over.

Next Georgie pretended to brush her long blond hair underwater while one of Sarasota's many church groups looked on, licking cones of vanilla ice cream, pointing at her.

How does she use the bathroom? Can she walk in that thing? Hey, sunshine, can I get your number?

The next afternoon, as the sun crested in the cloudless sky, Marlene, Georgie, and Joe had lunch on Femme Beach. Marlene wore an enormous hat and sunglasses and reclined, topless, in a chair. She pushed aside her plate of blackened fish. Joe, after eating her share and some of Marlene's, kicked off her shoes and joined Georgie in the water, dampening her khaki shorts. Neither of them spoke for a moment.

"Marlene needs a place where she can be herself," Joe said eventually. "She needs one person she can count on, and I'm that person."

"Oh," Georgie said, placing a palm on top of the calm water. "Is it hard being a movie star?"

Joe sighed. "She's been out pushing war bonds, and she's exhausted. She's more delicate than she looks. She drinks too much."

"You're worried?"

"Sometimes she's not allowed to eat. It's hard on her nerves."

"Is this why the other girls left?" Georgie asked, looking out onto the long stretch of water. "You could have mentioned her, you know. You could have told me."

"Try to be open-minded, darling."

"I'll try," Georgie said, diving into the water, swimming out as far as she ever had, leaving Joe standing knee-deep behind her. Maybe Joe would worry, she thought, but when she looked back, Joe was in a chair, one hand on Marlene's arm, and their heads were tipped toward each other, oblivious to anything else.

What exhausted Georgie about Joe's guests was that they were all-important. And important people made you feel not normal, but unimportant.

That night the other guests went on a dinner cruise on the *Mise-en-scène*, while Joe entertained Marlene, Georgie, and Phillip. They were seated at a small table on one of the mansion's many balconies, candles and torches flickering, bugs biting the backs of their necks, wineglasses filled and refilled.

"How do you like Whale Cay?" Phillip asked Marlene.

"I prefer the drag balls in Berlin," she said, in a voice that belied her boredom. "But you know I've been coming here longer than you've been around?"

Marlene leaned over her bowl of steamed mussels, inspecting the plate. She pushed them around in the broth with her fork.

“Tell me how you got to the island?” she asked Phillip, who, to Georgie, always seemed to be sweating and had a knack for showing up when Joe had her best liquor out.

“After Yale Divinity School—”

“He sailed up drunk in a dugout canoe. I threatened to kill him,” Joe interrupted. “Then I built him his own church,” she said proudly, pointing to a small stone temple perched on a cliff, just visible through the brush. It had two rustic windows with pointed arches, almost Gothic, as if it belonged to another century.

“He sleeps in there,” Joe said.

“I talk to God,” Phillip said, indignant, spectacles sliding down his nose. He slurped his wine.

“Is that what you call it?” Joe said, rolling her eyes.

“What do you have to say about all this?” Marlene asked Georgie.

“About what?”

“God.”

“Why would you ask me?” Georgie felt her face get hot.

“Why not?”

Georgie remembered the way sitting in church made her feel pretty, her mother’s hand over hers. She could recall the smell of her mother, the same two dresses she wore to church, her thrifty beauty and dime-store lipstick and rough hands and slow speech and way of life that women like Joe and Marlene didn’t know. Despite Phillip, the church at Whale Cay still had holiness, she thought. Just last week Hannah had sung “His Eye Is on the Sparrow” after Phillip’s sermon, and it had brought tears to Georgie’s eyes, and taken her to a place beyond where she used to go in her hometown church, something past God as she understood Him, something attainable only when living away from everyone and everything she had ever known. Even if He wasn't a certain thing, He could be a feeling, and maybe she'd felt Him here. That day she'd realized she was happier on Whale Cay than she'd ever been anywhere else. She'd been waiting all her life for something big to happen, and maybe Joe was it.

"I suppose I don't know anything about God," she said. "Nothing I can put into words."

"You aren't old enough to know much yet, are you? You haven't been pushed to your limits. And you, Joe?" Marlene asked. "What do you know?"

Joe was quiet. She shook her head, coughed.

"I guess I had what you'd call a crisis of faith," she said. "When I drove an ambulance during the First War. I saw things there I didn't know were possible. I saw—"

Marlene cupped her hand over Joe's. "Exactly," she said. "Those of us who have witnessed the war firsthand—how can you feel another way? We've seen the godless landscape."

Firsthand, Georgie thought. What was firsthand about seeing a war from a posh hotel room with security detail, cooing to soldiers from a stage? Firsthand was her brother Hank, sixteen months dead, who'd been found malnourished and shot on the beach in Tarawa.

"That's exactly when you need to let Him in," Phillip said, glassy-eyed.

"You have a convenient type of righteousness," Joe said.

"Perhaps."

"I don't see how a priest can lack commitment in these times," Marlene said, scratching the back of her neck, eyes flashing.

Phillip rose, flustered. "If you'll excuse me, one of our native women is in labor," he said, "and I must attend." He turned to Joe. "Celia's been going for hours now."

"Her body knows what to do," Joe said, lighting a cigarette.

Joe and Marlene smoked. Georgie poured herself another glass of wine, finding the silence excruciating. Nearby a peahen screamed from a roost in one of the small trees that flanked the balcony. The island had been a bird sanctuary before Joe bought it, and exotic birds still fished from the shore.

"Grab a sweater," Joe instructed, standing up, stamping out her cigarette. "I want to take you girls racing."

The water was shiny and black as Joe pulled Marlene and Georgie onto a small boat shaped like a torpedo. It sat low on the water and had room for only two, but Georgie and Marlene were thin and the three women pressed together across the leather bench seat.

"Leave your drinks on the dock," Joe warned. "It's not that kind of joyride."

Not five minutes later they were ripping through the water, Georgie's hair blown straight back, spit flying from her mouth, her blue eyes watering. At first she was petrified. She felt as if the wind was exploring her body, inflating the fabric of her dress, tunneling through her nostrils, throat, and chest. A small sound escaped her mouth but was thrown backward, lost, muted. She looked down and saw Marlene's jaw set into a tight line, her knuckles white as her long fingers gripped the edge of the seat. Joe pressed on, speeding through the blackness until it looked like nothingness, and Georgie's fear became a rush.

The bottom of the boat slapped the water, skipped over it,

cut through it, and it felt as though it might capsize, flip over, skid across the surface, dumping them, breaking their bodies. Georgie's teeth began to hurt and she bit her tongue by mistake. The taste of blood filled her mouth but she felt nothing but bliss, jarred into another state of being, of forgetting, a kind of high.

"Enough," Marlene yelled, grabbing Joe's shoulder. "Enough! Stop."

"Keep going," Georgie yelled. "Don't stop."

Joe laughed and slowed the boat, cutting the engine until there was silence, only the liquid sound of the water lapping against the side of the craft.

"Take me back to the shore," Marlene snapped.

Georgie stood up, nearly losing her balance.

"What are you doing?" Joe demanded.

"Going for a swim," Georgie said.

Georgie kicked off her sandals, unbuttoned her sundress, leaving it in a pool on the deck of the boat. She dove into the black water, felt her body cut through it like a missile.

"We're a mile offshore! Get back in the boat!" Joe shouted.

Joe cranked the engine and circled, looking for Georgie, but everything was dark and Georgie stayed still so as not to be found, swimming underwater, splashless.

"Leave me," she yelled out. "I'm fine."

"You're being absurd. This is childish!"

Eventually, after Marlene's repeated urging, Joe gave up and headed for shore.

Georgie oriented herself, looking up occasionally at the faint lights on the island, the only thing that kept her from swimming out into the open sea. It felt good to scare Joe. To do what she wanted to do. To scare herself. To do the one thing she was good at, to dull all of her thoughts with the mechanics of swimming, the motion of kicking her feet, rotating her arms, cutting through the water, dipping her face into the warm sea and coming up for air, exerting herself, exhausting her body, giving everything over to heart, blood, muscle, bone.

continued . . .

A Scribner Reading Group Guide

Birds of a Lesser Paradise

Megan Mayhew Bergman

Introduction

Megan Mayhew Bergman's *Birds of a Lesser Paradise* captures the surprising moments when the pull of our biology becomes evident, when love collides with good sense, and when our attachments to an animal or wild place can't be denied. In "Housewifely Arts," a single mother and her son drive hours to track down an African Gray Parrot that can mimic her dead mother's voice. A population control activist faces the ultimate conflict between loyalty to the environment and maternal desire in "Yesterday's Whales." And in the title story, a lonely naturalist allows an attractive stranger to lead her and her aging father on a hunt for an elusive woodpecker. As intelligent as they are moving, the stories in *Birds of a Lesser Paradise* are alive with emotion, wit, and insight into the impressive power that nature has over all of us.

Topics & Questions for Discussion

1. How much of a role does nature play in the lives of the heroines of Mayhew Bergman's stories? How do their relationships with the natural world affect their decisions?

2. Whether it is an African Gray parrot or a lemur, animals are central to each of these stories. How do the characters identify with or distinguish themselves from animals? Do any of the characters share certain qualities with the animals described?

3. In "Housewifely Arts," what did her mother's parrot represent to the narrator while her mother was still alive? How did the parrot's importance change after her mother passed away?

4. How did you react to the veterinarian husband in "The Cow That Milked Herself" examining his pregnant wife in the same way he examines animals? Do you think his clinical take on his wife's pregnancy reveals any universal truths about motherhood?

5. "For centuries people had used the swamp to hide from their problems," says the narrator of the title story. Does Mae use the swamp to hide from her own problems? If so, how? How does her father's scare in the swamp change her priorities?

6. Lila feels ugly and damaged after her face is disfigured in "Saving Face," and goes to great lengths to isolate herself. How do you think her experience with Romulus and the sickly calf will change her? Can she reclaim the person who she was, despite her new challenges?

7. Lauren, the population control activist in "Yesterday's Whales," has a crisis of faith when she becomes pregnant. Have you ever experienced an event that's challenged your long-held convictions? Is there any way to reconcile two wildly different points of view?

8. Do you think the narrator of "Another Story She Won't Believe" realizes the mess she's made? What do you think propelled her to self-destruct? Do you think her treatment of the lemurs represents an insurmountable character flaw?

9. What does it take to forgive yourself after an act of negligence? What kind of mother do you think the narrator of "The Urban Coop" will turn out to be, if she can become pregnant?

10. "My mother once told me: Never underestimate avoidance as an effective coping mechanism," says the narrator of "The Right Company." Is her retreat to the small Southern town of Abbet's Cove an effective way to deal with the collapse of her marriage? When she tries to free Mussolini's dog, the animal refuses to make an escape. What does this juxtaposition say about the narrator's circumstances?

11. In "Night Hunting," a young girl must come to terms with her mother's declining health. How does her walk through the cold Vermont night force her to confront her fears? Do the ever-threatening coyotes represent a more primal danger than her mother's cancer?

12. Could a hunter and an animal lover ever have a functional relationship? Do you think the woman in "Every Vein a Tooth" uses her relationship with animals to avoid the messiness of human intimacy? Or does her extreme devotion to the animals she rescues come from a purer, more optimistic place?

13. "The Artificial Heart" is the only story in *Birds of a Lesser Paradise* that's set in the future. How do you think it fits in with the rest of the stories in the collection? Do you think it's a natural impulse to want to prolong life, even if the quality of that life becomes less than ideal? Or do we become lesser versions of ourselves if we try to cheat death?

14. The narrator of "The Two-Thousand-Dollar Sock" is a fighter, as is her husband, and ultimately her dog, Vito, who attacks a bear to protect the family. Do you think humans have a similar compulsion to fight and defend?

Enhance Your Book Club

1. Find a local animal shelter where all members of your book club can volunteer and have some fun in the process.
2. The swampland setting of the story "Birds of a Lesser Paradise" is exotic, but bird-watching is a fun pastime that can be done just about anywhere. Get a few pairs of binoculars and head into the great outdoors—record what you see and cross-reference with a bird-watching guidebook.
3. "The Right Company" takes place mostly in a mom-and-pop restaurant in Eastern North Carolina, where the narrator's food writer friend explores Southern comfort food with glee. Prepare your own Southern-inspired comfort food and invite your book club over for a meal!

A Conversation with Megan Mayhew Bergman

You live with a variety of animals on a small farm in Vermont, and your husband is a veterinarian. How have your interactions with animals informed your writing of these stories?

Interacting with animals draws me into a physical world, which is where I want to be. I've always been an animal person, and my husband is basically an enabler—now I can get access to all the one-eyed cats and neurotic beagles I want. In fact, we kind of maintain a secular, downtrodden version of Noah's ark in our farmhouse. But instead of beautiful beasts, we have decrepit, incontinent dogs, rescue goats, and vicious cats marauding around.

My husband can break my heart any day with shop talk. I spend time in the clinic with him after hours, and when I leave, each patient weighs on me. How did the cat with liver failure end up? What choice did the owner make about the old lab with the lung tumor? There is constant tension in his work, an ethical dilemma around every corner. That, in addition to our emotional investment in companion animals, is the stuff narrative is made of. Love, choice, grief, change.

You're clearly an animal lover, but you also write extensively about the menace of animals—often it can't be helped, it's their nature. Do you think humans also have a wild, brutal side?

I'm attracted to, and interested in, primal innocence. I think it's a quality animals and children share.

When I was writing this collection, I was grieving the death of my mother-in-law and acclimating to life with my first child. The following questions often occurred to me: What will we do for survival? The protection of our offspring? I'm fascinated by the primal self—though we operate in an industrialized society, I figure our bodies and minds haven't evolved at the same breakneck pace. I think vestiges of our animal selves bubble up more than we realize. Are our drives and needs really that different from those of our ancestors?

I have a background in anthropology, which I can never manage to shake. When someone brings me a casserole, I can hear my professor's voice: *there is no such thing as altruism*. Or if I get lost driving, I think: *that's okay, Megan, your female predecessors stayed near the yurt and gathered berries. Your brain wasn't designed for complex navigation.* (The feminist in me quickly raises an objection.)

And there you have my interior dialogue . . . a messy business.

Has motherhood impacted your understanding of the natural world, and if so, how has that influenced your writing?

The act of having children did not completely agree with my environmental and feminist beliefs, yet I determined it would be biologically and emotionally satisfying. And it was, which wreaked havoc with my belief system. Suddenly 95 percent of my being was directed to promoting my child's welfare. The other 5 percent mourned my loss of freedom, and in between feedings I was growling at my husband, mumbling lines from de Beauvoir's *The Second Sex*.

Motherhood is a whopping dose of humility. It takes you out of your head and puts you back into the world; you must invest in others. There is less time, in the early years, to dwell on bleaching your teeth or promoting your work.

Nothing, I think, returns you to your body more than childbirth. It's a violent, primal act, and sublime. My heightened awareness about potentially dangerous people and objects in my peripheral vision made me feel downright animal. The urge to protect my children at all costs permeates every moment of my life. Motherhood does something strange to the self; it makes you a little wild. The urge to exist and persist is a struggle all living things share—this idea is at the heart of all my stories.

How biographical are these stories? Are there pieces of your personality in each of your female characters?

No one of these stories is completely biographical, but there is a piece of me in every protagonist: the woman who worries if she should become a mother at all, the woman who struggles to conceive, the mother who finds purpose in her children and fears failure. There are women who want a wilder life, women who struggle to be dutiful daughters, women who are suspicious of human exceptionalism. Women with good intentions and a history of mistakes. Women who are homesick, nostalgic. Women eager to make sense of the world who are occasionally struck with human guilt, a sense of culpability in the earth's deterioration. Women who, in the face of grief, become reliant on a sense of humor or a companion animal for comfort.

Many of your characters seek solace in certain places, whether it's the North Carolina swamplands in "Birds of a Lesser Paradise" or the small seaside town in "The Right Company." Have you ever felt such a pull to a particular location? How does where you live define who you are?

I'm pulled toward places that have an air of mystery: wilderness, abandoned or historic houses, rural towns. These places have different rules. You lose a sense of control, and that's exciting to me.

I think a lot about places I passed driving the rural roads of North Carolina in my youth, the way an empty, paint-stripped farmhouse could jumpstart my imagination for hours. Who lived there? What happened? What still happens there?

A lot of times we self-select where we live, which says something about a character. But sometimes we're pulled to a place for a job or a person, which is also revealing. I think it's possible to find yourself partially defined by a place; location can impact your internal rhythm, food intake, friendships, proximity to family. When people are away from family, they are away from habits and watchful eyes, and able to make a life of their own. I'm always fascinated by the pull of home, even on people who opt to leave.

We come to place by a series of choices, and ultimately choices make characters interesting.

Many of your stories take place in the South, where you grew up, though you now live in Vermont, a life you often chronicle on your blog at www.mayhewbergman.com. Do you think Southerners have a different relationship with nature than Northerners do?

I can't speak for others, but I have a different relationship with the outdoors up north. In the South, I took the outdoors for granted; it was almost always accessible. But part of the reason we moved to Vermont is that we wanted to be outside more; we wanted acreage, gardens, ruminants.

In North Carolina, our historic house backed up to a donut shop, and vagrants drank beer behind our fence. We were close to the small town I grew up in, the tea-colored ocean I love. I knew the sandy soil, the tall pines, the crops growing in the fields, the soundscape: people talking slow, cicadas buzzing. During the building boom, I watched high-density housing developments consume my childhood landscape. I knew how to get into a hot car without burning myself. We hiked well-groomed trails and picked up after our leashed dogs.

In Vermont, the animals must be fed regardless of the two feet of snow outside. The garden must be weeded in spring and summer. I've gotten into bird watching, primarily because Vermont is a quiet place and I notice the birdsongs, the swooping flight of a pileated woodpecker. I run lonesome roads, and often encounter stray cows, deer, porcupines, groundhogs, rabbits, and unleashed dogs. My neighbors in Vermont boast as much about their gardens as they do their children.

I've been fascinated by my adaptation process. I finally figured out how to dress for the winter (down everything). I learned to run in the snow. I can drive in conditions I once considered apocalyptic. In Vermont, we are *religious* about the weather. You have to know whether or not there is going to be a snowstorm—especially if childcare and airport logistics are involved. But I always feel a twinge of homesickness as the winter settles in, or when I step off a plane in North Carolina and feel the humidity on my skin. I miss the violence of southern storms. I wonder if this will change as years pass, and the idea of "home" shifts.

THE STORY "THE ARTIFICIAL HEART" IS A BIT OF A DEPARTURE—IT TAKES PLACE IN THE YEAR 2050, AFTER ALL FORMS OF LIFE IN THE WORLD'S OCEANS HAVE DIED OFF, AND AN ELDERLY MAN'S FAKE HEART KEEPS TICKING EVEN AS THE REST OF HIS BODY IS SHUTTING DOWN. HOW DID YOU EXTRAPOLATE THESE PLOT POINTS FROM THE PRESENT MOMENT?

Hospitals often suggest you write a living will before you give birth—cheery, right? When told to do so, I started asking myself questions about quality of life, and what I would want for myself and my family. Recently, an elderly person whom I love made a request that the nursing home not take any dramatic measures to revive her if she should fall seriously ill. I thought it was a brave and definitive statement. This person, well into her nineties, was frank, saying: *I'm tired and I'm ready.*

With our increasing ability to prolong life with technology, it is possible that, in many cases, minds will increasingly outlive bodies, and bodies, minds. Taking care of aging parents results in emotional and financial pressure, joy and heartbreak. What do we owe each other? Ourselves?

My husband and I talk constantly over the dinner table about his thought process when it comes to euthanizing animals. Judging quality of life—especially when a patient can't talk to you about it—is a subjective business. So is mercy, and all that big-idea stuff.

I want to be clear—I have no prescriptive opinions to add, only questions to ask, scenarios to imagine. "The Artificial Heart" probes issues of guilt and accountability. How will we feel when we discover we've pushed people, and our natural resources, too far? I'm fascinated, also, by our capacity to forgive, and to love broken things.

About the Author

Megan Mayhew Bergman grew up in Rocky Mount, North Carolina, and attended Wake Forest University. She has graduate degrees from Duke University and Bennington College. Her stories have appeared in the 2010 *New Stories from the South* anthology, *The Best American Short Stories 2011*, *Ploughshares*, *Oxford American*, *One Story*, *Narrative*, *PEN American*, the *Kenyon Review*, *Shenandoah*, *Gulf Coast*, the *Greensboro Review*, and elsewhere. She lives in Vermont with her veterinarian husband, their two daughters, three dogs, four cats, a horse, goats, and chickens.